EXTINCTION C-14

AN ALEX MASON THRILLER

DAVID ARCHER

BLAKE BANNER

RIGHTHOUSE

ISBN-13: 978-1-63696-445-4

ISBN-10: 1-63696-445-1

Cover design by: Damonza

Printed in the United States of America

www.righthouse.com

www.instagram.com/righthousebooks

www.facebook.com/righthousebooks

twitter.com/righthousebooks

PRAISE FOR ALEX MASON

"It is brutal, wastes no time, and is full of action."

AMAZON REVIEW

"Better than Bond, Bourne, or Reacher."

AMAZON REVIEW

"For fans of Clancy, Mitch App, and Brad Taylor."

AMAZON REVIEW

"Same level as Patterson or Baldacci."

AMAZON REVIEW

"This book is filled with action, intrigue, espionage, and everything else lovers of a good thriller want."

AMAZON REVIEW

ALEX MASON THRILLERS

Odin (Book 1)
Ice Cold Spy (Book 2)
Mason's Law (Book 3)
Assets and Liabilities (Book 4)
Russian Roulette (Book 5)
Executive Order (Book 6)
Dead Man Talking (Book 7)
All The King's Men (Book 8)
Flashpoint (Book 9)
Brotherhood of the Goat (Book 10)
Dead Hot (Book 11)
Blood on Megiddo (Book 12)
Son of Hell (Book 13)
Merchant of Death (Book 14)
Extinction C-14 (Book 15)
A Vengeful God (Book 16)

PROLOGUE

BILLY SQUIRE HAD an IQ of 170, equivalent to that of Einstein or any of the great physicists of the technological era. He was also intelligent enough to know that your IQ was not a constant, and tested while you had the flu or a dirty contact lens irritating your eye, you would generate a lower result. Not because the test was faulty but because your intellect was functioning less efficiently as a result of the distractions. Intelligence was not something you had but something you did. He did it, he knew, exceptionally well.

Which was why he liked to think that if he could persuade Apsara to come away with him and leave San Jose, then he might be able to teach her how to use her intelligence more efficiently. She was beautiful, and she was really smart—especially when it came to money. He had to pay for every minute he spent with her, even though they were only talking. "Yackety-yak cost same as gin gan! My time, my money!" she would say to him.

He smiled at the thought of her. 'Gin gan' was a vulgar Thai expression meaning to have sex. He had never had sex with her, though that was her job. Secretly he wanted to, and he had paid her thousands of dollars over the months, but he had always felt that if they descended into sex, it would sully their relationship and make him just like everybody else for her. He knew that was naïve, but he didn't care. She was more than a whore for him, and he believed he was more than a trick or a score for her. They could talk for hours.

He had talked to other girls in the past, and they all did the same thing. They would look at him with dreamy eyes and shake their heads and say, "Wow, Billy, you're so smart...!" Which he found humiliating and deeply embarrassing.

But Apsara was different. She sometimes frowned at him and snapped, "That make no sense!" in her high, nasal voice, and forced him to explain it—whatever it was. And when he did explain, she would listen with great care, frowning, assimilating as much as she could of what he said.

At other times, she would bark a laugh, like she knew better. When he tried to explain to her what particle-waves were and the phenomenon of superposition, she did that. She barked a laugh and said, "Everything mind! There your supaposishon! Everything just maybe possible! But when you concentrate—" And she frowned and clenched her fist tightly in front of his face. "Then you collapse the maybe into particular reality."

Of course she was a Buddhist, and that was her Buddhist teaching coming out. Still, it took some smarts to realize that parallels existed between what Buddha had said and what particle physics was saying.

He dialed her number. He'd been to see her often enough that they'd made him her personal client and let him have her private number. That had been a special moment for him. He knew well enough that for the club, it was just the money. But for him, for a woman to have held his interest that long, that meant they were communicating. And *that* made her special.

"Hallo, lover boy. You want gin gan or you want yackety-yak?" The laugh that followed was coarse and crude, and he loved it.

"I would just love to see you if you're free."

"I always free for you, Yackety-Yack Boy. You come now."

He was smiling as he pulled on his leather jacket, as he clattered down the stairs and out into the limpid glow of the street lamps on Orleans Drive beside the Bay. His Honda was parked just outside. The lights flashed, and as he climbed behind the wheel, he failed to notice the headlamps of the SUV that came on fifty yards behind him. That was probably because he was still thinking about Apsara, who right then would be waiting for him at the P̃hû Hying Lew Club on West Santa Clara and South Almaden Avenue, just five or ten minutes away along the Bayshore Freeway.

He drove south, unseeing, along Orleans Drive, among the abundance of plane trees and Jerusalem pines that grew along the sides of the roads, to right and left, and the low, sleepy space-age buildings that lay in the peaceful shade of the trees like forgotten sets from *The Next Generation*.

At one time, it had troubled him that the information technology giants accrued such fantastic wealth and power, and yet so far from using that technology and that wealth to drive the world toward a more enlightened state, they had become complicit in the steady erosion of fundamental values and freedoms and the equally steady creation of a hive mentality where he saw his fellow humans degenerating into little more than emaciated androids. But since he had settled here in Silicon Valley, he had become kind of desensitized to the issue. His hyper-focused mind had room only for his work, which he knew would change the world, and for Apsara, who had already changed his world.

At the airport, he took exit 390 to join the Guadalupe Parkway. Pretty soon he was in town and turning into South Almaden Avenue among what Billy thought of as a curiously Californian mix of hyper-modern glass and steel towers, vast empty lots, and rundown, seedy structures from the early 20th century which had probably served ex-cowhands seeking gold. He turned right onto West Santa Clara Street and came finally to a large, grotesquely ugly two-story building on the corner. It had a shabby door with peeling green paint, and the drapes were drawn across the two windows at the front. So it always looked closed.

Above this was written in ancient fluorescent tubing *Phû Ħying Lew Club,* and there were two glowing images of Oriental women, one of which winked at you every five seconds. He pulled into the parking lot at the side of the club. There was little traffic, but still he didn't see the SUV with tinted windows that now pulled in just twenty feet behind him.

He climbed out and made his way back toward the sidewalk. His car bleeped as he slipped the keys in his pocket. At the door, he pressed the intercom, and a voice said, "*Phû Ħying Lew,* private club. We don't want none."

"It's me! Billy, Billy Squire. I'm here to see Apsara."

"She know you comin'? You got appointment?"

He knew she was teasing, but it still gave him an adrenaline jolt. "Yeah," he laughed, playing along. "She knows I'm coming."

The door buzzed, and he eased through into a kind of reception hall that looked like it had been decorated from the Buddhist Temple Budget Store: 'Samsara to Nirvana—we provide for your needs every step of the way! Buy two singing bowls and get a meditation mat free!'

The room was in semi-darkness, but on the far side, maybe twenty feet away, he saw a door open and warm light spilling out. Silhouetted against that light was the unmistakable form of Apsara. She came to him, smiling and holding out her hands with that inimitable, unaffected swing of her hips. She was graceful, he thought. Her face was beautiful, the proportions of her small, neat body were exquisite, and there was a sense of peace and inner beauty that radiated from her like gentle light.

She took his hands, and to his astonishment, she went up on her toes and placed a lingering kiss on his lips.

"Tonight I got special surprise for my Yackety-Yack Boy." She brushed his ear with her lips. "Tonight I gonna teach Yackety-Yack Boy special gin gan."

So it was in a state of burning confusion and conflicted

passion that Billy allowed himself to be led by the hand, through the red and gilt reception into the warm, opulent bar, heavy with tobacco smoke, festooned with lions rampant, smoldering dragons, and paper lanterns. There, men, mostly Western men, sat in dark corners and cubicles with exquisite Thai girls drinking Bolinger.

She led him across the room. Several of the girls winked at him, like they were telling him he had a special treat in store that night. Apsara, holding his hand tightly, led him then up the red-carpeted stairs to the rooms on the second floor. At a door halfway along the corridor, she stopped, turned to him, took hold of his face, and gave him a long, lingering kiss that was everything he had ever imagined it would be. She then opened the door and ushered him in. As he brushed past, her expression became a little sad.

"I sorry, Yackety-Yack Boy," she said. He frowned at her, confused, then saw the four men in the room. They were powerfully built, with big arms and thick thighs. They were not Thai or Oriental. One swarthy man in a suit looked Italian. Two were taller and fair-haired. The fourth was tanned and fair-haired, with pale blue eyes, and Billy thought for some reason that he looked South African. They stared at him with no expression on their faces. He returned the stare for a moment but turned quickly to look behind him when he heard the door click closed.

Apsara had left him, and he heard the soft rattle of the key as she locked the door. He turned slowly back to face the four men. The one who looked South African was holding a pistol. Fear lurched and burned in Billy's belly as the man extended his arm and aimed. There was no hesitation. The canon exploded, and the weapon kicked. Billy felt his chest burn, then the stab of searing pain like a needle piercing deep inside his rib cage.

And then nothing, just the eternal darkness that enfolded and engulfed everything.

ONE

I WATCHED Nero across his desk. I knew what he was thinking. Occasionally his left nostril would dilate, and he would curl his lip. Then his lips would purse, and he would grunt softly and look at the door. It was what he did when he was getting irritated because somebody was late for an appointment, and his mind was drifting in the direction of very cold Krug and oysters.

He glanced at me and arched an eyebrow that seemed to blame me for the delay. "Is your Captain Gallin always this late? If I had known..." He trailed off, drumming his fingers. I knew better than to answer. "I should have thought in her position, punctuality would have been a consideration."

I toyed with the idea of suggesting maybe her father, an old friend of Nero's, was holding her up but dismissed it.

"Her father is punctual to a fault," he said, like he'd read my mind. He stabbed a button on his desk. "Lovejoy, have we any word from Gabriel?"

"They've just arrived, sir. They are on their way up."

He grunted, and the resentment in his face grew. Now as well as having been made to wait, he had no excuse for his champagne and oysters. He concealed it with difficulty a few minutes later, when the door opened and Gabriel Gallin, the head of the Mossad mission in London, and his daughter, Captain Aila Gallin, entered. He stood and smiled and held out his hand to the captain first, while her father spread his arms.

"Nero, my dear friend! Forgive our lateness. We were delayed by a phone call from home just as we were arriving. You know how it is."

"Think nothing of it, Gabriel. Captain, a pleasure to see you again. You both know Alex, of course."

Gabriel made effusive noises about how he knew me, and the captain, who to me was plain Gallin, smiled with her eyes but left her mouth out of the operation, which was oddly disturbing.

We sat. I could tell Nero was still thinking about Krug and oysters, but he said, "You have probably heard something."

Gabriel shrugged and pulled down the corners of his mouth. "Chatter."

Nero opened his hands like a lotus bud over the bulge of his belly. "I am afraid I am to some extent constrained as to how much I can tell you—even Alex."

Gabriel shrugged elaborately, involving most parts of his body in the process. "Politicians, Nero. Don't worry about it." He laughed. "The things you can't tell me are probably the same ones I can't tell you!"

Nero arched an elaborate eyebrow. "Perhaps," he said. "No doubt you have your own sources."

Gabriel gave a smile that managed to blend modesty with smugness and gave a less elaborate shrug. "We did not survive six thousand years of persecution, my dear Nero, as you well know, by not having our sources. We haven't got the ephod back yet, but I hear something to do with the ZPE Corporation...?"

He trailed off. Nero grunted.

"As you know, Moschid Robles is something of a visionary who at times seems to have more money than sense."

"His fortune stands at some two hundred billion dollars, I believe."

"Precisely. The man is a fool, however, as he tends to employ the best and invests both his money and his boundless enthusiasm with little or no restraint. But occasionally he strikes gold."

Gallin spoke for the first time, arching an eyebrow that rivaled Nero's. "Where did he strike it? Intelligent taxis that play chess with you while discussing comparative religion and the counter-culture of the sixties? Or the mining colony on Mars?"

If I'd asked the question, he would have accused me of being facetious. When she did it, it made him smile. Which just goes to show that however big your IQ is, a beautiful, intelligent woman can still make a sap out of you.

"Precisely, Captain. The man is, as I say, a clown, but also a visionary. But where he has most recently, and most potently, struck gold is in that other field of research which fascinates Mr. Robles, the generation of energy." He gave a small sigh, like it was an effort trying to adapt his vast thoughts to our tiny minds. "Energy," he said. "It is one of those words that we all use, but few —if any—actually understand." He spread his hands in a gesture that was oddly reminiscent of Gabriel. "There are essentially two types of energy. There is what we might call mechanical energy, which is caused when one force acts upon another, such as gravity, friction, thrust, inertia..." He spread his hands again so that we could contemplate all the other possible examples he might come up with. "But then there is that other energy which nobody understands. That energy which is the underlying substance of sub-atomic particles. I do not refer solely to the strong force and the weak force but also to the very substance and nature of the particles and their flow. We experience it as the flow of electrons in the electric currents that sustain our civilization, but there may be many others. These are the forms of energy that fascinate Robles.

"He, and every industrialist on the planet with more than a single neuron, is aware that our energy needs and consumption have become unsustainable. Not only is the population growing out of control, but our massive use of energy is causing irreparable damage to the very environment which sustains us. This is of course the precise definition of a parasite, which is what we have become."

Gabriel cleared his throat. Nero nodded once. "I am coming to the point, Gabriel."

Gabriel winced and shrugged at the same time. "I never thought I would meet someone more verbose than me and who rambles more than I do when he talks. But here he is."

Just for a moment, I thought I might be getting a rare glimpse into an old friendship, but Nero just raised an eyebrow at him and went on.

"Spain, Portugal, and France showed us last April how fragile our renewable energy supplies are and how vulnerable they render us to attack. And Tesla has shown us—repeatedly—all the reasons why electric motors do not, cannot, and will not work. The principal ones being that the batteries are dangerous, dirty, and expensive to make, and their charge runs out far too soon."

Gabriel gave a small shrug. "So Moschid Robles became fascinated with the idea of finding a source of clean energy that would last a long time and be as reliable as coal and petrol."

"Indeed, and to that end he created the ZPE Corporation."

"The Zero Point Energy Corporation."

"Precisely. He also recruited a raft of very brilliant physicists whom he screened to make sure they all suffered, as he does, from either Asperger's, dyspraxia, dyslexia, or some form of information-processing syndrome that would make them think in lateral, unconventional, and original ways. It was a valuable and interesting experiment that has produced some very promising, indeed exciting, results.

"First among these was Dr. William Squire, a young man of colossal intelligence, born in the slums of London, whom he recruited out of no lesser place than Harvard. In fact, Squires was kicked out of Harvard while working on his doctoral thesis there. It seems he made a speech during a debate, in which he stated that the principles of freedom of speech and freedom of expression were more important than the sensibilities of, and I quote, 'a bunch of pansies who can't face up to reality.'"

Gallin and Gabriel both chuckled.

"Robles sponsored him, pulled strings, and had him finish his thesis at Princeton. Once Squire had his doctorate, he recruited him directly into the ZPE Corporation and gave him his own department and staff, working on a highly confidential project partly funded by the Pentagon which involved a source of energy of exceptional duration whose output could be measured in giga-joules. That is billions of joules."

Gabriel grunted. "I was aware of some of this, naturally, but I have read his doctoral thesis, and there was very little in it that suggested this kind of research. It was good but hardly earth-shattering."

Nero nodded. "I know. Robles recognized something in him, and from what I have heard, they had many late-night discussions about the feasibility of certain projects Robles had lying around. He is himself a talented scientist, and it seems he and Squire had a meeting of minds. It would seem the thesis at Princeton was a front for the real research they had going on. A fact which speaks to the size of Squire's intellect."

Gallin spoke up. "Cutting to the chase, the chatter out there is that one of Robles' leading scientists has gone missing. I am guessing that is Dr. Squire."

Nero nodded several times slowly. "He was at the San Jose Company Headquarters in Silicon Valley, working late last Friday night. There is no record of his leaving, and the CCTV cameras do not show his car as having left. There is some suggestion that they may have been tampered with, though how or by whom is not clear. All we know for a fact is that he was there when every-body else went home. He was seen, and he spoke to people. And then, at some point, he wasn't there anymore."

"His car was gone? But it doesn't show up leaving on the CCTV footage?"

"Correct. As you know, Robles is a major defense contractor. The Pentagon has charged the director of intelligence with finding out what has happened and where precisely Dr. Squire is. We need to know whether he has absconded, whether he has been abducted, or..." He faltered a moment. "Whether he has been murdered." He shrugged and shook his head at the same time. "Or it may be something entirely different. As things stand, we have not a shred of evidence, either forensic or otherwise. All bets are off."

Gallin said, "This is an American issue. American corporation, American defense contractor, American jurisdiction. So why have you invited the Mossad to be part of this investigation, sir?"

"Because I am covering my bases, Captain. Let us not forget that energy covers a very broad field, especially in particle physics. Nuclear energy does not only power submarines and towns, it also devastates cities and countries in the form of bombs. If China or Russia are behind this, with the cooperation of Iran, the threat to Israel could be significant, not to say existential." He arched his eyebrow at Gabriel. "I don't need to tell you that Putin, Xi Jinping, and the Ayatollah Khamenei are subtle, devious operators, Gabriel. So we discussed this at the Pentagon, and it was agreed that you should be involved in the investigation from the outset."

Gabriel gave a gracious nod. "What has the president to say on the matter?"

"As you know, the president is very sympathetic to Israel, but he has not been read in on this operation. It is strictly need to know, and because we don't know how hot it's going to get out there, we need plausible deniability—in industrial quantities."

Gabriel made an O with his mouth but said nothing. Gallin said, "And what is the operation, exactly?"

Nero gazed at his fingers for a moment, where they lay on his desk. His nostril and his lips twitched.

"Initially the mission is to find out what has happened to Dr.

Squire. However, clearly it cannot be that simple or straightforward. As an integral part of that initial mission, we need to know" —he held up one pudgy finger—"A, *precisely* what he was working on, B, how far advanced he was, and C, whether that work had any bearing on his disappearance. Once those four questions have been answered, then we can look at the full operation."

He turned to me and gave me a kind of once-over as he spoke to Gallin. "You will act as special agents of the Federal Bureau of Investigation. Lovelock will supply you with your accreditation and your tickets to San Jose and hotel reservations. She will also give you each a file on Dr. Squire." He turned to Gabriel. "Is there anything you or the Mossad wish to add?"

"No."

"In that case"—he turned to me—"let me just stress to you both that for all his antics in the media and in politics, Moschid Robles is an immensely powerful and dangerous man. He recognizes no limitations and sees himself as some kind of god. He has the classic delusions of a man who abuses cocaine, but on the kind of grand scale you would expect from him. I would stress also that Dr. Squire is a genius in the class of Einstein, Heisenberg, or Niels Bohr. He is the kind of man whose thinking changes the course of history. That makes him at least as dangerous as Moschid Robles. This operation begins as a mere missing persons inquiry, but there is no telling where it will end. You must know that you are dealing with something far more..."

He trailed off, apparently for the first time in his life lost for a word. Gabriel, his old friend, supplied it.

"Deadly," he said.

Nero nodded. "Yes, deadly."

Somehow Gallin and I knew we had both been dismissed. I stood, and Gallin stood with me. She and her father rarely display affection in public, but she gave him a brief 'I may never see you again in this world' hug and a kiss, and I said to Nero, "We'll be packing and getting ready then, sir."

He almost smiled. "I was wondering why you were still here."

Gallin and I stepped out. Lovelock was talking to Nero on the intercom as she handed us our manila envelopes and winked at me.

"Two dozen?" she was saying. "And the Krug, very cold, yes, sir. Coming right up."

TWO

ON THE COMPANY plane to San Jose, we watched DC fall away beneath us as we headed west across the vast continent. I sipped my martini and put a peanut in my mouth. I watched Gallin a moment as she watched the surface of the planet slip by forty-five thousand feet below. She was always good to look at, even—or especially—in a military shirt with her hair tied in a knot at the back of her neck.

"What?" she asked the window. "You're staring."

"How come you were late?"

"Like Gabriel said, we got a call from home just as we were arriving."

"You told me once the only time you would ever be late was when you were dead. You'd be the late Captain Aila Gallin."

She shifted her eye from the window to look at me. "If you'd said that, it would be almost witty. Coming from me, it's just a statement of fact."

"So how come you were late today?"

"Again?"

"Sure. You didn't answer. What, the director of the London field office of the Mossad can't say, 'Listen, I am about to go in for a meeting with the US director of intelligence in DC, I'll call you back'?"

"No. He couldn't do that."

"Huh!" I nodded with my eyebrows halfway up my forehead. "So that makes it a pretty serious phone call, and two gets you twenty it was about this very job."

"Two gets you twenty." It was neither confirmation nor denial.

"We're not sharing?"

"Sure we are." She said it to the window. "Look. We're in the same Bombardier."

I frowned. "Hey, come on! We're partners, and last time I checked, in Goa if I remember right, we were pals. What's this about?"

She shifted in her seat so she could face me.

"Mason, bottom line, you work for the Pentagon, and I work for the Mossad. Most of the time, we're on the same page and we have the same objectives. Sometimes we don't." She shrugged and spread her hands. "What can I tell you? A rocket falls in a suburb in northern Israel and kills Mrs. Mizrahi taking her groceries home from the store. In Israel it's an outrage, and we all feel it. In the US, especially in DC, it's another day in Israel. It doesn't make the news. Why should it? But when the next round of talks and negotiations comes around, the priority for the Israelis will be to stop any more Mrs. Mizrahis; the priority for the US will be to secure a deal that looks good at home, even if it means leaving Hamas and Hezbollah in a position to send more rockets into Israel." She pointed at me with her finger like a gun. "You and me, we're pals. If you were Jewish, I might even marry you. You're a mensch, you've got balls of steel, and my dad loves you. But the US and Israel are not pals. They are allies whose interests usually align."

I was quiet for a long time, feeling like reality had shifted slightly and I might fall over if I stood up or not fit through doors anymore. "That is," I said, finally, "probably the strangest thing anyone has ever said to me."

She drained her glass. "Yeah, but don't go getting ideas, Mason. You will *never* convert to Judaism, believe me." Then she smiled. "But can you imagine what our kids would be like? They would be *bad*ass!"

"Balls of steel?"

She shrugged. "Metaphorically. Obviously, I don't know..."

"Stop." I called the stewardess and had her bring me a very dry martini.

A little later we were served lunch, and we ate in silence with Gallin looking slightly smug.

We touched down at San Jose International mid afternoon and collected a rental Mustang convertible from the Avis desk.

"I'll drive," she said and winked at me as she drew the keys from my jacket pocket and rasped, "Your raw, masculine animality scares me when you get behind the wheel."

She was still laughing when I slung the cases in the trunk and climbed into the passenger seat beside her.

It was a short drive from San Jose Mineta International Airport to Orleans Drive, where ZPE had their head offices near the banks of the bay. It should have taken fifteen minutes, but with Gallin at the wheel, it took only ten.

It was one of those buildings, in one of those neighborhoods, where it looks like all the concrete and glass are not merely not harming the environment; they are actually benefiting it. The correct word would be 'healing.' All the concrete and the plate glass and the electricity actually *heal* the environment in these places. And the geeks and the nerds who populate these places, in their *Star Wars* T-shirts, Legolas-long hair, and skinny jeans are actually proto-elves on a path of fast-track evolution where they will become custodians of the planet once the level of vibration rises and we shift to the next level.

That is what these places look like: portals to a better, saner world where AI does all your thinking for you and problems are just challenges you built AI to take care of.

Actually, all that concrete and glass came from factories that used just as much fossil fuel in the manufacturing process as any other factory in the construction business, and the enormous draw on the power grid caused by the massive, twenty-four/seven use of hugely powerful computers means that Nerd Havens probably cause more atmospheric pollution than, say, a fish canning factory or a car factory, but they cause it off site, at the power generating plants.

We parked in the ample lot, among the fleet of Teslas, and stepped through the automatic plate glass doors into a large reception area that felt like the arrivals area of a *Star Trek* space station with marble floors and marble walls. There were also trees growing out of the floor and a fountain. The reception desk was a green, marble square in the middle of the floor, and as we approached it, Gallin's heels echoed off the walls and came back to us. My own Ninja steps were silent and did not echo.

I leaned over the marble counter and smiled at the girl on the other side. She had a pretty face untroubled by thought.

"Good afternoon," she said. "How can we help you today?"

I wanted to tell her my tribe was being depleted and I needed a woman with good, child-bearing hips and strong teeth to help us survive. Instead I said, "I am Special Agent Alex Mason, this is Special Agent Aila Gallin. We are here about Dr. William Squire."

Her eyes went round, and she said, "Oh" like it didn't compute. "Well, he hasn't been in for a couple of days. We don't know—"

"That's why we're here."

"Shall I call Ms. Steiner? She is the manager—"

Gallin answered, "Don't bother her yet. We'd actually like to talk to his friends and colleagues, the people he had most contact with day to day. We'll talk to Ms. Steiner later."

"Oh, um…"

"Are you friendly with Dr. Squire..." I looked at her badge. "Esme?"

Her eyes went even wider. "Oh, no! He would never speak to me!" She laughed at the sheer craziness of the idea. "I don't think he even knows..." She trailed off. "No, I'm not sure who he speaks to, but I guess the people in his department?" She frowned. "Is he in trouble?"

Gallin smiled without feeling. "That's what we are here to find out. Where is his department?"

"E-1, on the top floor. But security won't let you up. Everything here is very confidential. You'll need passes, and I *have* to let Ms. Steiner know you're here."

Gallin said, "Mason and Gallin, special agents."

Esme nodded and picked up the phone. "Ms. Steiner? Special Agents Mason and Gallin from the FBI are here..." She gave a nervous laugh and glanced at us. "About Dr. Squire... Yes, they want to talk to his colleagues... I told them... Yes, Ms. Steiner, I'll tell—"

She stopped because I had reached out and taken the phone from her. I put it to my ear and said, "Ms. Steiner. This is Agent Mason. Do I understand you are unwilling to cooperate with the Bureau in this investigation?" As an aside to Gallin, I said, "Call the office, tell Director Nero ZPE is not willing to cooperate with the investigation." On the other end of the phone, I could hear an icy voice saying, "Now hold on just one moment there, Agent Mason—"

"I'm holding, Ms. Steiner."

"Dr. Squire has not gone missing. He is an unpredictable genius, and he hasn't shown up for a couple of days. What the hell are the FBI doing—"

"Ms. Steiner, with all due respect, the Bureau does not have to explain to you why it decides to conduct an investigation. Dr. Squire is engaged in research for a defense contractor, and neither we nor his employer know where he is right now. So we can come in and conduct our investigation with your assistance, or we can get a court order and bring an army of agents to comb through every office, desk, drawer, computer, laptop, safe, and pocket in the building. Make a choice."

She was silent for a beat. Then, "I'll be down to get you. Give me thirty seconds."

"Make it twenty-nine."

There was a momentary hesitation before she hung up.

Over on our left, there was a green marble staircase consisting of green marble steps that projected from the wall but had no other visible support or banisters. This staircase climbed the wall in a semicircle and was contained within a pale green glass wall. Above, the steps reached a landing that continued in a semi-circular gallery affording a view of the entrance lobby. At the far end, I saw a door open, and a woman in a gray suit came striding out and clattered down the stairs. She emerged from the green glass wall and strode toward us, making more echoes than Gallin had. She could have been attractive, but you got the feeling if you touched her, she'd snarl and bite your fingers off. And her hair was pulled back so tightly you could almost see it baring its teeth. I figured her height at five-three in heels. A megalomaniac.

"Agents Mason and Gallin?"

I was damned if I was going to dance to her tune. I said, "Are you Ms. Steiner?"

"Yes. Are you—"

"I am Special Agent Alex Mason. This is Special Agent Aila Gallin. We are from the Federal Bureau of Investigation. We need to talk to some of your staff."

"I am very busy, Agent Mason, and so are my staff."

"Like I said, we can come back with a warrant."

"That won't be necessary. Neither is it necessary for you to keep threatening me. We are happy to cooperate with you, Special Agent, but will you please be aware that we are always working to a schedule."

"I don't plan to waste your time, Ms. Steiner, or ours. Can you show us to Dr. Squire's department?"

She sighed through her nose, loud enough to make it sound like a snort. She turned her back on us, and we followed.

"Dr. Squire's department is upstairs." She pushed through the door to the green stairs, and we started to climb, watching her contracting calf muscles just ahead of us. She spoke over her shoulder as she went.

"The bulk of Dr. Squire's work is highly classified, as you well know. They will not be able to discuss it with you."

I watched her calves a moment, and the swing of her hips, and asked her, "What was your relationship with Dr. Squire like, Ms. Steiner?"

She had reached the landing and stopped and turned to face us as we climbed the last steps. "Would you care to clarify that question, Agent Mason?"

"No. I would like you to answer it."

"Our relationship was strictly professional."

"You didn't socialize?"

"No."

"What about professional events, Christmas parties, conferences...?"

She gave her head a little shake and shrugged. "We were civil, we greeted each other, exchanged a few comments..."

"Are you telling me you weren't friends?"

"I am telling you, Agent Mason, that we did not interact socially beyond the limits of work."

"Lead on."

She actually scowled. "*What?*"

"To his department, Ms. Steiner. Lead on."

She spun and marched on. She led us, by way of a couple of passages, to an elevator which she opened with a card, a code, and an iris scan.

Inside, as the doors hissed closed, I said, "Your security is pretty tight. I'm surprised you're unfazed by Dr. Squire's disappearance."

"That's because you think of it as a disappearance. The

average IQ on our staff is a hundred and fifty, Agent Mason. Dr. Squire is close to two hundred. You cannot expect a mind like that to abide by rules or observe protocol. They write their own rulebook, and we have enough experience to know we have to work with that. Anything else would kill their creativity."

Gallin said, "You're not concerned that might get them killed or abducted?"

"Like your partner said, we have strict security." The elevator stopped, and the doors hissed open. Ms. Steiner stepped out and turned to wait for us. "But short of moving the whole operation to Area 51, there is not a lot we can do if they choose to have a private personal life."

We followed her down another long, antiseptic corridor with cream walls and a cream carpet, toward a set of double doors with a scanner panel beside it. Ms. Steiner placed her card on the scanner, typed in her code, and had her palm scanned. The door opened, and we stepped through into a short tunnel, where we were scanned before a second door opened and we stepped into another corridor.

This one ran for maybe thirty feet before it made a dogleg and had a couple of doors on either side.

Steiner went to move on, but Gallin stopped her. "Are you telling me that despite the sensitivity of what Dr. Squire was working on, you had no supervision or control over the people he met or hung out with? You didn't keep tabs on him or the people who were close to him?"

Steiner stopped and returned a couple of paces. She looked Gallin square in the eye. "No, Special Agent, I am not telling you that. I am telling you that we respect his privacy, and because we understand the extremely difficult nature of his work, we give him space."

"He has gone missing."

"So you say. It would not be the first time Bill didn't show up for a couple of days because he'd been disconnecting or letting off steam. I don't know why the Pentagon has gone off the deep end this time. I guess they, and you, just don't know Billy."

I was about to tell her she'd just gotten through telling us she didn't know Billy either but decided there was nothing to be gained from that, so I let it pass. I was also wondering, as she was, what was different about this absence without leave that had triggered a panic attack among the brass.

Instead I said, quietly and half to myself, "I guess that's the thing, isn't it? None of us knows." She stared at me. I went on, "And with a man like Dr. Squire, we should know."

THREE

SHE SHOWED us into a small conference room that had a long, oval table, cream walls, and no windows. She said, "Your passes are being printed. Citta, that's our AI, has read your biometrics on the way up here, and she is printing your passes. I'll get Krishna, he is a friend of Bill's. He'll bring you your passes" and left.

Gallin sat at the table, and I smiled and shrugged. "Citta, spelled C-I-T-T-A but pronounced Chitta, is the Pali term for mind."

She returned the smile. "Pali, huh?"

"Working man's Sanskrit."

"Huh, with those looks and that manner, I'd expect her to go for Wotan or a Valkyrie."

"Krishna, Citta, I am detecting a distinct leaning toward Indian mysticism. But this is the age of diversity, Gallin. You never know. She might come back with a representative sample of all world deities. Do you think deities identify, Gallin? Could Jupiter, for example, suddenly identify as a goddess?"

She gave her head a single shake. "There is no filter, is there, Mason, between your brain and your mouth?"

"It comes from having been born into an overprivileged

family in the richest country in the world. I grew up believing I could do or say anything I wanted, and it would be OK. It really damaged me. I now identify as a poor, underprivileged single mother from Mengomeyén, in Equatorial Guinea. But do you think I can get my doctor to take me seriously?"

"Shut up, Mason." But I could see she was repressing a laugh.

The door opened, and Steiner came in with a man who could have been anywhere between forty and sixty. He had large, dark pouches under his eyes, the whites of which were slightly yellow. He was skinny and stood with a slight droop, but his belly protruded in a small bulge. His jeans and his Nike sneakers were dirty, and his AC/DC T-shirt had food stains. What there was of his hair hung over his ears and his collar, like it had died there and nobody had thought to remove it.

Steiner tossed our passes on the table.

"Special Agents Alex Mason and Aila Gallin, these are your passes. Please wear them at all times. This is Dr. Krishna Das." She stood at the door while Dr. Das scrutinized us. "Dr. Das," she went on, "was Dr. Squire's personal assistant and collaborator. If you need to talk to any other members of Dr. Squire's team, Dr. Das will arrange it. If there is nothing else...?"

I expected her to say, "Close the door on your way out." She didn't, so I said, "We'll close the door on our way out. Thanks for your help and cooperation, Ms. Steiner."

She didn't answer. She closed the door, and Gallin said to Dr. Das, "Please, Dr. Das, won't you sit down?"

His eyes flitted over the seven available chairs before he sloped over and dropped into one with his back to the wall. He didn't say anything. He sniffed, glanced at me, and looked back at Gallin.

She said, "As Dr. Squire's personal assistant, you must have known him quite well."

His face broke into a surprising smile with lots of very white teeth. His laugh was like a couple of deep, inward gasps, which he delivered staring at the table top.

"Does anybody—" he said. "I don't think anybody, how can

you ever…" The laugh faded, but he kept staring at the table. "I mean, how would you ever know somebody?"

Gallin sighed. "Dr. Das, I am going to need you to come down a few levels from the sublime to the day-to-day. I am not asking you whether you had an absolute ontological integration with Dr. Squire, simply whether you had significant epistemological interactions with him."

His eyes had become round and shifted from the table to Gallin, like he thought she was worth a second look. "Oh," he said. "We had quite a lot of detailed epistemological interactions."

"Right, now I am going to need you to come down another couple of levels so we can talk like normal, stupid people talk. Can you do that for me?"

His face broke into a grin, and he giggled. "OK, I can try. Like in the movies."

"Exactly, like in the movies."

"My friends are calling me sometimes like Sheldon."

"That's funny." She didn't smile. "So if you were Sheldon, who was Billy?" She didn't let him answer. She plowed on. "Did you hang out a lot, in the canteen, maybe go out for a few beers?"

He raised both hands and tilted his head to one side. "Well, I have to say, we do not drink. I know some people drink. Some colleagues even tell me a little drink sometimes helps the flow of ideas." He indicated with his hands, in a repeated sweeping motion from his head down, what a flow of ideas was. "Some colleagues even use ayahuasca and other psychotropic and hallucinogenic substances to optimize the functioning of their minds." He leaned forward toward Gallin, and there was a boyish cheekiness to his expression. "I ask them, 'Have you tried thinking?'"

Then he leaned back, with his head thrown back and his mouth open, and after a bizarre count of four, he began to laugh. The laugh resolved itself into a humorous "Hmmmm…" and he added, "Of course they are sometimes struggling with concepts of space and time, and to embrace these plastic relativities, they feel they need to break down the rigid structures of the mind." He shrugged. "It's OK. But I tell them, a receptive, open mind is not the same as a state of fantasy."

I cleared my throat and sat opposite him. "I'd have to agree, Dr. Das, but I'm afraid you've kind of lost me. Who are these people who are indulging in so-called mind expanding drugs? Are they part of the team here? Were they friends of Dr. Squire?"

Nothing much changed in his face except that it became expressionless. "Nothing illegal," he said.

"We're not interested in that, Dr. Das. Let me ask you straight out. Do you know where Dr. Squire is?"

"No." There was no inflection or expression. It was a flat statement. "But Billy is always like this. Just like his mind is free and wild, so is he." He waved his hands at us. "People want him to sign here, sign there, have an office, make a job, drive a car—he don't care! It is their problem. He says, 'Yes,' they give him a house, an apartment, a place to do his experiments. But if tomorrow he doesn't feel like coming to work, he will not. And you can shout and threaten and do what you like. He is not interested and not listening." He gave another strange laugh. "He is god in his own universe. He does as he pleases. His product is his genius. He sells it to the highest bidder. The price"—he raised a long, brown index finger—"is his freedom."

It was an interesting insight, and I could see from Gallin's frown she thought so too, but I wasn't sure how it was helping us.

"So you and Dr. Squire don't drink. Did you hang out when you weren't working?"

He gave a little sigh and repeated, "When we weren't working" as though it was a meaningless phrase. "In this kind of work, Special Agent Mason, there is no strict separation between work and not work. We work twenty-four hours a day, seven days a week, because our work is life itself."

Gallin spoke up. "I'm not sure if we are being stupid or you are being evasive. You know in *Big Bang*, sometimes they sit down and play video games, or talk, or have lunch in the canteen. For basic carbon life forms like us, that's called hanging out when you're not working. If you have an IQ of over one-sixty, you know that. So again, did you and Billy hang out when you weren't working?"

He drew breath three times before he finally said, "Yes."

She went on, "OK, so when you aren't discussing the finer points of the fabric of the universe, what do you talk about? Does Dr. Squire have some place he likes to escape to? Is there a cabin in the woods somewhere? Does he go fishing? You think he's just letting off steam somewhere? We are concerned he's gone missing. So based on conversations you've had, hobbies you've discussed or shared, things he's told you about his life, where should we look to see if we're right and he's gone missing or you're right and he's just chillin'?"

He thought for a long moment, then asked, "Have you tried his house?"

I smiled on the unpleasant side of my face. "That's what I call being a wiseass, Dr. Das. We wanted to talk to his team before we went to his house so we would have some context."

"Yes, that makes sense. I ask not to be a wiseass, Special Agent, but because it was where he spent most of his time." He spread his hands like he was appealing to me and tilted his head on one side. "Office, home. Office, home." He smiled like it was sad but true.

I said, "Bars, restaurants...?"

Gallin interjected, "Girlfriends?"

He kind of gurgled and showed his teeth. "No, no, no girlfriends. Maybe virtual, but not tangible, three-dimensional one. He, we, our few friends, we are not really restaurant people, you know. Some takeaway. Going out to dinner very expensive in this area. Too many billionaires. And bars." He shrugged. "We don't drink." He laughed. "Stereotype nerd. Stereotypes exist for a reason." His eyes widened as part of a big grin. "So stereotype or archetype? Huh?"

He rounded off with his little gasping laugh, and Gallin smiled. "Right. Good question. So who is 'we'— your few friends who don't drink and don't go to restaurants?"

"Ah, well, OK, I shouldn't, without..." He made a strange gesture pointing with both index fingers toward the door. Gallin said, "We are the Federal Bureau of Investigation, Dr. Das, so you should. But if it makes you feel better, we won't tell."

He simpered and shrugged. "Well, I suppose. So there is Gizmo. That is Dr. Clara Belle Epstein. She is Jewish and makes robots. So we call her Gizmo. Pete Chidester, he is English. We call him the Raj because he is an imperialist. He says, 'Britain gave India railways and hospitals!'" He squealed with laughter for a moment. "So we call him the Raj. So funny."

"Yeah, that's funny. Anybody else?"

"Yes, Moo. He is from Texas. We call him Hagar because he looks like a Viking. He is very big with very long, blond hair."

"His nickname is Hagar. So what's Moo, his real name? His parents called him Moo?"

"His name is Chet, but his surname is Muse, so people call him Moo because he does not like Chet. But his real nickname, with us, his friends, is Hagar."

"OK, Chet Muse, otherwise Moo or Hagar. What's in a name, right? A moose by any other name would smell as sweet. A couple more questions, Dr. Das, and for now, we are done. I want you to think hard about this one—"

"That might take weeks!" He glanced from Gallin to me and back again with an open mouth and a big grin on his face, then burst out laughing. Gallin laughed too. She thought it was funny.

"Right," she said. "Not that hard. Just like a Muggle thinking hard. Is there anyone you can think of, either in your immediate circle or in the wider circle, who might wish Billy harm or want to abduct him? Let's say we go look for him and find we are in fact right and he has gone missing. Who would you first think of as a suspect?"

"Ooooh, that is a very serious and complex question, Special Agent Gallin."

"Yeah, that's why I am asking it, Dr. Das."

He nodded and said with no hesitation, "Ayatollah Khamenei."

"Ayatollah Khamenei? You think Ayatollah Khamenei has abducted Dr. Squire?"

"No. I don't think nobody has abducted Billy. But if he was abducted, I would suspect Ayatollah Khamenei. Because Russia, China, and Iran form a loose unit, and Iran has both"—he raised a long index finger and tilted his head on one side—"highly active terrorist branch and also, ironically, branch with deepest penetration in Western society. And these unit of Russia and China and Iran are very much wanting the kind of stuff Billy is..." He trailed off. "The kind of stuff Billy *knows how* to make."

"The kind of stuff..."

He was shaking his head. "I have said too much already. I cannot tell you more about this."

I stepped in. "OK, Dr. Das, we won't press you on that point, but let me ask you this. Assuming we go and look for Dr. Squire, and he turns out to be missing—"

"Hypothetical situation."

"Exactly, hypothetically, is there any individual that you would be looking at for that connection with Iran? I mean" —I gave a small laugh—"climbing down the ladder of abstraction a bit, somebody more immediately involved with Dr. Squire and you guys than the Ayatollah Khamenei."

He nodded. "Like for example Ali working in the canteen, or Dr. Ahmed in Department X."

"Really?" I glanced at Gallin. She glanced back. Dr. Krishna Das shook his head. "No, they are just hypothetical people. Nobody comes to my mind immediately, but I will think about it and get back to you with my thoughts."

I sighed and sagged back in my chair. I gave Gallin another glance, and she said, "Dr. Das, you have been very helpful, thank you. It has been a very useful epistemological exchange. Could you ask Dr. Clara Belle Epstein to come in?"

He stood and grinned. "Of course, I will tell Dr. Gizmo you are waiting for her. With bated breath!"

He let himself out and closed the door behind him. Gallin and I stared at each other. She frowned and said, "Did you ever get the feeling you had been wading through fascinating treacle?"

I nodded. "Just now. One of the fascinating things about it was the way a guy that intelligent can play the fool so convincingly. Was he playing us? Or is he just a crazy genius?"

"I don't know. Maybe one thing is genius and another thing is smart, right?"

I smiled. "Is that a stereotype or an archetype?"

She grunted. "So this *Big Bang* bunch divide their time between Orleans Drive and Billy's place. They don't drink, and they don't go out, except to get the occasional takeout. He can't think of anyone who would want to harm Billy, except Ayatollah Khamenei. And yet Billy goes missing."

She raised an eyebrow at me. "Don't take this the wrong way, but you know what US intelligence can be like sometimes. I mean, OK, you guys are amazing, sometimes, but sometimes you can make a storm in a teacup because you misread the intelligence. So some kid doing surveillance expects Billy to go home at five-thirty, but Billy doesn't leave the office. The building closes up. No sign of Billy. He calls Billy's cell—he's going to pretend it's a wrong number—but Billy doesn't answer. Red alert, Dr. William Squire has gone missing. He's been abducted by the Iranians. Meanwhile, it turns out Billy never went to work that morning. Because he was busy hanging upside down from a rafter to see how bats perceive the time-space continuum. Your vast intelligence establishment is too busy categorizing people and doesn't always get that the biggest threats come from people who can't be categorized."

"Wow. Not a bad point. So you want to interview Gizmo, you want to go and check out Billy's house, like Sheldon suggested, you want me to do one or either of those things...?" I spread my hands and waited.

"We interview Dr. Gizmo, then we go check out his house. Then we come back and interview Dr. Pete the Raj and Dr. Chet Muse, otherwise Moo or Hagar. Plan?"

"Plan."

FOUR

GIZMO, Dr. Clara Belle Epstein, was not what I had expected. Perhaps my stereotypes had won over my archetypes, but I was expecting an emaciated neurotic genius with bottle-base glasses and ratty hair who lived on a diet of Chinese noodles and black caw-fee. Archetype or stereotype, that was not Dr. Gizmo.

Dr. Gizmo was tall, almost six foot. She was slim and graceful, and in black jeans and a plain black T-shirt, there was something tenuous about her. As though if you reached for her, she would waft away like a shadowy vapor. Her hair also was long and black, and the only way to describe her face was to say it was perfect. It was tempting to say she was expressionless, but that would not be right. Her expression was one of mild curiosity, like she didn't really belong here and she found the rest of us a little odd. She didn't wait to be asked. She crossed the room gracefully and sat. She eyed Gallin a moment, then looked at me.

Gallin didn't say anything, so I said, "Dr. Epstein, I am Agent Mason, and this is Agent Gallin. We are from the FBI. Do you know where Dr. Squire is right now?"

"No." Her voice was quiet, pitched low.

"Does he often miss days at work?"

"No, never." She gave a small sigh, like she realized she had to clarify but it was boring to do so. "Bill works all the time, twenty-four hours a day. Sometimes he works here, sometimes at home, sometimes in the park or the mountains. He doesn't follow a fixed routine."

"So when he didn't show up, you weren't concerned?"

"No."

"We have reason to believe Dr. Squire has gone missing."

She studied my face a moment before answering, then glanced at Gallin. "Then you have access to data I haven't got."

Gallin asked, "Are you and Dr. Squire close?"

Her eyes strayed to the wall. She took another deep breath, and her shoulders rose slightly. "Forgive me, Agent Gallin. I don't want to be obstructive, but your question doesn't mean anything. Close is, at best, vague. It is totally subjective, and when used metaphorically to describe a human relationship, it is practically meaningless. Can you please be more precise?"

I could sense Gallin's irritation without looking at her and said, "Dr. Epstein, when we talk about people being close in law enforcement, we refer to there being a degree of intimacy. Now we don't want to get lost in a maze of semantics here. So giving the words their plain meaning, were you and Dr. Squire close friends? Did you confide in each other? Did you meet when it wasn't necessary, to eat, play, relax..." I spread my hands. "You know what we are asking."

"Bill and I were friends. We would meet often, here, obviously, but also at his house and sometimes for some cultural activity like an exhibition or a conference."

I felt a stirring of curiosity and again, sensed it in Gallin too. She said, "Would these meetings include other people, like Dr. Das, Dr. Chidester, and Dr. Muse?"

"Sometimes." She gave a small shrug. "Often."

I said, "But not always."

"No."

I leaned forward with my elbows on the table. "Dr. Epstein, was your relationship with Dr. Squire more than friendship?

Please don't play semantics. I mean what you think I mean. Were you intimate? Do I need to clarify what I mean by that?"

Most of the time, her face wasn't easy to read, but right then, just for a second, it was an open book. She said, "No, you don't need to elucidate. And no, it was not intimate. We were work colleagues and friends, no more."

I held her eye for a moment. She tried to hold mine, but after a couple of seconds, she looked away.

"Have you any idea where Dr. Squire might be now?"

The faintest color touched her cheeks. "He's probably at home or with—" She bit back the word. I said, "With whom?"

She shook her head. "I don't know. How should I know? A friend, maybe. It's his life, I have no idea."

For someone who had come in having left their expressions and emotions at the door, it was quite an outburst.

An instinct told me not to pursue it—at least not yet. "We understand that Dr. Squire had a small number of close friends among whom he counted you, Dr. Chidester, Dr. Das, and Dr. Muse. Would you say that was correct?"

"Yes."

"Is there anyone you would add to that list? Do you know of anyone else he was close to, in the sense we have used that word so far?"

Her face seemed to close down. Her eyes shifted from mine to the tabletop. I was struck by the extraordinary beauty of her face. With a smile it must have been radiant, but when you looked at it, you knew it very rarely smiled.

The passing of time was acutely noticeable in the silent room. Eventually Gallin said, "Dr....?"

Dr. Gizmo blinked and took a deep breath.

"I'm sorry. I was thinking. No, I can't think of anybody else he was close to, in the sense you use the word."

"You were thinking pretty hard." She didn't answer. She just watched me and waited. I leaned forward. "Dr. Epstein, I can't force you to speak to us, but I will tell you this: The more you open up, the less interest we'll have in you. The more you clam up and hide, the more interest you'll generate until we are all over you twenty-four seven like a rash. Now we all three know that when I asked you about other people in Dr. Squire's life, you clammed up, and you are hiding something. Do you want to reconsider your answer?"

There was not a flicker of emotion on her face. She just said, "No. I don't know of anybody else he was close to in the sense you have used that word."

Gallin looked at me, and I shrugged. She turned to Dr. Epstein. "We're done here. You have not been helpful, Doctor. You have left us both with the impression you are hiding something. I am pretty sure we will want to talk to you again—and again." She pulled a card from her jacket and tossed it across the table to Dr. Gizmo. "If you change your mind and decide to be more cooperative, call us."

"Is there anything else?"

Gallin shook her head. "No."

Dr. Clara Belle Epstein stood and left the room with all the grace the gods had endowed her with but without Gallin's card. The door closed softly, and I turned to Gallin.

"What was that?"

She raised her shoulders an eighth of an inch and leaned back. After giving her head a small shake, she said, "Less than it seemed to be, I'm guessing. She has a big crush on Billy. Billy's got neurons instead of testicles and hasn't realized there is a beautiful face and a smokin' hot body behind Gizmo's brain. And she, rightly or wrongly, suspects that Billy has what we call in England a bit of crumpet on the side."

"OK, but just answer me this. Is that ontological crumpet or epistemological crumpet? Also, is that body smokin' objectively or subjectively?"

"Let's get you out of here before you blow a fuse. We'll leave a message with Steiner that we're coming back."

I stood as she made for the door. "Sure," I said. "Whatever

you say, but in the end, what *is* a fuse and who *is* Steiner? You know, in the greater ontological context of existence, or not."

"Keep it up, Mason, keep it up..."

We found Steiner in her office and informed her that we had to go out but would be back to finish interviewing Billy's colleagues. She looked about as pleased as a turkey listening to "Jingle Bells." We left her making plans for AI to take over the world and delete people like me and Gallin and went out to where our Mustang was waiting. It beeped and bleeped at us until we obeyed and put on our seatbelts, and we pulled out of the parking lot and headed south to Moffett Park Drive and then Route 237.

It was a ten-mile drive to the suburbs to the west of Cupertino. Normally, Gallin would have done that distance in less than ten minutes, but this time she was cruising with the hood down and the California sun lying lazy on her aviators.

"It's too soon to try and analyze this yet," I told her.

She ignored the comment and asked me, "Tell me something: What do you think we are going to find at Billy's place?"

I gazed out at the Sunnyvale Municipal Golf Course as it glided by and spread my hands. "There is no way of knowing. I don't want to sound like the *Big Bang* brothers, but we have insufficient data."

"Right, so go with your gut. What do you *feel* we will find there?"

"I'm a man, Gallin. I have trouble feeling. You should know that. But for you, I'll pretend I am French..."

I turned my attention back to the rolling green hills of the golf club and tried to shut down my intellect and just feel. What did I feel as I imagined us approaching the house, opening the door, and stepping inside...?

"Nothing," I said. I turned to look at her. "He won't be there, but there will be no sign of burglary, violence, home invasion. There will be nothing."

She nodded. "Let me ask you something else. If you have a passion for a subject, something you are investigating and developing, where do you do your best work: with a small group of like-minded colleagues, at home alone in your office, or in the mountains?"

I frowned. "That's a good question, Gallin. Study, books and reports et cetera, home in my study, let off steam and regenerate, mountains, but actual productive, creative work, with colleagues at the workplace."

"Right, and we are not talking about some introverted loner. This guy likes the company of his gang, and he has them over to his house a lot by the sounds of it."

"I agree." I nodded. "But what's the point you're making?"

"That the behavior Steiner, Das, and Gizmo alluded to, his repeatedly going AWOL, is anomalous and must have a reason."

I thought about it. "The third party Dr. Gizmo was mad about." She glanced at me to nod, and her mouth was a tight, thin line. "That's good, Gallin. It makes a lot of sense. So what are we saying? Do we think he's eloped?"

She didn't answer. We'd come to the Mountain View inter-change, and she turned onto Route 85. Shortly after that, we came off the highway onto Homestead Road in Cupertino and wound our way out to the semi-countryside setting of Cristo Rey Drive. We found Manzanita Court and pulled up outside a large, rambling clapboard house with a number of gabled roofs and chimneys at odd angles to each other. There was a driveway with a Honda in it and a set of rambling steps that wound through an unkempt yard with a giant oak tree that obscured most of the front of the house. Beyond it, I could just make out a porch and a rocking chair.

I pointed at the Honda. "His car. I memorized the license plate from the report."

"Good boy. That gets you one brownie point."

"If he's inside, I am going to laugh all the way back to DC."

She nodded with little humor in her face, and we climbed out of the car.

We ducked past the huge oak tree and climbed the broad

steps through the lawn, then the narrow, wooden steps to the porch. The porch was about seven feet deep and took up the whole front of the house, maybe some thirty feet. There was a wide, wooden door with a window on either side. While Gallin leaned on the bell and knocked, I strolled to the end of the porch and looked down at the Honda. The only thing that was remarkable about it was that it was at his house. It led to two obvious possible conclusions: either he was at home or he'd been abducted from his home. If the latter was right, it narrowed the time frame from when he was last seen at work until the next morning, when he was due at work. I turned back to Gallin. She was standing with one foot over the threshold, watching me.

"Anything?" I shook my head. "Coming?" I nodded and followed her into the house.

The ground floor was taken up almost entirely by a single open space that included a vast living area and an open plan kitchen. It was minimalist in style, with parquet floors and animal skins strewn here and there. There was a vast TV bolted to the far wall and five big black easy chairs with control panels on the arms angled around a big, rustic coffee table, with the TV as their focal point. There was little else in the room aside from a couple of small bookcases with an eclectic mixture of books including Mickey Spillane, Roger Penrose, Ian Fleming, Yogi Ramacharaka, and John Milton's *Paradise Lost*. I noticed the car fob was on the bookcase by the door.

Rising up the left-hand wall was a pine staircase. Gallin followed me up to a large landing carpeted with a thick rush mat. There was a study containing a desk with no drawers and a computer, and there were five bedrooms— each with a made bed, chairs, chests of drawers, desks, and closets, two bathrooms (one en suite), and little else. We spent five minutes examining them. Gallin checked all the wardrobes and chests of drawers in turn.

"The only one with clothes in it is his," she said, holding the doors to his closet open. "But there's a black pair of jeans, a black

Snoopy sweatshirt, and a pair of black lace panties in the chest of drawers next door."

"You think they might belong to Dr. Das? Or maybe Chet Muse, the Horrible Hagar?"

She didn't react for a moment, examining the contents of the closet.

"You're funny," she said eventually. "No, seriously, you're inappropriate, but funny."

Then she sighed and closed the wardrobe doors. She turned to face me, crossed her arms, and leaned against the wardrobe.

"It is exactly as I said; there is nothing here." I gave a single nod and shoved my hands in my pockets. "The car outside says he is either home or he was abducted from home, but there is no sign of struggle."

"There is no sign of *anything*, Mason. It's like a team of OCD cleaners went over the place."

"Except that Clara Belle Epstein has left her jeans, her sweatshirt, and her panties here. Nobody else left anything, though each of them has a room and a chair."

"They're like a family of nerds."

"Only Clara doesn't want to be a sister. She wants to be more." I sighed and ran my fingers through my hair. "I know this is all significant," I said. "But..." I raised my shoulders and shook my head. Gallin supplied the words.

"It signifies absolutely nothing," she said.

I nodded. "Nothing."

FIVE

IN BANGKOK, it was early morning, noisy and already sultry under a cloudy sky that was breaking apart here and there to show patches of clear blue. The air was dirty with fumes and rich with honking horns and shouting voices.

The woman Billy Squire had known as Apsara was making her way through the crowds on Phaya Thai Road. She looked good in an expensive blue business suit, strappy high-heel shoes, and a string of real pearls around her neck. She had a swing to her hips that said she was sexy, but she had a look on her face that said she also had class.

At the Unicorn, under the raised walkway, she turned left and made her way to the Eastin Grand Phayathai Hotel. She approached the big glass doors, and the doorman, in his top hat and tails, opened the door for her and gave a small bow. She ignored him and crossed the lobby to the elevators. The doors slid open, and she pushed in through the exiting crowd and rode up to the Sky Lounge on the thirty-eighth floor.

There, she passed through the arch and stood by the palms in the giant earthenware pots, scanning the bar. She found him quickly. He was sitting by the huge, arched windows overlooking the city with a tall drink in front of him. He was reading papers and had a brown attaché case beside him. She crossed the room, pulled out the chair, and sat opposite him.

"Hello, Mr. Smith."

He looked up and smiled. It was a dirty smile that failed to hide the meanness behind it. "Oh, hello, Angel," he said. "How's tricks?"

She knew the term and knew it was intended as a putdown. "Boring," she said.

"Name of the game," he said and laughed.

She smiled. "We gonna talk a lot of bullshit or we gonna talk business?"

A waiter in a burgundy waistcoat came up. She glanced at him briefly and said, "Gin tonic, Bombay Sapphire, and Schweppes. Don't give me no Nordic shit!"

"Yes, ma'am."

He bowed and went away. Mr. Smith chuckled. "Same old Angel. Don't hold back. Say what you *really* mean." He laughed.

"Many kinds of angel, Mr. Smith." She said it as she leaned back in her chair. "There are angel of mercy, archangel, angel of justice, angel of vengeance and retribution, and angel of death."

The laugh faded, and his face went hard. "I hope that's not a threat, Angel. Threats will not help your cause."

"Is no threat, Mr. Smith. Is a fact. Now we talk business. You promise me, I do this one job, you gonna give me what I want and take me off the books. Now you got what you want, I want get what I want."

Mr. Smith made a face of mock astonishment. Outside, a hawk circled, thirty-eight stories above the crowds.

"Angel, Angel, what is this? Is this any way to treat a colleague and a friend? First threats, now demands... What has happened to my darling Angel?" He looked around with his arms open, like he was searching. He raised his voice. "Has anybody seen my Angel? Has anybody seen the real Angel? Please bring her back to me!"

She watched him with no expression on her face. When he

was done, he chuckled. "You know it's not that simple, Angel; and besides, that decision is not for me. It comes from Mr. O."

"Then what the fuck I am doin' here?"

"Just chill and relax a bit, will you? Enjoy your drink and let's talk."

He said it gazing over her shoulder. The waiter appeared and set her glass down in front of her, then departed.

"Talk 'bout what?"

"Money?"

She picked up her drink and sipped, then set down her glass carefully, like there was one precise place where it had to be. "You know what I want, Mr. Smith. Mr. O know what I want."

"And you shall have what you want, Angel. Hey, a promise is a promise, and we are not going to let you down. You know that Mr. O really cares about you." He grinned and winked at her. "That's why he has sent you a little bonus."

He reached in his jacket and pulled out a fat envelope, which he slid across the table for her. She picked it up and looked inside, then raised her eyes to study his face.

"Ten thousand dollars, Angel. You're welcome!"

"I don't want money. You know what I want."

"I told you, sweetheart, this is a bonus. You will get what you're asking for—"

"Not asking for. It was part of the deal."

"And you will get it. Like I said, this is just a bonus to say thank you for a wonderful service. And..." He nodded slowly and spread his hands. The gesture was almost apologetic. "Mr. O realizes that you can never go back to the States. After all, the risk of their finding out your involvement is far too high."

The threat was clear, but she didn't rise to the bait. "When you gonna give me what I want?"

"That's not for me to decide, and you know it."

She picked up her glass and stared at the slice of lemon for a long time before she put the glass down again and asked, "OK, Mr. Smith, what I gotta do for him to give me what I want?"

Mr. Smith didn't so much smile as leer. "*Now*, see? Now we are being cooperative. Now you're asking the right questions."

"OK, now I askin' the right questions. You gonna give me an answer?"

He observed her a long moment. Then he wet his lips and gave a sigh.

"There is somebody we need you to take care of."

"'Take care of' mean a lot of things in English."

"True. That's true. But in this case, we mean it in the best sense. Feed, provide loving care, listen to, console." He gave a small shrug. "You know the routine."

"I know the routine."

"We'll give you the usual pay, plus another bonus—"

"I don't want fuckin' usual pay an' bonus. You know what I want. I want what we agree."

"And I can promise you—and Mr. O has instructed me to promise you—this will be the last job we give you. He will person-ally give you what he has agreed to, and you will then be free to pursue your life as you wish."

She was aware of a hollowness in her gut. It was debilitating, but she knew better than to let it show. She reached for her glass and took a long pull. As she set down the glass, she spoke the two words with more bitterness than she had intended. She said, "Ten years."

She studied his face to read his reaction. Instead of under-standing, what she saw there was an alertness: an alertness to see if he had secured what he wanted from her or if he had lost her. Let him worry.

"Ten years I bin fighting to get what I want. Maybe you think, 'She bin ten years, she go on forever, doin' what I tell her, and I not need to give her what she want never.'"

He didn't answer. He just watched her.

"That what you and Mr. O thinkin'?" She didn't let him answer. "That what you thinkin', you makin' a mistake, Mr. Smith. Sometimes you keep doin' the same thing over and again, and it become you life habit. But other time, when you want something so real bad, you keep doin' what you need to do to get what you want so bad, and you don't get it, and you don't get it..." She trailed off, holding his eye. "In the end you go crazy, Mr. Smith, and you do something crazy."

"Crazy?" he said quietly. "Crazy like what?"

"I don't know, Mr. Smith. I not crazy yet. But if I go crazy, you and Mr. O better have somebody shoot me. Because if I no get what I want, life mean nothing to me. I die, I don't care. You know what worry me, Mr. Smith?"

"What?"

"How much I can hurt the people around me." She smiled at him. It was a smile devoid of all feeling. "How much I can hurt friend and colleague who have help me so much in the last ten years, that is what worry me."

She looked down at the glass on the table that might be half full or half empty. He watched her do it. After a moment, she said, "You know how many whore in Thailand?"

"I have no idea, Angel."

"No less than three hundred thousand, maybe as much as three million. You know how many are successful business woman?"

"Tell me."

She held his eye for a long moment. "One. Me. You know why I am one in three million, Mr. Smith?" She waited. He didn't answer. So she went on. "Because I not stupid. Because I see an opportunity and I am take it. Maybe I use it today. Maybe I use it tomorrow. Maybe I use it in five, seven, ten year... I am the opposite of stupid, Mr. Smith. I am smart. Very smart. More smart than you think."

She picked up her glass and drained it, then set it down on the table again.

"I goin' to look after your patient. Two month. When I finish, you and Mr. O give me what I want. You give me bullshit instead of what we agree, I go crazy. I go crazy, my friends and colleagues get hurt bad, maybe die, or worse."

He had developed an ugly look on his face. He drew breath to speak, but she raised a hand to silence him.

"You gonna ask me, am I threaten you?" She held his eye for a count of three. "Yes. Yes, Mr. Smith I threaten you and Mr. O. And you be smart if you take notice because today you done somethin' very stupid. Bad move. You leave me with nothin' to live for, but you got everythin' to lose. Bad position for you. Bad move."

She stood. "You send me instructions where I got to go. Something happen to me, people gonna cry at my funeral. Nobody gonna cry more hard than you and Mr. O. Next move, you better make a good move, Mr. Smith."

She turned and walked out through the arch with a sexy swing of her hips and an expression on her face that said she had class.

SHE DIDN'T GO HOME. She rode the elevator down thirty-eight floors and crossed the lobby out, past the Unicorn and onto the busy, noisy bustle of Phaya Thai Road. She hailed one of the thousand green and yellow taxis and told him to take her to the Wat Prayurawongsawas Worawihan Buddhist temple on the south side of the river, across the Phra Phutthayotfa Bridge. It was just four miles and should have taken no more than ten minutes. But the traffic in Bangkok was always heavy and chaotic. Reckless, she thought, reckless and with no regard for human life. Human life in Thailand, she thought, with a bitterness that had turned sour with the passing years, human life in Thailand was cheap. Like the luxury hotels, the whores, and the drugs on the streets. Human life was cheap, and death was easy.

Quietness enveloped her mind at the thought of death. She was a Buddhist, and she took her religion seriously. Billy had told her Buddhism was not a religion but a philosophy. He had explained to her why, in his cold, Western empirical way. And she had explained to him that the answer to life could not come just from the intellect. It had to come from the heart and the soul too. She smiled at the memory. He had wanted to understand, but he was too intelligent, and his mind would not let him.

Though she was only a few years older than Billy, he reminded her of her son. She smiled again a private smile. He was nothing like her son, in any way. Yet somehow he reminded her of him. Perhaps because Billy had stirred very special feelings in her. The feelings of a mother. She had loved her son with a depth and a passion only a mother could know and understand, and the only person she had ever come close to loving, aside from her son, was Billy. Billy, with his crazy, fascinating ideas about how the universe worked, about what was energy, about the survival of the human soul.

He did not believe in the survival of the human soul.

Death, he said, was death.

They had stopped. She looked and saw the driver watching her in the mirror. Outside was the vast, circular shape of the temple, towering high and conical, gleaming white against the blue sky.

She paid him and climbed out. She didn't pause to gaze at the temple. The outside was for the milling tourists, for the curious and for the vain. They had traveled thousands of miles to see the outside of the temple, to see what it looked like. She had traveled only a couple of miles, but her intention was to go inside.

To go inside.

She found her way through the crowds and the dark echoes of the temple to the Turtle Mountain Garden. There she sat on the faded blue bench opposite the small pagoda on the rock. She closed her eyes and took three slow, deep breaths. Then, quietly, privately, with barely an external sign, she began to weep. She wept as she had wept for the last ten years, with a torn soul that could never be healed, with a heart broken and bruised but still living, with a blackness at the center of her being from which flowed endless emptiness, solitude, and pain.

She wept, quietly and almost invisibly, not because of her son's death, but *from* her son's death. Because that was the place she inhabited. That was where she lived: in the bloody, repulsive, unbearable, intolerable image of his body, so young and beautiful and vibrant, lying in that alley among the trashcans and the spilled garbage, sticky and red with his spilled life. His eyes open but empty; he was empty. There was no soul in him. And it was that emptiness, that dead, empty place where she lived—in the agony of that emptiness.

SIX

SUPERINTENDENT CHAKRI ANCHALI played his flashlight over the corpse. The stench was dense and sickly. The sultry atmosphere was oppressive, and the relentless sawing of the cicadas made an almost claustrophobic prison of the black rainforest around him.

Inspector Boonya pointed at the corpse's leg, which lay severed some six inches from the body. He went to speak but turned suddenly and ran a few steps to vomit violently into the undergrowth. Superintendent Anchali did not react. He knew from personal experience that the dehumanizing of human beings could be nauseating and even traumatic. It seemed to strike at something basic and fundamental inside us. Even seeing a cripple or a person born with a deformity was unsettling and at times disgusting. To see a woman like this, with her limbs severed, with staring eyes and lips pulled back over her teeth, grotesquely grinning in terror, it was more than most men could tolerate.

His thoughts lingered for a moment on the village boys who had found the corpse that morning. The image would haunt them all their lives. He knew that. He knew that from bitter experience. These images became ghosts, and they lingered, watching you from the half-shadows of your mind until your own death and dehumanization.

He turned to his inspector, who had returned and was wiping his mouth on his handkerchief.

"Seal the area. We'll need—" He sighed and shook his head, thinking. "We need a thousand square meters. Mark the location of the other three bodies. We'll bring spotlights and equipment tomorrow. It is too dark to do anything more tonight."

His subordinate nodded. "Yes, sir." Then he started bellowing orders to his men. Superintendent Anchali made his way back along the path, through the undergrowth, toward the village of Hmŭbān pā. When he had sufficient signal, he called headquarters.

"This is going to be 2015 all over again. We were able to find three bodies before the sun went down. It is impossible to say how many more there are. In Songkhla and Perlis there were twenty-four bodies. Here it is even more remote. We need forensic teams and a helicopter—perhaps two—to take the bodies to Bangkok. I want them identified. I want to know who they are and why they have been murdered."

Why they had been murdered. He knew why they had been murdered. They had been slaughtered because they were involved in trafficking opium and heroin across the border into Myanmar, where it would be smuggled into India and then start its long journey either north and west to Europe or east to America.

Superintendent Anchali was very familiar with the people who trafficked opium and heroin. They were psychotic and ruthless, and these men, women, and children whose bodies lay mutilated in this mass grave had been killed because they were suspected of informing, because they had asked for more money, or simply because they had become loose ends who knew too much and needed to be eliminated. The brutality and cruelty of the killing served the simple function of inspiring terror and ensuring that they would always be obeyed.

He paused as he reached the entrance to the small village and looked back along the path. The moon was rising over the trees, casting a faint silver on the leaves as they moved gently in the breeze.

It was a beautiful scene, a beautiful image. It was a beauty which was in stark contrast to the black hatred he had inside him, his loathing for those who trafficked not only the opium and the heroin but also human beings—slaves. Women, girls, and young boys were enslaved to provide sex in infernal clubs right there at home in Thailand, but also in a whole network of evil places across India and Pakistan, Kuwait, the Middle East, Turkey, Poland, and finally into Europe and North America. It was a web of evil and corruption that enveloped the world. And the very men whose task it was to stamp out this evil were feeding on it and becoming rich.

Anxiety twisted his gut. He should inform the Special Operations Unit. Even if human trafficking and narcotics came within his jurisdiction, the fact that the mass grave—for he had no doubt that was what it would prove to be—was in the rainforest near the border with Myanmar meant that the Special Operations Unit should be informed, but he also knew that once they were informed, the case would be removed from his hands and suppressed. Too many people, powerful people in the military, in the police, and in government were making far too much money from the sex and drugs trade for them to leave a case like this in the hands of a known troublemaker like him.

He turned back and moved into the village. At the door to one of the shacks was a woman, old and gnarled like an ancient tree. He glanced at her, and she held his eye.

"Did you know what was out there?" he asked her.

She had the sunken, caved-in look of those who had lost their teeth long ago, and she moved her wrinkled lips and jaw as though chewing her own gums. She nodded once, regarding him with care.

"Why didn't you inform the police?"

She opened her toothless mouth and laughed one shrill laugh.

"And join my body to those in the grave? You think I'm crazy? I told the boys not to go there, and I told them not to report it! Now they will come and kill us too, as a warning to others!"

He approached her. "Who?" he said. "Who will kill you?"

She shook her head at him. "They will kill us all if I talk to you."

He nodded. "Yes, old woman. Exactly. And now it is too late. They will come for you, and they will kill you all when we leave. So your only hope now is for me to protect you. Tell me who they are."

"Pah!" She spat her contempt at his feet. "You can do nothing!"

"Fine!" He said it savagely. "So it is too late! So what have you got to lose?" She stared at him, and he repeated, "*What have you got to lose?*" She continued to stare. He drew close to her and spoke in a hoarse whisper. "*I cannot promise you your safety. I cannot promise you we can protect your village. But I can promise you one thing, old woman. I can promise you revenge!*"

Something happened to her eyes. A hard glint came into them, like two dark diamonds. He saw in them a reflection of his own hatred. They flitted over his face, as though reading what she might find there, then she looked away.

"They come from down there." She pointed south. "Sometimes they pass through, and we do not see them again. Other times we hear guns, and we know they have left bodies. Sometimes we see them pass, and they have men, women, sometimes children, and they are tied with ropes."

"Who are they?"

She shrugged her bony shoulders. "I don't know who they are. I just know they come from down in the valley. I know they drive up the track and leave their cars in the clearing. Then they walk past our village, going toward the border. That is all I know."

He sighed. It was not much. In fact, it was practically nothing. "I will do my best to protect you," he said.

"Pah!" she said again, more quietly, and spat.

As he went to step away, she said, "I heard something, one time, when they came."

He turned back to her. "What did you hear?"

"There was one in a hat. I see him often. He has a red beard and white skin, like a European or an American. He was talking to another one. I was hiding, watching, listening, and he talked about a doctor."

A jolt of adrenaline made him draw closer to her again. "A doctor? Did he mention a name?"

She nodded. "Yes, he called him Dr. Olan."

"Olan? Are you sure?"

She shrugged. "You know the Americans. They talk funny. Wowwowwow, like they have a cat in their mouth!" She cackled. "It sound to me like Dr. Olan or Oclan. Something like that."

"And the man with the hat?"

"Big. Not fat, big. Big red beard, white hat, big boots."

He left her with more promises that he would do everything he could to protect her and the village and made his way toward the house where he was lodging. He could feel the first, hot stirrings of hope in his belly. A useful description of a man, possibly an American, who approached from the south with a white hat and a red beard who was talking about a Dr. Olan or Oclan. It could be a Scandinavian name: Olaf? Olafsen? Or it could be a name the old woman was not able to pronounce. In any case, it was useful. It was not conclusive, it was not probative, but it was useful. It was enough to make a start, and he was under no obligation to pass these particular details to Special Operations. The grave he had to inform them about; the ramblings of an old woman he did not.

Back in his room, after a modest meal of chicken and rice, he spread a map of the area on his bed. He circled with a pen the location of the village and the site of the grave and then began to scrutinize the deep, broad valley that descended toward the river Pai. There was little to see but millions of trees. Satellite imagery would have been useful, but up in the rainforest, in the mountains, there was barely enough signal to make a call or send a text message. It had to be old school.

And as the word crossed his mind, he saw the tiny image almost on the banks of the Pai river. The name caught his attention. Samnaksong Pai Nam Jai. Samnaksong was a temple or a monastery awaiting state approval. Pai Nam Jai was the river of heart water—of generosity. He smiled. Pai was the name of the river, but the word meant 'to go,' even to journey. So it was the journey of generosity, of heart water.

A temple awaiting state approval in such a remote place. To the north, there were large, cultivated areas with several samnaksong, but they were on flatlands, close to farms and schools and villages. This one was deep among inaccessible mountains with no roads. It was hard to imagine that it would have survived.

The germ of a thought took root in his mind, and the more he scanned the valley to the south of this tiny village, the stronger did his suspicion become. For there was nothing to the south save dense rainforest and eventually the River Pai.

The River Pai, which flowed from north to south through the sprawling town of Pai and then turned west to flow through the mountains to the border with Myanmar. He paused in his scrutiny of the map to sip from a stone cup of tea. The land to the north of the town of Pai would be ideal for the cultivation of poppies. And the river would provide a fast and simple method of transportation.

But not all the way to Myanmar. It would make them too vulnerable crossing the border. With dense jungle on either side, it would make them sitting targets. Plus it would not take them anywhere useful, with roads or further forms of transportation. But if they left the river at Samnaksong Pai Nam Jai, a three-day march along simple tracks in the rainforest would bring them to the border town of Loi Tai. There nobody would give them problems, and they would have access to road transport to move their product on, north and east.

The short trek through the rainforest would provide them also with a convenient place to dispose of people who had become an inconvenience. It was surprising how many people could become an inconvenience in that trade. It was not just informers and suspected informers; it was also potential rivals within your own gang and, most frequent of all, the white-slaves. Women abducted and forced into prostitution who refused to conform, who rebelled or collapsed emotionally and were not able to perform their jobs. Sometimes they were given an overdose and left in the street; more often, they were brought out to the forest, to the miles of rainforest wilderness, and shot. And the forest was left to close in and do its job.

The jungles and rainforests, the mountains, the lack of resources, and the high-level corruption in the area had made it almost impossible to hunt and shut down these gangs. But now, here at last was a chance, a single opportunity, and he intended to use it.

SEVEN

"IT SIGNIFIES ABSOLUTELY NOTHING," she said.

I nodded. "Nothing. And yet..." I looked around the room. "It's almost like *Monk*, isn't it?"

"A *monk?*"

"No, *Monk*, the old TV series. Everything has its place. Minimalist and neatly ordered. Even his friends. A place for everything, and everything in its place." I pointed at the five chairs angled at the TV. "I lay you a hundred bucks that each of those chairs is allocated to a particular friend."

"What's your point, Mason?"

I pointed to the small bookcase by the door. "The fob for his car. It's in the wrong place. I don't know where it belongs, but there is no way this guy just drops the keys when he comes in. I'd say he has a leather wallet, or a keychain, and he keeps his keys in his pocket where he will never lose them."

"So the car was driven home by somebody else, who dumped the keys inside the door, in haste, and scrammed."

I found a sandwich bag in the kitchen, dropped the fob in the bag, and slipped it into my pocket.

Outside, we opened the car, and while Gallin had a look, I called the office. After being put through voice recognition,

Lovejoy answered in that voice that sounded like dense hot chocolate liberally laced with expensive brandy.

"What can I do for you, lover boy?"

"Quite a lot, I should imagine."

"You probably shouldn't imagine, sugar."

"You have my location, right?"

"I got you pegged."

"I need this car taken to the lab."

"OK, sweetheart. Leave the keys in the glove compartment. The boys will be there in about half an hour."

I hung up. Gallin was climbing out of the car. She was wearing a latex glove and holding a small, gold cylinder. I frowned.

"What's that?"

She held it up for me to see. "A lipstick. Chanel Rouge Allure, fifty bucks a shot."

I was still frowning. "What's that on your hand?"

"A latex glove, Mason."

"You carry evidence gloves with you?"

"You never know when a latex glove might come in handy."

I nodded, feeling oddly disturbed. "I never thought of it that way."

She eyed me a moment. "Focus. So far nobody has suggested that Bill is gender fluid, right?"

"Right."

"Now we've got black lace panties in the room next to his, and we've got Chanel Rouge Allure at fifty bucks a shot under the front passenger seat of his car."

I gave a small shrug. "Could the lace panties and the lipstick belong to the same woman?"

"Let me ask you a question. Can you imagine Dr. Gizmo in black lace panties?"

"Well, now that you mention it, yes."

"Correct. You know why? Because it's a secret thing only her chosen man is going to get to see, *if* he gets his act together. Now

—" She held up the lipstick and opened it. It was a deep, brilliant, luxurious red. The kind of thing you'd expect to see on the cover of a dime thriller in the fifties.

"Can you imagine her wearing this?"

I winced. "I'm trying, I want to, but no. It's not her."

"So it is not part of Billy's secret, transgender wardrobe because he hasn't got one, it is almost certainly not Dr. Clara Belle Epstein's, so whose is it?"

"The woman Dr. Clara Belle Epstein refused to acknowledge existed." She nodded, and I wagged a finger at her. "I'll tell you something else. That lipstick you are holding, Gallin, is the only trace of her in the—" I hesitated and shrugged. "I was going to say in the house, but it isn't even in the house. It was under the car seat."

"It was in the car by accident, because of a slip-up."

In the end we waited for the lab guys. They showed up twenty minutes later in a tow truck. Two guys swung down. One went to hook up the car. The other approached us with a clipboard. I recognized him as Joe, the head of ODIN's Forensics Department in San Francisco. "They have you driving trucks now?"

"Nero asked nicely, so I thought I'd come along personally and have a look. How's it hanging?"

"Perpendicular. I really need to know who was in that car, Joe. Also"—I handed him the fob and the lipstick—"who handled the fob. The owner of the car is Dr. William Squire. He works for a defense contractor, so his prints and DNA will be in a database somewhere, and they should be on the fob. The million dollar question is who else's prints are on there. They should be the most recent prints on it." As an afterthought, I added, "See what the GPS can tell you, too. Theoretically, this guy goes from home to work and back again. Any significant variation could be of interest."

"You got it."

"Also, who used this lipstick? Is it the same person who used the fob? And for the sake of completeness, is the person who held the lipstick the same person who wore it?"

He smiled. "I'd like to be at *that* party! You're covering your bases. Nero said it was top priority. I'll get right on it. Should have some answers for you by this evening."

Ten minutes later, we watched them drive away with the Honda and made our way back inside and closed the door. We both wanted a final look around. Gallin went upstairs, and I rummaged through his books. It's surprising what people will use as bookmarks sometimes. But on this occasion, there was nothing but printed words.

I put the last book away and stood looking at the room. To say it was minimalist would be an understatement. What you saw at a glance when you came through the door, that's what there was in the room. Added to that, I didn't exactly know what I was looking for.

I heard Gallin's feet on the stairs. She came down holding a pair of black lace panties in her hand. I pointed at them.

"What do you intend to do with those?"

"Ask Dr. Gizmo if she recognizes them. This house has nothing left to tell us. Let's go." As she said it, her eyes strayed to the window, and she shoved the panties into her pocket. "Hello," she said. "Who's this?"

It was a Tesla. It pulled silently into the Honda's recently vacated parking spot, and a tall man climbed out. He had a big head with long, wild hair, big shoulders, and the build and movements of an athlete. We watched him mount the steps to the porch, cross in front of the window, and a moment later, the lock rattled and the door opened.

He stood framed in the doorway, scowling. "I guess you guys are Mulder and Scully from the FBI."

I pulled my badge and showed it to him. "Special Agent Alex Mason. This is Special Agent Aila Gallin. We're from the Federal Bureau of Investigation. Who are you?"

"I'm Dr. Chet Muse. I worked with Billy."

I glanced at Gallin. "Past tense? You're the first person I've come across since we arrived here who's used the past tense. Everybody else insists this is normal. He disappears all the time."

He stepped inside and closed the door. "Not all the time, and never for more than a day or so. Besides, it was something that had started happening recently. We, his friends, were worried about it."

He made his way to the dining table and sat. Gallin pointed at his hand. "You have a key."

"We all have keys."

"All is...?"

"Krishna, Clara, Pete, and me. We used to hang out here with him."

I pulled out a chair and sat. "Used to. Again the past tense. Your colleagues are all taking this view that it's normal, but you're stuck in the past tense. How come?"

"In our line of work, you really don't want the Feds getting involved and drawing attention to you. So they are giving you the brush-off. But I think something has happened to Billy. I think he's been assassinated."

I sagged back in my chair, and Gallin sat.

"Can you substantiate that?"

"No. But I'll tell you what has me worried."

Gallin said, "Shoot."

"Billy's behavior started to change about three months ago. It's hard to be exact because that kind of change usually starts a little before you notice it, right?" We both frowned and nodded. "So maybe three months ago, maybe a bit more, maybe once a week he'd go out in the evening. That's probably normal to you guys. But we'd get here on a Tuesday or a Thursday, and he wasn't here. His car wasn't here, and he wasn't here, and he wouldn't turn up till next morning."

"And how was he when he showed up?"

"Good!" He nodded. "Cool, relaxed, normal, only maybe a little happier than usual. Buoyant, know what I mean?" He twisted his face, like he didn't like the taste of his own thoughts. "I actually checked out his arms to see if he was shooting up drugs or something. But he had no needle marks, and his health was fine. If anything, he was a bit more snappy, funny, cheerful. Like his neurotransmitters were charged up to maximum, right?

"So after he did this a couple of times, I asked him. You know, 'What are you doing? You're not showing up, you're out all night, this is anomalous behavior. What's going on?'" He hunched his shoulders and looked genuinely bewildered. "He said he'd found someone he liked to talk to. I told him he had us. He could talk to us. He said we were too smart. He said the person he was talking to was not so smart, but she listened, and she had wisdom from experience of living in the real world. That's what he said."

I said, "And that worried you."

"Yeah, it worried me a lot. I am not a leftwing liberal intellectual, Agent Mason. I am a patriot, and I believe in what we are doing. If Billy was out in the small hours of the morning talking to some woman whom he described as not smart but with real world wisdom, there was a damn good chance he was being played and giving up defense secrets without even knowing it."

"Did you talk to him about that?"

"Yeah, of course. He said I was being paranoid and I should have more trust in him. So it became a regular thing. Once a week, he just wouldn't show up till the next day. And maybe that day he would not show up at the lab."

Gallin cleared her throat. "You said you thought he'd been assassinated. That is very specific. What makes you think that? Isn't it more likely he was abducted?"

"No. If he was abducted, it would be by Iranians. And if you ask me, that was what they intended to do. But he was assassinated, A"—he held up a large thumb—"as a punishment, B to stop any possible leak, and C"—he held up his index and middle finger—"as a warning to anyone else who might be thinking about chatting with our nation's enemies."

I said, "You think he was assassinated by our own government?"

"No."

"By who then?"

"By the Mossad."

Gallin couldn't help her reaction, though she covered it well. She let out a startled laugh and sat forward. "The Mossad? Assassinate an American citizen on US soil?"

He gave an ironic smile. "You don't know the Mossad, Agent Gallin."

She smiled. "I guess not. You do?"

"I've worked with one of theirs for a few years now."

"You need to explain that, Dr. Muse."

"I do?" He looked surprised. "Dr. Clara Belle Epstein is Mossad, planted here for the very purpose of keeping an eye on Billy. He strayed, and she either killed him or had him killed."

EIGHT

THE ROOM WENT VERY QUIET. I watched Chet as it dawned on him that he had said too much, and Gallin watched the tabletop like she had all her thoughts laid out there.

"You're telling us that what Dr. Squire was working on was of interest to the Israelis?"

His cheeks flushed, and he swallowed hard. "Well, uh, no, not especially. You know, Israel lives with her back against the wall. So they are always interested in defense developments in the USA. We cooperate a lot with Israel. So you know..."

He was talking himself into a corner, and he knew it, but he couldn't see a way out. Gallin pressed him.

"Are you saying, then, that very defense project in the USA has an Israeli scientist planted there who is also a Mossad agent?"

"No, that would be ridiculous."

"I agree. So we're back to square one. Dr. Squire was working on a project which was of extreme interest to Israel. So much so they planted an agent who was also a robot scientist and a genius to boot."

"You know I can't discuss the project. It's classified. Besides, it was a stupid notion on my part. I didn't think it through."

I said, "I don't think there's a lot you don't think through,

Dr. Muse. I just think you were hoping for a different response from us. Aside from being Israeli, what makes you think Dr. Epstein is a member of the Mossad?"

He hesitated a moment, then leaned forward with his big forearms laid flat on the table in front of him.

"From the time she joined the team, she was always working hard at getting close to Billy. She'd use every excuse she could find to be close to him, like physically, working at the same bench, sharing his desk, sitting opposite him at lunch, that kind of shit. But also, she was forever engaging him in conversation about everything and anything, from famine in Africa to climate change, James Joyce and Ulysses, the travesty of the *Lord of the Rings* movies, red wine..." He rolled his hand in the air. "On and on and on. And she's smart, so she knew what she was talking about."

Gallin asked, "How did Dr. Squire respond to these advances?"

"He loved it. He was the most sexually innocent person I ever met. He thought she was brilliant—which she is—and a great conversationalist. So he welcomed her and included her in our group."

"That doesn't make her an Israeli spy, Dr. Muse. It just makes her a highly intelligent woman fascinated by a brilliant man."

He ignored her. "Then, once she was in, she started coming on to him in a more subtle way. She managed to wrangle the bedroom next to his for when she stayed over. None of us ever leaves clothes or toiletries or shit like that here because we are aware—it's an unspoken rule—doing that is encroaching on another person's space. But she starts leaving seductive underwear and stuff. Like, 'Look what you're missing, Tonto!' And then she starts coming around on the days when the gang isn't here. Because she has stuff she needs to discuss with him. Like she can't discuss it at the lab during the day. It has to be here in the small hours."

I raised both hands. "Dr. Muse, I am going to have to stop you. You said you had evidence to substantiate the claim that Dr.

Epstein was an agent for the Mossad. All you have done is lay out all the reasons she irritates you. There is nothing in what you have said that suggests she is an Israeli agent. It is just the behavior of an infatuated woman who is perhaps a little intense."

He grunted, sighed loudly, and spread his hands. "OK, from where you're sitting, that is what it looks like. From where I am sitting, I guarantee you she is Mossad, and she either killed Billy or had him killed."

Gallin cut in suddenly. "Did you ever see her wear makeup? Lipstick, for example?"

He stared at her a moment like she was crazy. "No, strictly jeans and T-shirts kinda gal. No jewelry, no makeup."

I scratched my head. "I'm having trouble squaring something up, Dr. Muse. You just got through telling us that Dr. Squire had started going AWOL till the small hours, now you're telling us that Dr. Epstein was coming on to him and he liked it. Which is it?"

"Both. Because when he started going AWOL, as you put it, she started getting mad. She didn't like it one bit. A couple of times she stormed off and left Krishna, Pete, and me on our own. When he told us all he'd met someone he loved to talk to, like I told you before, she could hardly contain her anger. She gave him a lecture about not talking to strangers outside the group, confidentiality and national security."

"How did he react?" It was Gallin.

"He laughed at her. That made her real mad. It was shortly after that he disappeared."

I looked at Gallin. She didn't look happy. She looked mad, but like she didn't know who to be mad at.

I said, "This is really very helpful, Dr. Muse. Please think very carefully about this. Was there any clue, any indication, any comment he ever made that might suggest who this person was?"

He started to answer three times, and three times he made a face like he really didn't like what he was about to say. Finally he said, "Oh, man... Once," he said, looked me in the eye and nodded. "Once—and you know, it's the kind of comment that is real easy to misinterpret, but once he said he was having some of the best conversations he had ever had, and he didn't care that he had to pay for them." He stared at us, and we stared back at him. "I know," he said, "the first thing that springs to mind—"

Gallin shrugged. "The first thing that springs to my mind is a psychoanalyst."

He blinked and after a moment held out his hand, palm up, like he was introducing her. "That," he said, "is a possibility that had not occurred to me."

I said, "In the small wee hours of the morning? I can only think of one kind of conversationalist you'd pay to see after midnight."

She gave a reluctant nod and turned to Dr. Muse. "Was there any hint or indication where he was meeting this professional conversationalist?"

"No." He shook his head. "He was real close about that." He took a deep breath and let it out as a sigh. "I know you're skeptical about what I said about the Mossad. But I know that Clara works for Mossad, and I know that she suspected a honey trap. I can't tell you what we were working on, and if I did, you'd have to arrest me. But I can tell you it's the kind of thing Israel would be interested in and would not want to fall into the hands of Iran, Russia, or China."

Gallin echoed his sigh and nodded. "We'll certainly keep that in mind, Dr. Muse. Is there anything else you can add to this? Was there anyone else he was close to, anyone else he had regular contact with?"

"No, as far as I am aware, that's it. And I knew him about as well as anyone."

We talked for another fifteen minutes, but nothing new emerged, and eventually he left. When he was gone, Gallin pulled out her phone and made a call. While it rang, she stood and walked across the room toward the five black chairs. She spoke with her back to me.

"It's me... No, nothing. Listen, I'm pretty pissed. Did the institute put a watcher on Dr. Squire?" She waited, listening. Then, "That's not what I am hearing this end. I just got through being told Dr. Clara Belle Epstein works for us and either executed or arranged a hit on Dr. Squire." Another pause. "Please do."

She hung up. When she turned, I asked, "Your dad?"

"He's not my dad when I'm working."

"Well, what did he say?"

"They'll get back to me. Let's go talk to Dr. Pete Chidester. After that, I want a long, cozy chat with Dr. Gizmo."

She opened the door and went outside. I was still sitting at the table. After a moment, I heard her voice from outside.

"Are you coming or what?"

WHEN WE GOT BACK to the ZPE Corporation on Orleans, Dr. Chidester was not there. He had taken a bunch of work home with him but had left word for us to go see him at his house in Vineyards-Avalon, a ten-minute drive along Route 237 and then north five minutes on I-680.

As we left the reception and stepped back out into the California sunshine in the parking lot, I held out my hand.

"Give me the key."

She stopped dead and stared at me. "What, you don't like how I drive now?"

"Give me the keys, Gallin. Or I rent my own car."

"*What?*" She screwed up her face. "That's childish. What's the matter with you?"

"This is the third time I'm going to tell you. There won't be a fourth. Give me the keys."

She tossed me the fob and climbed in the passenger seat. Fifteen minutes later, we pulled up outside one of the more modest houses on Upper Vintners Circle. It probably had only five bedrooms. There was an ample lawn out front and a garage with room for three cars, maybe four. Right then there was a Tesla parked on the drive, outside the garage. I parked across the drive so the Tesla could not reverse out, killed the engine, and climbed out. Gallin followed me along the crazy paving to the porch, and I leaned on the bell.

The door opened, and a woman who might have been from anywhere in the Indo-China area of the Pacific smiled at us without feeling. She was maybe five two, with an apron, wet hands, and eyes like flint.

"I am Special Agent Alex Mason; this is Special Agent Aila Gallin. We are with the FBI, and we would like to speak to Dr. Peter Chidester, please."

"Dr. Chidester expecting you." It could have been an affirmative statement or a question, but she stepped back and gestured us in.

It was a modern house that, for once, was not divided into spaces but into rooms. We were in a hall maybe ten foot square with a hat stand, a coat stand, and an umbrella stand. There was also a small table where you could put your gloves and a mirror where you could check the angle of your hat. If I hadn't known already, I would have guessed this was the house of an English bachelor.

"This way, please."

She led us through a door on the right into a comfortable drawing room with an open fire and lots of bookcases, down a short passage, and knocked on a solid oak door with no iron studs in it. She knocked, waited a beat, and opened the door.

"FBI here, Doctor."

There was a mutter, and she stood back to let us in.

The house had suggested a man of middle age, but I was surprised to see that Dr. Chidester was barely in his mid-twenties. He was on his feet and coming around his large oak desk with a big smile on his face. He had that pleasant, clipped speech of the English upper class, plus the bashful good manners.

"Good of you to come," he was saying as he grabbed Gallin's

hand, like we were doing him a favor. "Agent Gallin, I gather. Aila, not"—he blinked and stammered slightly—"not, not a man's name yet!" He laughed. "And Agent Mason." He grabbed my hand. "How do you do? Dr. Peter Chidester, but please, call me Peter. Can't be doing with all the titles."

We took a couple of chesterfields, and he folded all scrawny six foot four of himself onto a sofa. He was still laughing his bashful laugh.

"Ancestor was Earl of Chichester, but the Cicestrian peasants with their linguistic burr pronounced Chichester Chidester, and so, over time, we became the Lords of Chidester. So the story goes. My father is now Lord Chidester, which just goes to show how silly titles are."

"Your father is Lord Chidester?" It was Gallin. "Titles can be powerful symbols and rallying points."

"You're—" He pointed at her. "You, the accent, somewhat...um..."

"I am English, Peter. But I am working with the FBI."

"Right, good. Super. Excellent. Well, um, I thought I would rather meet you here. I scan the place for bugs routinely, latest generation stuff, as you can imagine, and stuff to tell you I wouldn't want anyone else listening in on. So could I see your badges please?"

We showed him our badges, and he took them over to his desk, where he dialed a number on an old Bakelite telephone with a rotating dial.

"What is life without the odd frivolity?" he asked us as he listened to it ring. "Ah, yes, good afternoon. Is this the Federal Bureau of Investigation?" He looked at us, pointed to the mouthpiece, and mouthed, *F-B-I*.

"Yes, now this is Dr. Peter Chidester, and I have two special agents here with the names Alex Mason and Aila Gallin. Their badge numbers are..." He read out our badge numbers. "I wonder if you could confirm that they are in fact genuine special agents and that they are tasked to investigate a disappearance at the ZPE Corporation?"

We waited silently for a couple of minutes. Then he nodded a few times and said, "Thank you very much. You have been most helpful."

He hung up and gave us his bashful smile.

"Well, unless you have the real Agents Mason and Gallin bound up somewhere and you have had extremely good plastic surgery, I must assume you are who you say you are. May I offer you a drink? Tea? Coffee?"

We told him coffee would be great, and he buzzed the kitchen, then came and sat back down on the sofa and returned our badges.

"Dr. Chidester, Peter, are you always this careful, or—"

"No. It is more a case of what I have to tell you is so sensitive that I am being a tad OCD about it. Clearly I cannot reveal the nature of our work, which is highly confidential, but I can tell you that several governments and organizations would kill without batting an eyelid to get their hands on it."

Gallin said, "You don't share the view that Dr. Squire has gone AWOL for a few days?"

"No. Billy was a bit out there, like a lot of men with high genius, but he was also a very responsible, dedicated scientist, and he absolutely did not indulge in this primadonna nonsense which is being attributed to him. In this kind of work, it is true that we work twenty-four hours a day. Some work we do at Orleans Drive, some we do at home, and some we do in each other's houses. We do not go down to Mexico to do ayahuasca, as some people are suggesting. And we certainly don't just take off and not let anyone know where we are. We don't, and that certainly is not Billy."

"So what do you think has happened to Dr. Squire?"

"I think he's been killed."

NINE

I FROWNED AT HIM. "Based on what, Peter? From what I can see so far, the people who didn't know him are worried that he seems to have disappeared, but half his colleagues say it's normal behavior in him, and now you believe he's been killed. The one thing that is consistent is that nobody seems to have any grounds for what they believe. All we do know is that he seems to have vanished."

He took a deep breath and sighed. "It's not simple, Agent Mason. I'll grant you that. The thing is, Billy confides—or at least used to confide—in me more than the others. Possibly because we are both English, we had a kind of rapport. Whatever the reason, he used to open up with me when we were alone. Anyway, a while back, he told us all he'd met someone he had great conversations with.

"We all thought it was a bit odd, and oddly unprofessional for him. So I tackled him about it in private, and he opened up. He told me she was in fact a prostitute from Thailand. He'd met her online and then gone to meet her downtown. He swore there was no sexual relationship between them, they just talked—"

He stopped and looked past me at the door, which had

opened. He smiled. "Ah, Nanny with the tea. Just put it on the table here, Nanny. I'll do the honors."

She had approached and was standing by my side holding a large tray in front of her laden with tea and coffee, milk and sugar, and a plate of biscuits. I looked up at her, and her face turned crimson. Then she opened her mouth and began to scream a long, steady, high-pitched scream. As she screamed, her left hand went under the tray to support it, and her right went onto the tray to grab a napkin. Chidester was on his feet, shouting, "Nanny, what on Earth...?"

The whole thing only took about three seconds. She let the tray drop. The napkin fell away, and she was holding a semi-automatic in both hands. She was still screaming. The metal tray crashed on the table, shattering the cups, the saucers, and the milk jug. Gallin and I were scrambling to our feet as the Glock exploded once, twice, three times. Peter's chest seemed to implode, while his back erupted in blood and gore.

She was still screaming as he collapsed on the sofa, still wearing an expression of astonishment, though he was too dead to be astonished anymore.

She started backing away toward the open door. He eyes were wild, staring first at Gallin, then at me and back again. She was babbling in what I took to be Thai, thrusting the weapon at us. Gallin was talking, low and calm, "Take it easy, Nanny. Nobody else needs to get hurt. Take it easy..."

But Nanny wasn't listening. He voice was getting shrill again, and she was jabbing the gun around at us like she was trying to make us go away. I took a step toward her, and she turned and ran. I snapped at Gallin, "Call an ambulance!" and I took off after her. I heard the front door open as I scrambled down the corridor. I made the porch in time to see Nanny running across the road toward a guy on a big motorcycle. He was in black leathers with a black helmet, and when she was halfway across the road, he pointed at her with a semi-automatic. There was a flat crack, like a firecracker, and the back of her head erupted, blowing gore and matted hair across the blacktop.

I stopped dead in my tracks and watched the bike accelerate from zero to sixty in a couple of seconds and vanish toward I-680.

Gallin came up beside me. She stared at the corpse a moment, then said, "Peter is dead. The cops are on their way."

I stared at her for a long count of five. She ignored me and looked away. Eventually I said, "Tell me something I don't know, Gallin." She didn't answer. I pressed her. "Why don't you tell me whether Dr. Clara Belle Epstein works for you? Why don't you tell me why you and your dad were late for the meeting with Nero in DC, partner?"

"I can't."

"You can't." I loaded the word with sour irony.

She turned to look at me. "I can't because I don't know whether she works for us or not. I am waiting to find out."

"And when you find out, Gallin, will you tell me?" She didn't answer. I went on, "This is not how partnerships work. I am being real patient, but my patience is running out, and right now there are at least two people dead who did not need to die." I pointed at her. "If the shoe were on the other foot, you would have dumped me by now, and you know it. This is *not* going to work!"

I went back inside and called the office. They put me through voice recognition, and I told Lovelock, "Put me through to the chief, will you?"

A moment later, Nero's voice came through. "Alex."

"Sir, there is a possibility that Dr. Clara Belle Epstein, a member of Dr. Squire's team, is working for the Mossad. The allegation was made by Dr. Chet Muse, who also believes she had Dr. Squire executed." I turned and saw Gallin in the doorway, watching me and listening. "Captain Gallin has checked with her superiors but is unwilling to share their reply. It seems they want her in on the investigation but are not willing to cooperate with us."

He grunted. I went on.

"While I have you on the phone, it seems Dr. Squire was engaged in lengthy conversations—that is not a euphemism—with a Thai prostitute downtown. While we were talking to Dr. Chidester, who gave us that information, his Thai servant came in and shot him. She was shot as she made her escape by a guy who was waiting for her on a motorcycle."

"I see." I might have told him rain was forecast for the afternoon. "I'll have a chat with Gabriel."

"Thank you, sir."

I hung up. Gallin's voice came to me across the room from her dark silhouette in the door.

"There is nothing I know that would have saved his life."

"That's not the point."

She sighed. "We're soldiers, Mason. We work undercover, but that doesn't change the fact that, bottom line, we are soldiers. We do what we're told."

"Like the prison guards in Auschwitz and Belsen?"

"Come on! There is no com—"

"Remember when you were abducted and taken to Iran?"[1] She went quiet. "*Do you remember that?*"

"Yeah, I remember."

"I was ordered to leave it. I was ordered not to go after you. I was told the Mossad would take care of it."

"That's not fair, Mason."

"What is not fair, Gallin, is that we collaborate on a job where people's lives are at stake, and you cut me out and don't share the intelligence you have." I threw my hands in the air. "You tell me the intelligence you have would not have saved his life if you'd shared it. But we don't know, do we? We don't know what situations are going to arise. The next guy to get shot might be me. And maybe *that* time the intelligence you have might have saved my life. We don't know. *That* is the point."

---

1. See *Mason's Law*

"I'm sorry."

"Yeah, me too." I went to the door and handed her the key fob to the Mustang. "We're either partners or we're not." Outside, I could hear the sirens approaching. "If Nero wants me to stay on, I'll rent my own car. If ODIN and Mossad decide to work together, they can send you a different partner. I am not working with you as long as you're holding out on me."

I brushed past her and walked out into the sunshine to wait for the cops.

We spent twenty minutes or so with them, explained it was an active FBI investigation, and had them secure the scene while ODIN, in the guise of the FBI, sent in a forensic team to inspect the site.

When we were done, Gallin jerked her head at the Mustang and said, "A word."

I followed her to the car, and she opened the driver's door. "Ride with me," she said. "We're supposed to check in to the hotel. I don't know what you aim to do, but let's talk about it on the way."

"Can you? Talk about it?"

"Enough, Mason. Get in."

It was a twenty-minute drive down I-680 to the San Jose Hilton. She took it easy, and for the first few minutes, she didn't say anything. When I made a question with my face and showed it to her, she said, "I'm thinking."

A couple of minutes after that, she said, "In answer to your question, if you did to me what I am doing to you, you're right. I'd be mad as hell." She held my eye a moment, then added, "But I would also understand that it was not you doing it. It was your boss, or the organization behind your boss."

I drew breath, but she raised her right hand off the wheel to silence me.

"Let me talk. You gave me a mouthful back at the house. Now you get to listen. You were going to tell me that's a copout. And up to a point, you're right. I know you broke the rules in Iran to come and get me. I'll never forget that. And you *know* that if your life was on the line, I'd break every rule in the book and then some to get you safe."

I sighed and grunted because now she'd said that, I couldn't be mad at her anymore. So, ungraciously, I said, "But?"

She nodded, watching the road. "The USA is an impregnable fortress, Mason. To the south you have Mexico, who can't even invade their own country, let alone the States. To the north you have Canada, whose most aggressive act would be to put you in the naughty corner and have a meaningful exchange with you about your gender."

"Funny."

"Your only serious enemy is more than six thousand miles from DC, literally on the other side of the world. You couldn't get much farther away without going into space."

She fell silent for a moment, and I waited, watching the wind whip her black hair across her face.

"Israel is exactly the opposite. We are the size of New Jersey, and we are surrounded on all sides by various huge countries that constitute a spiritual and religious *nation*—Islam—which wants more than anything else to annihilate us. To wipe us off the map and make us cease to exist. Yes, we have truces with many neighbors now, but only because of our military strength and because we have the United States behind us." She took a deep breath. "So what happens now? The White House makes the biggest arms deal in history with Saudi Arabia, turning, at a stroke, the Saudi army into the most powerful army in the Middle East, after our own. It does an AI deal worth billions with Qatar, a country that refuses even to acknowledge our existence, AI being potentially the most formidable weapon in history. In the same week, it is announced that the US is going to be more lenient with Iran's nuclear program, and the president snubs Israel by negotiating directly with Hamas without informing us to release an American hostage. So do we feel safe? Do we feel our ally has our back?"

She studied me a moment. "Mason, when *you* keep a secret, it is to protect that secret. When *we* keep a secret it is to ensure our very existence and survival as a people. I need you to understand that if the head of the Mossad tells me, 'Do not talk about or discuss X, Y and Z,' I have to take his orders very seriously indeed."

I sighed loudly. "Fine." I spread my hands and nodded. "Fine, I get it. But we cannot cooperate as partners if you are holding out on me—however good your reasons may be."

"And I cannot disobey a direct order from my superiors. So what do I do?"

I studied her face a moment. "That's why you were late for the meeting. That was the call."

She shrugged. "You might well think so. I couldn't possibly comment." She sighed again. "Listen to me, Mason. You know as well as I do that Israel's enemies are America's enemies. Oddly enough, it does not follow that America's friends are Israel's friends. But the bottom line is, we are not going to do anything to hurt the US. We need the US as an ally. So whatever secrets I am required to keep will not benefit Iran, Russia, or China, or any terrorist group out to attack the States. They will simply protect Israel."

We had reached the hotel and pulled up outside. She killed the engine and studied my face. "Don't walk out on me. I need you."

She climbed out and threw the keys to the parking valet. To me, she said, "Come on, let's get a drink. We need to make a plan."

I climbed out of the car and followed her inside, telling myself I was smart and cool and immune to women who tried to wrap me around their little fingers. At least, I always had been.

TEN

WE CHECKED IN, had our luggage sent up to our rooms, and went to the bar for a drink. We ordered a couple of dry martinis, and when the waiter had left and we were secluded at a table behind a palm, she sat dunking her olive for a long moment. As I drew breath to ask her if she was going to be doing that for the rest of the evening, she said, "Don't break up our partnership."

I came back fast. "Ask yourself a question."

She looked up, surprised. "What?"

It wasn't a question about what she should ask herself. It was more a *What the hell are you talking about?*

"Ask yourself," I said, "whether I am breaking up our partnership, or whether you already broke it by not trusting me."

"That's below the belt, Mason."

"Yeah, maybe so. But ask yourself that question anyhow."

"OK, I'll ask myself. Now will you shut up a moment and listen?"

"To what?"

"Dr. Peter Chidester just got murdered by his Thai maid. Now I propose to you we need to consider two things. One, what was the purpose of killing him? And two, what was the *style* of his killing?"

"The *style*?"

"Yes, exactly, the style. Let's take them in turn. First, the purpose. Now I think it is safe to say he was killed because he was talking to us—"

"They all talked to us. Only he was killed."

"Exactly. Try not to interrupt. The difference was that Peter was giving us information the others were not. And that was because Peter knew Dr. Squire better than the others and had information the others did not possess."

"The prostitute he was talking to."

"Right. Now let's just set that on one side for a moment and look at the style of the killing."

"Bizarre?"

She raised her shoulders a fraction. "Yeah, but maybe that wasn't planned. I got the impression, looking at Nanny's face, that she didn't want to do it, and the screaming was part of psyching herself up to do the deed. What I was most interested in was the fact that the execution was carried out right there in front of two FBI agents. There was absolutely no attempt to hide it."

"Huh..."

"Now, Mason, contrast that with what happened to Squire. It's pretty stark. Almost like the two were carried out by two different people."

"Except," I put in, "that they are connected by two links— a Thai woman and the motive for Peter's execution."

"Right." She sipped her drink, and as she set down the glass, she said, "What is different is the motivation behind the execution. They didn't give a damn if the killing was right out in the open, because the killer was herself going to be killed. The trail ended with her. But with Squire, we don't even have a body. Practically every trace of what happened to him has been erased. And that raises the next question. What would make a person want to erase every trace of that event? Why not just gun him down, the way they killed Peter?"

"Because they didn't kill him. They abducted him."

"Maybe. Probably." She picked the olive out of her drink and put it in her mouth. "We really need to talk to his whore."

"We should get the results of the prints pretty soon. The DNA will take longer. But now let me ask you a question."

"Shoot."

"What about Dr. Clara Belle Epstein? Is she with Mossad?"

She held my eye a moment. "I don't know. Neither does Gabriel. He told me he was going to make inquiries and get back to me." She saw the skepticism on my face and sighed. "I might bullshit you, Mason, but I wouldn't lie to you."

I nodded once. "Now I just have to decide whether that is bullshit or a lie." I softened it with a smile and added, "But we need to resolve this, Gallin. If we don't, it is going to become a problem."

We talked some more without reaching any kind of conclusion. Outside, through the window, late afternoon was turning to dusk when my phone rang.

"Alex, Joe from the lab. I got something for you. I'm going to email it to you, but I thought you'd like the gist of it right away."

"You're not wrong. What've you got?"

"The prints on the lipstick are also on the front passenger door handle and on the seatbelt. They are *not* on the fob. The prints on the fob belong to a man. I'll come back to that. The prints on the lipstick belong to a woman."

"There was a time that would have been obvious."

There was a brief silence during which I remembered I was in the San Francisco Bay area. Joe said, "Happily, we are in a more enlightened age now."

"Right."

"They belong to one Emon Chaiya, a Thai national. She came here as a refugee about five years ago claiming the Thai police wanted to kill her because of family involvement in the narcotics trade. She was arrested a couple of times out east, in New York and Philly, for prostitution, but the charges didn't stick, and she moved out west, first to Nevada, then to San Francisco, then San Jose about a year ago."

"Have we got an address where she lives or works?"

"Her last place of employment was an escort agency called the Phû Hying Lew Escort Agency, run out of a private club on West Santa Clara Street. Her home address seems to be an apartment on the same street, above a bagel shop. I'll send you the addresses by Whatsapp."

"Thanks, Joe. That's really helpful."

I hung up. Gallin jerked her chin at me in a question. I said, "We have a light supper, then we go and visit Emon Chaiya, a Thai prostitute, at her apartment on Santa Clara. If she's not home, we go and visit a clip joint on the same street."

She fluttered her eyelashes at me. "I love it when you're masterful."

I wagged a finger at her. "Never say I didn't know how to show you a good time."

"You're the best, Mason. But out here, I think they are called sex workers."

"Even though it's illegal."

"But it's illegal with dignity, Mason. You don't get it. It's all about dignity. The dignity of crime."

"I think I need another martini before dinner."

WE HAD A LIGHT SUPPER, and at eight-thirty p.m., we took a short drive up South Almaden Boulevard to Santa Clara and turned right. A couple of hundred yards on, we passed a low, unassuming building that had a neon script over the door that, if you weren't looking for it, you'd never notice. It said, *Phû Hying Lew* in a red scrawl that occasionally flickered like it was dying. I continued on down the road while Gallin pulled out her phone and started typing. Pretty soon I saw the bagel shop on my right and pulled in. I killed the engine, and Gallin said, "Bad girl."

"That's no way to talk to your phone. It does its best."

She gave me that blank look and said, "P̄hû H̄ying Lew, the name of the club, in Thai it means *bad girl*. The club is called Bad Girl."

"Thailand. We keep coming back to Thailand."

"And bad girls."

"Let's go up and see what P̄hû H̄ying Lew Emon Chaiya has to say for herself."

I climbed out, but Gallin sat there with pinched lips. I made a face that asked her what she was doing, and she sighed and got out, slamming the door.

"She won't be there, Mason. You know she won't."

"You're probably right. But if she's not there, maybe something she left behind will be. Like her lipstick."

She grunted. "Alex Longshot. OK, let's go have a look. But the place will be antiseptically clean. You know it."

"Like Billy's car?" I asked as we trotted across the road.

The street door was next to the bagel shop. It was open, and we pushed in and climbed the narrow steps to a narrow, carpeted landing and a single door. Gallin went ahead because her lock-picking skills were better than mine. My technique was to ram in the screwdriver on my Swiss Army knife and turn. She seemed to whisper to it, coaxed it a little with a couple of pins, and it let us in of its own accord.

The door swung open onto a dark, silent place. On the left was a door open on to an ample living room. It was gloomy because the drapes were drawn across the large windows, but bright shafts split the gloom here and there, highlighting particles of drifting dust.

She turned to me with the faint light touching the planes of her face. "You want to take the living room? I'll take the bedroom." She pointed to her right, where a door opened onto darkness. I nodded.

The living room reminded me of Billy Squire's living room. The most remarkable thing about it was that there was absolutely nothing remarkable about it. There was a suede, three-seater sofa and two large, overstuffed calico armchairs, all positioned around a large, heavy, ethnic coffee table. There was a large TV against the wall and a dresser behind one of the armchairs that almost reached the ceiling. It had glass paneled doors flanking shelves, and the lower half had long drawers. From the smell and the stains, you could tell it had once contained glasses and bottles. Now it contained nothing but air and dust. Forensics might find something here, but it would take that: an expert with a microscope.

The kitchen told the same story with a strong smell of bleach thrown in. Whoever had left this place had not wanted to leave a forwarding address.

I found Gallin in the bedroom. She had the mattress up against the wall and was checking the underside of all the drawers.

"You were the one who said we weren't going to find anything, remember?"

She grunted and muttered something about her dad and for the sake of completeness.

I checked the en suite bathroom and found the same kind of nothing we had found everywhere else. I leaned on the doorjamb and watched Gallin. She was kneeling inside the wardrobe.

"It's not just that she, or they, have obliterated every trace of her habitation here—"

She leaned out of the wardrobe and squinted at me. "Habitation here?"

"Yeah. Even when she inhabited the place, she was hardly ever here. You could not say that she *lived* here in any meaningful sense."

"I agree."

"This is where she slept and had breakfast. That's about it."

"I agree."

"We are wasting our time here."

She nodded, raised her eyebrows, and spread her hands all at the same time. It was a very Mediterranean gesture. "I am not going to say that I hate to say I told you so. I enjoy saying I told you so. So I told you so."

"Yup. But now we know that it's a waste of time, whereas before we would have been wondering, what if she had pasted a travel brochure under her underwear drawer with a hotel in Thailand circled in red ink and the legend, 'I am going here'? So you see, I have given us certainty and clarity."

"Right. So as you have given me that, big guy, in gratitude, let *me* take *you* to a brothel."

"If you feel you need to do that, Gallin, don't let me stand in the way of your free self-expression."

"Jerk."

I followed her out and down to the car.

It was a two-minute drive down the road, going back the way we'd come. We pulled into the parking lot in back of the building and climbed out of the Mustang. The doors slammed and echoed like two shots in the darkness. There was an iron staircase that climbed to a dark door. A little to the left, there was a window with the drapes closed, but a little light escaped through the folds. There was silence but for the muffled rhythmic sigh of the traffic on Santa Clara.

We made our way around to the front of the building. It had a shabby green door with peeling paint revealing a pale, orange undercoat. There were a couple of windows with wrought iron bars over them. The drapes were drawn across on the inside, with only razor thin strips of light showing. Above the door, stretching across the front of the building, was a neon sign in fluorescent tubing reminiscent of the fifties, when smoking was good for you and girls wore flared skirts and really short socks. It read, *Phû Hying Lew Club*, and there were two glowing images of Oriental women, one of which winked every few seconds and reminded me of the movie *Blade Runner*.

Gallin leaned on the bell and hammered with her knuckles. After a minute, maybe more, the door opened a couple of inches, and a face peered out over the top of a chain. Contrary to the stereotype—or the archetype—the face was not inscrutable. I could scrute it very easily. It had had enough of life, hated us on principle, and wanted us to go away.

"Who you?" it said. "What you want? You go away. Private club!"

I was about to tell the scrutable face that we were the FBI and wanted to talk to the manager, but Gallin got in ahead of me and said, "How can we join? This place was recommended by a friend, and we are just crazy to join. We don't care how much it costs. We just really want to join. Please?"

The eyes became doubly narrow. "What friend? Who friend? Recommend who? Who name?"

Gallin put her finger to her lips like she was really alarmed. "Shshsh," she said. "Inside! I'll tell you inside. He asked us to be *very* discreet. Please? I am telling you, price is *not* an issue."

The door closed. We glanced at each other. A moment later, the door opened, and the Scrutable One stood back and beckoned us in. It was hard to tell what gender, if any, the Scrutable One had. He, she, or it closed the door as we entered the foyer and scowled at us.

"Who recommend? Who name? Who you are?"

I smiled at him or her or it. "Do you know Emon Chaiya?"

The scowl deepened. "Apsara!"

"Emon Chaiya?"

"Apsara!"

We clearly weren't getting anywhere, so I went out on a limb. "Dr. Peter Chidester. He told us to ask for—"

Gallin cut across me and said, "Apsara. He told us to ask for Apsara. Is she here? He said she was really wonderful."

The Scrutable One stared at us for five long seconds, then said, "You wait here. I go find Apsara. I find Apsara good for you. Yeah."

We sat on some crimson fake Rococo chairs, and the Scrutable One pushed through a crimson padded door and vanished. Gallin and I stared at each other in silence.

ELEVEN

WE SAT in silence for several long moments. I studied Gallin's face and spread my hands a little.

"Apsara? You speak Thai? Maybe Apsara means, 'get outta here,' or 'I don't understand what you're saying,' or 'speak up, I'm deaf.'"

"You had a better plan?"

"No..."

"You were going to tell her Dr. Chidester said we should ask for a name that was getting a knee-jerk reaction." I couldn't think of a wiseass reply, so she plowed on. "Emon Chaiya, Apsara, Emon Chaiya, Apsara, Emon Chaiya, Apsara..."

"I get it."

"You know what I think?"

"Most of the time, yeah."

"I think it's like Zena, or Cheri, Coco, or Lulu. Emon Chaiya is what figures on her birth certificate. Apsara could be her working name. You know what it means? It's a celestial being in Hindu and Buddhist culture, a spirit of the clouds or water, seductive, irresistible."

"Seriously?"

She nodded. "The Buddhist temples of Southeast Asia are

covered in them. You know those Thai dancers with the disjointed necks? They represent Apsaras."

"You knew that? Son of a gun."

"Getting old, Mason. Slipping. Falling behind. Not keeping up. You'll be in the home for retired wiseasses soon. I'll come visit you on the first Sunday of every month and feed you gruel. As long as you don't drool. You can't drool the gruel. If you start drooling gruel, you're on your own."

The red door opened, and the Scrutable One came in, followed by an exquisite young woman who, though not naked, could not really be said to be dressed either.

"Apsara. Nice for you. Good, good. You take to Room Five. She make you happy."

I studied Apsara's face a moment and smiled at her. "You speak English, Apsara?" She returned the smile and gave a little bow. I turned to the Scrutable One. "Does she speak English?"

"You want yack-yack or you want gin gan? You got two nice woman!" She pointed at Gallin and the frail Apsara. "Two good woman! Why you want yack-yack? Gin gan! Gin gan!" She made a motion like she was riding a galloping horse and laughed. "Gin gan! Gin gan!"

Gallin stood and smiled. "Hey," she said. "The language of love is universal. Let's go do a bit of gin-gan yack-yack."

The Scrutable One pointed down the corridor. "Room Five. You pay now. No pay no gin-gan! No yack-yack!"

Gallin shrugged at me. "You pay, big guy. This could be the high point of your entire life. See you in Room Five. We'll start without you on the gin-gan yack-yack."

Ten minutes and three hundred bucks later, I joined them in Room Five. It followed the same theme of the rest of the place: Ming Dynasty Rococo with lots of crimson and gold tassels. The bed was four-poster, and Apsara was sitting on it watching Gallin as she scrutinized the walls and the ceiling, looking for concealed cameras. It had to be the first time government agents searched for hidden cameras so they wouldn't film what they *didn't* do in a brothel.

"We're clean," she said.

I pulled up a chair and sat opposite Apsara, looking into her eyes. "Do you speak English?"

She smiled a really pretty smile, nodded, and pointed to the bed next to her. I turned to Gallin. "You knew about Apsaras. Do you speak Thai?"

She sighed. "I visited Southeast Asia in my gap year."

"Your what?"

"It's a thing we do. You don't do it. Go and travel, see the world before they start shaping your mind at university. So I went to Southeast Asia. I was in Thailand for three months. I remember practically nothing."

Apsara had been watching us like she was watching a tennis match. Now she looked at me, waiting for my reply, but Gallin said what sounded like "*Khun phud phas'a xangkvs' di him?*"

The girl giggled and said, "*Lekh thi.*"

"She doesn't speak English."

"No kidding."

The girl said something long and cute, patting the bed beside her. She made it seem like a good idea. Gallin shook her head, still smiling. "*Khun rucak Billy him?*" The smile faded from the girl's face, and she shook her head. Gallin pressed her, "*Khun rucak Emon Chaiya?*" She added gestures like hugging and linking fingers to suggest friendship and closeness. The girl dropped her gaze to the floor and shook her head.

"You want to tell me what's going on?"

"'Do you know' is about all I remember in Thai because, from what I remember, they don't say, 'Do you speak English?' They say, 'Do you know English?'"

"So you asked her, does she know English, Billy, and Emon Chaiya?"

When I said the name, the girl looked up at me. She looked scared, but she also looked sad. I repeated the name, giving it the inflection of a question, "Emon Chaiya?" and nodded. She gave a tiny nod back.

I pressed her gently, "Emon Chaiya, Apsara?" and I pointed to her. She nodded again and held my eye. I fancied we had a telepathic moment, and I told Gallin, "Emon Chaiya was the kind of enchantress Apsara, and now this kid has taken over."

I hunkered down in front of her, took out my cell, and searched for 'where in Thai.' It told me it was *Thīhịn*. I showed it to her and said, "Where?" I made elaborate question gestures. "*Thīhịn* Emon Chaiya?"

She smacked her hands together like she was beating dust off them, then made her hand rise gracefully into the air. "*Kherǔxng bin*," she said, and stuck out her arms like she was gliding, making a fair imitation of the sound of jet engines.

I found a world map on my cell and asked her again, "Where? *Thīhịn?*"

She stared at my cell a moment, then put her finger on Bangkok and said, "*Bân*."

I looked at Gallin. She said, "Home."

The door opened behind me, and the Scrutable One came in with two guys the size of large refrigerators. One had long black hair tied in a ponytail and a large hooked nose. He had a chest like a beer barrel and oddly slim legs. The other one was your classic Viking turned Hells Angel. The Scrutable One was screaming.

"*You no come yack-yack! This not yack-yack shop! You come here do gin gan! Gin gan! This gin-gan shop! You go! You go get out! Go get out! Go!*"

We both got to our feet, and as though by telepathic accord, we both reached for our fake IDs.

"I'm Special Agent Alex Mason. This is Special Agent Aila Gallin. We need to talk to the manager."

The Viking sneered. "Yeah, and I'm Special Agent Trump, specializing in taking out the trash. Now how's about you walk out of here while you can still use your legs?"

I stepped close to him, so we were just inches away from each other. "You are a very stupid man, and you are going to cause your boss a lot of trouble, asshole."

His cheeks colored under his wispy beard. He telegraphed the right hook about a week in advance. So I turned my left foot in, bent my knee, and drove a devastating left hook into his liver. A powerful blow to the liver is one of the most cripplingly painfully blows you can receive. He gaped in astonishment. His pupils turned to pinpricks, and he crumpled to the floor, whimpering, curled up in the fetal position.

The big Indian guy suddenly had a knife the size of a machete in his hand, and he was scowling as he reached for Gallin's head with his left hand, pulling back the knife with his right, ready for the deep plunge.

My piece was in my hand, but I was too late. Gallin had spun and smashed her heel into his left knee. I heard the crack, and I heard his breath wheeze in his throat. She had him, but she wasn't compromising. What happened next happened too fast to see it. She took a wide step to her left, rammed her knuckles savagely into his arm just below the shoulder, so he was numb and wouldn't resist. Then her left arm was around his neck in a lock, and with the right, she drove the long blade he was still holding deep into his belly. It all took less than two seconds.

The Scrutable One ran from the room, screaming for the police. Gallin said, "You got anything else you want to ask? I don't think we want to be here. We have what we came for. If the cops show up, it gets complicated. You good?"

I thought about finding the Scrutable One, or the management, and asking them some questions, but I decided the chances of their knowing anything useful were outweighed by the complications attached to explaining ourselves to the cops. I nodded.

"I'm good."

"Let's go, then." To Apsara, she said, "Go to Nevada. It's legal there. Girl like you can make a lot of money, and you don't need to put up with assholes like these guys. Nevada, understand?"

We left her sitting on the bed, pale and weeping.

Outside, in the parking lot, while Gallin got behind the wheel, I called the office. Nero answered with his mouth full.

"Alex."

I outlined the situation for him, then said, "It might be an idea to get local law enforcement to stand down and for our guys to move in. Have the management interrogated and see who owns the club."

"You say that as though you plan to be somewhere else."

"Yeah." I glanced at Gallin. "I was thinking Gallin and I should take a trip to Bangkok, sir. We haven't got enough data at present to extrapolate hard facts, but subjectively, based on the raw data we have, it is possible to postulate a working hypothesis that there is a close connection between Emon Chaiya, AKA Apsara, and Dr. William Squire."

"Are you being facetious, Alex? I can't tell. However, I agree. Very well put. Make arrangements for Bangkok. Send me an interim report before you leave, and I shall acquaint you with what the team finds at the bordello."

I hung up. Gallin was laughing. She fired up the engine, shaking her head and said, "You're such an asshole."

"Why? What did I do?"

"Postulate a working hypothesis..."

"You want to book the flights and the hotel? I have to write Nero a report. But we have a problem, Gallin. Before we fly anywhere or take another step, I want to know what gives with Dr. Gizmo."

The laughter died on her face as we turned onto Almaden Boulevard. "I told you I don't know."

"Then we have to find out."

"How do you propose we do that? I've asked for a report. What more can I do?"

"We can talk to her, bluff. She doesn't know you're Mossad—"

"We don't know that." She had a point. I grunted, and she

went on, "If you ask me to push this, you put me in an impossible position, Mason."

I sighed. "I know, but if she killed Dr. Squire…"

"She didn't. Why would she? It makes no sense."

"If his work posed a threat—"

"Where's the body?" She cut me dead. I stared at her. She went on. "Let me ask you this, Mason. What is easier to hide, a living person or a dead body?"

"OK, a living person is easier to hide."

"So if Squire has dreamed up some super weapon that threatens Israel, why kill him and hide the body, when you can simply abduct him and use his expertise? If she is Mossad, she did not kill him. Plus, they would not have put me on this team with you if they already had someone here. Especially if she was briefed to eliminate him."

I nodded, watching the night slide by.

"Let it go," she said. "I'll tell you what they tell me—and I've got your back, Mason. I am not going to betray you. Relax, will you?"

As she said it, her cell began to ring.

"Yeah, Gallin. Who is this?"

She glanced at me with a small frown as she listened. "Dr. Epstein? It's good to hear from you. I thought you didn't pick up my card."

As she listened, she slowed and pulled up outside the center for the performing arts and stopped. She said, "Where are you now?" She listened, then, "That's about five minutes away on Alameda? OK, we'll be there in five minutes."

She hung up and frowned at me. "Speak of the devil. Dr. Gizmo wants to talk. She apologized for her attitude earlier today and said it's a lot more complicated than it seems."

"You think head office has told her to cooperate?"

Her phone rang again. She looked at the screen and said, "We're about to find out. Hi, Gabriel. You have news for me?"

Her father was also her boss. When she was working, she

called him Gabriel. When she wasn't, she called him Dad. She was saying, "She just called. She wants to talk. She says it's complicated. Is she with the Academy?"

She studied my face while she listened, then said, "OK. Listen, while I have you. I'm going to have to share with ODIN. I know what Head Office said, but it is going to hamper the investigation if we can't share. Also, Mason is pissed, and I don't blame him. We are going to get a lot of hassle and recrimination from ODIN and the Pentagon. We need—*I* need—to be flexible."

She winked at me while she listened to his reply. "OK, I hear you. Thailand in the morning. I'll send you a report from there."

She hung up, scratched her forehead while she looked at her phone, and pursed her lips.

"She's not a katsa[1]. We have no file on her. She is just a very talented robotics engineer with a PhD in robotics and another in particle physics. But she is not employed by the Mossad."

I raised my shoulders a couple of inches. "Good. So what did Dad say about sharing?"

She spun the wheel and eased into the traffic. "When you call him Dad like that, it makes me feel like we are married. It's weird, but it's kind of nice."

"Cut it out. What did he say?"

"I should use my professional discretion, and he'd have my back if Head Office gets difficult."

"That's nice," I said. "The only problem is that you have no professional discretion."

"But you know we have no secrets, darling. My heart and soul are naked for you."

"One day..."

"One day what? You'll realize what you're missing? She's on Morse and Freemont."

Five minutes later, we pulled up outside the house. It was set back from the road beyond a broad expanse of lawn with several

---

1. Mossad case officer

mature trees. It was on two floors and had a bright red door beyond a bizarre Ionic pediment supported on two fat, round pillars that reminded me of baobab trees from Africa.

Gallin killed the engine, and we climbed out and made our way down the winding concrete path that crossed the lawn. I noticed the house was dark, and no light filtered through the drapes on the living room window. The street lamps cast a dim glow, but the few trees and the house itself cast deep shadows.

I saw the tongue of flame in a timeless fraction of a second. Everything was held in a stillness that was more than motionless. Sick dread drained through my body. I heard Gallin say, "Oh!" Then her left hand was gripping my arm, and she was sinking to her knees. I bent to take her in my arms and heard a spitting splintering from the tree behind me. I gripped Gallin with one arm and reached for my piece with the other. I fired three times into the shadows where I had seen the flames, then dragged Gallin back toward the car as I heard running feet retreating into the dark.

I found the wound while I dialed for an ambulance. It was just above her left breast. It was oozing, not gushing. Her eyes found mine while I spoke into the phone. She said, "Is this how it ends?"

"No! The ambulance is on its—"

"So much..."

"What? Don't talk. It missed your heart."

She smiled. "My heart. So much we didn't say."

She took my hand and squeezed.

And closed her eyes.

TWELVE

THE CALL CAME at five in the morning. Angel was awake, sitting on her balcony looking down at the dirty, smoky town in the blackest hour before dawn. The town reminded her of herself. It was a whore making lots of money, but it had lost its soul, it had lost its way, it was searching for love, for something it had lost long ago. It searched for love but found only bitter cynicism.

She picked up the phone and pressed the green button. A man's voice said, "Are you Angel?"

"Yes."

"What kind of Angel?

"Angel of mercy."

"Rong Mueang Road, eight o'clock this morning. On the corner with Railway Station. You wait. A car will come for you."

The line went dead.

She collected her basic items, showered and dressed, and left the hotel without settling her bill. When they went to charge her American Express, they'd find it no longer existed. She took a taxi to the railway station and got there by seven-forty-five. Then she walked briskly to the corner of Rong Mueang, where she lit a cigarette and waited.

She didn't wait long. After ten minutes, a dark Audi saloon

pulled up, and the back door opened. She climbed in and slammed it closed, and the car took off. There were two men in the front and one sitting beside her. She didn't know him, but he regarded her with insolence, and she knew that at some point she would make him pay. Respect, she had come to realize over the years, was one of the three cornerstones of power. The other two were intelligence and violence. Violence used with intelligence brought you respect.

The driver had a beard and a military shirt and a face like a slab of concrete. The guy in the passenger seat was mostly hidden, but he had that similar ex-military air. She turned to the man in the suit.

"Where we going?"

"Nakhon Rachasima."

"Why? What is there?"

"You ask too many questions, woman. Mr. Smith told me, 'Take the whore to Nakhon Rachasima.' That is why. What is there you will find out when we get there."

It was supposed to be a four-hour drive along Route 304. It was a tedious trip through flat, unremarkable farmland dotted here and there with shabby, tumbledown villages that drifted by as though in another world.

But after three hours or so, they came quite suddenly to the fringes of the Khao Yai National Park, a patch of rainforest that covered over one thousand two hundred square miles. It lay side by side with the Thap Lan National Park, an even bigger expanse of rainforest, about twice the size. Route 304 ran between them for three or four miles before crossing another stretch of farmland and then plunging deep into the Thap Lan forest. Here the woodland was more dense and the trees taller and more abundant. She watched them slide past and longed to be among them, deep in their gentle shade. She smiled a private smile. Billy would have understood. Billy understood her as nobody ever had. But now he was dead.

She wondered about Mr. O's new patient. He'd called him a

patient, but he was not. He was just another person Mr. O would use and exploit. He would not be like Billy, but she would have to be sweet to him and make him feel good.

They began to slow, and the car moved into an inside lane to cross over the highway. There were a large number of tents set up, selling everything from fruit and vegetables to potted plants and dresses. In their midst, a broad dirt track led down among the trees. The driver nosed his way down the track, and Angel turned to scowl at the man in the suit.

"What this? This not Nakhon Rachasima."

"Take it easy, whore. This is where Mr. Smith said to take you. It's on the way to Nakhon Rachasima. You don't wanna go? That's fine. You can get out and start walking back to Bangkok. Is that what you wanna do?" He turned to the driver. "Hey, Frank, stop the car. The whore wants to walk back to Bangkok."

She turned away and stared out of the window and the trees as they moved by and the car crawled and occasionally bumped and lurched down the track. The light changed from bright sun to dappled green. After five minutes, they came to a large iron gate in a brick wall. They stopped, and the gate slowly swung open. From there on, the road was blacktop and wound past a well-tended, circular lawn with a fountain in the middle to a three-story rectangular building made of concrete and blue glass.

They pulled up outside the double glass doors. The three men got out, but she remained seated and watched Mr. Smith push out through the doors. The driver opened the door for her, and she climbed out of the car. The three men closed in, and Mr. Smith approached her with a big smile.

"Angel, it is always such a pleasure to see you. Mr. O has asked me to tell you how grateful he is and that he looks forward to meeting you in the very near future. I hope the journey was not too tedious."

She held his eye a moment, processing what he had said.

"Not good journey," she said, then turned her back on Smith

and looked into the suit's eyes. "This piece of shit call me a whore three times."

Nobody was expecting it. They were all too surprised by what she had said. Her right hand flashed out, and her long, crimson nails dug deep into the flesh of his cheek. She raked across and left deep gashes from his ear to his mouth. He cried out and backed off as the blood welled and oozed down his face.

"I not a whore, piece of shit!"

Rage turned his face crimson, and he went to lunge forward. Smith stepped forward, his hand held out, and the driver and his mate closed in. Angel sneered at the man in the suit. "You don't like it? Do something about it, piece of shit."

She turned her back on him and addressed Mr. Smith, who was struggling to hide a smile.

"You take me to patient."

"Mr. Smith!" It was the suit behind her. "She can't treat me like this!"

Smith released the smile. "Wrong. She can. You can't treat *her* like that. Next time be more respectful to the ladies. Get those cuts cleaned and get out of here." He put his arm around Angel and guided her toward the entrance. "Angel, my dear, come inside and have a drink. You must be hungry and thirsty after that long drive."

They crossed a bright, airy lobby to a bank of three elevators. He pressed the button to the third floor, but she noticed there were two more buttons to two basements, both of which required a key to get to.

"Who my patient?"

The elevator stopped, and he led her down a short corridor with a marble floor and white walls to a large corner office. "You'll meet him soon," he said.

He opened the door for her, and she stepped inside. There was a big, Castilian desk with a huge leather chair. There were floor-to-ceiling bookcases against two of the walls and an old Castilian credenza against a third, with a large silver tray of drinks.

In the center of the floor, there was a round coffee table sitting on a vast cowhide with four large, calico armchairs positioned around it.

He gestured at the chairs and said, "A drink before lunch. What will you have?"

"Gin and tonic. Bombay and Schweppes. You know."

She sat, and he spoke with his back to her. "The man we want you to care for, Angel, you should be flattered. He is a great man. He is of huge importance to Mr. O. I cannot stress enough how important it is for us that he is kept happy and well."

She watched him turn around, and the look in her eyes made him stop and hesitate before approaching and placing her drink before her. He sat and sipped his own.

She said, "That important?"

He sighed and smiled. "Yes, Angel, that important. Mr. O already has what you want so badly. He has it, and he will bring it to you personally, but first we need—*need*—you to attend to this man. He needs you, we need you, and you will be paid. We will give you what you want, and we will set you up for life so you never have to worry again."

"You know what going to happen if you betray me. If you try screw me or kill me."

"We are well aware of everything you can do, Angel. We want to see you as one of us, as a friend, as part of the family."

She smiled a smile that was as thin as it was cruel. "Oh," she said. "So nice to be in the family."

It was what her mouth said with its thin smile. It wasn't what her eyes said.

"How could you not be? You mean so much to us."

"I mean so much, we family, you tell me what this place is, what you doin' here."

She laughed out loud because she knew he would never tell her. She also knew she would find out some other way. Smith smiled and forced a good-humored chuckle.

"Some things only Daddy knows, Angel. Now how about

you settle into your suite, have some lunch, and then I take you to meet your charge?"

"Yeah," she said. "Is good."

———

So while Emon Chaiya, also known as Angel and Apsara, was stripping and stepping into the shower, four hundred miles to the north and a little bit west, Superintendent Chakri Anchali was coming to the end of a mile long trek. It had been an arduous trek down a steep canyon, from the tiny village of Hmŭbān p̆ā, where the bodies had been found to the Pai Nam Jai Buddhist monastery that stood on the banks of the Pai River.

There was a path which he had followed. It was well trodden, but it was narrow and bedeviled by roots, potholes, and muddy hollows and streams. It was clearly a track used by the smugglers —Dr. Olan's gang—which they wanted to keep as secret and invisible as possible. So the biggest creature to walk this path would be an ass or a mule.

He broke out of the trees onto a broad expanse of rocks and dirt that formed the bank of the river. And there, to the left, rising startling and awe-inspiring from the bank was the massive stone hulk of the temple. It was massive but also silent aside from the slight moan of the breeze among the towers and balustrades.

Behind him, he heard Inspector Boonya emerging from the undergrowth followed by three officers. They all stood staring at the great monolith of the stone temple. Boonya took two steps and came up beside his chief.

"Is it sacred?"

Superintendent Anchali glanced at his subordinate. He wondered briefly how someone who had seen so much death, depravation, and corruption could still believe that anything was sacred. He ignored the question and pointed toward the river. There a small pier and landing area had been built.

"Was it built by the people who built the monastery, or by somebody else. Boonya?"

His inspector stared at him. "How could we know, Chief?"

Anchali smiled. "Look at the monastery, Boonya. What is the first thing that strikes you?"

The three officers gathered around to listen. Boonya gave a small shrug. "It is *big!*"

Anchali grunted and nodded. "What else?"

Boonya thought a little deeper. "It is beautifully constructed. The masonry, with such huge rocks of granite, so far from the city. It's incredible, how did they do it? How did they get the cranes here?"

Anchali nodded and smiled again. "Beautifully made, and we don't know how they did it. But it is beautiful, meticulous craftsmanship. Now look at the pier and the landing area. Do you think the same person made it?"

Boonya sagged and smiled, and the three officers laughed. "So simple when you see it, sir, but not so simple to see."

"Empty mind, Boonya. An empty mind sees and hears everything."

They walked down to the river's edge, and while Inspector Boonya and his men examined the mooring, Superintendent Anchali stood staring at the façade of the monastery, some hundred and fifty yards away. It was massive and forbidding, with plain stone walls and no windows—at least in the outer wall. There was no external sign of life or habitation. No sounds, save the soft moan of the wind.

A slightly closer look showed him that the doors, vast, arched wooden doors twelve feet high, maybe nine or ten feet across, were open—only slightly but open nonetheless.

He turned to his men. "Come, we are going to the temple. The door is open."

They stood and turned, but they did not move. Boonya said, "Sir...?"

"Come! They are Buddhist monks. The worst they can do is offer you green tea! Come! Let's go!"

He started to walk, and for a moment he thought they would betray him, but he heard Inspector Boonya's voice shrill and furious.

"Come on, you lazy slobs! Do you want to still have a job when you get back home? Dogs! Or should I shoot you now? Move! Move!"

Superintendent Anchali smiled to himself as he trod the shingle and stone that separated him from the great doors. He would ignore his men's fears. He knew that Boonya shared them. They were all superstitious. They were ancient beliefs that were resistant to empirical science. Even the Westerners, brought up and educated in their empirical schools and universities, came here searching for answers that science told them did not exist.

Maybe when his men saw the inside of the monastery, they would see that their superstitions, their demons and magicians were just dust and the wind moaning in the towers.

He had arrived at the great doors and saw that a smaller door inserted into the great door in fact stood open. He stopped and waited for his men to catch up, though they seemed to walk with leaden feet.

When they stood around him, he wagged a finger at them with his other hand behind his back.

"There are ghosts, men, and there are demons and wizards, and all kinds of evil spirits. But they are not in there." He pointed at the monastery door. "Do you know where they are? Shall I tell you where they are? *They are in your heads!*" He pointed his index finger at his own forehead. "In here, in your imagination. And believe me, a man's imagination, when it is not controlled by his will, can turn his world into hell! But you are police officers. You are strong, and you have iron wills! So you will see, when we go inside, that there is nothing here but an old, disused temple. And we, the Royal Thai Police, are its masters!"

He turned, pulled his revolver from its holster, wrenched the door open, and stepped inside.

THIRTEEN

THERE WAS A LARGE SQUARE, maybe a hundred feet across, bordered on three sides by a covered walkway behind a colonnade. In the center, there was a round pond, easily ten feet across, and in the center was a large, golden statue of the Buddha meditating. Beyond the Buddha, on the far side of the square, two flights of stairs rose from right and left to a great door that stood open. The silence was absolute.

Superintendent Chakri Anchali turned to his men. He could see the fear in their eyes and felt a surge of anger.

"Inspector Boonya! You are with me. You men, search the walkway and the bottom of the pond."

One of the officers, Sub-Inspector Aroon, a young man known to be ambitious, saluted. "What are we searching for, sir?"

Anchali shook his head. He took a moment to answer. "I don't know," he said at last. Looking around him, he added, "Where are the monks? Why are the doors open? Where is the food, the drink? Where are the animals?" He turned his attention back to the young sub-inspector. "You are looking for answers."

"Yes, sir!"

He turned to Inspector Boonya. "Come, you take the left, I will take the right."

They drew their weapons and ascended the thirteen steps to the broad, granite landing outside the huge doors. They stood half open, and through the gap they could see only darkness. Anchali holstered his pistol, grabbed the door nearest him with both hands, and heaved it open. Inspector Boonya, seeing what his chief was doing, did the same, and the sunlight spread across the pink marble floor of the chamber and up onto the walls, where there were vibrant frescos depicting the life of Gótama Buddha, from his birth in the gardens of Lumbini, in Nepal, to his death in Kushinagar, in India.

Ahead of him on a pedestal, rising to some twelve feet in height, was a huge statue of the Buddha in the lotus position, deep in meditation. The statue was gold, with blue curling hair. The face showed the eyes closed and the mouth in a smile that inspired peace and tranquility.

As he approached it, his steps echoed against the walls and seemed to roll up into the domed ceiling. He heard the inspector behind him. "I don't like this place, Chief. Why is it so quiet?"

"It's a Buddhist temple, Boonya. Aren't you a Buddhist?"

"Yes." The inspector's voice came to him across the shadows. "But all the temples I know are noisy and full of people. This place..."

His voice trailed off. Anchali glanced at him: a black silhouette in the brilliant frame of the massive doorway. He moved to his right, to the Buddha's left and stood looking down at a large mandala contained in a glass case. It depicted the eternal cycle of life, moving relentlessly through suffering to joy, and back to suffering again, and then joy again, through endless lives, rebecoming eternally, never dying, being forever reborn into new lives until enlightenment was reached, and with it freedom from pain and suffering.

"There are doors."

The words seemed to roll, echoing through the shadows. He frowned at his inspector. "What?"

The shadow in the doorway pointed to the far corner, to the Buddha's right. "There is a door, and also stairs that go down."

"Come!"

"Yes, sir."

The door was not locked. They passed through and found a long, stone passage that led to a number of very basic bedchambers, a large kitchen, a large dining room, workshops for masonry and carpentry, offices, and eventually a large back yard with corrals for goats and sheep and chickens.

But they found no people and no animals.

Returning back through the maze of passages, Anchali stopped again in the office and found ledgers and files. These would go for forensic analysis, but on impulse, he spent fifteen minutes photographing what he could.

When he was done, Inspector Boonya, who had watched him from the open door, asked in a hushed voice, "Where are they, Chief?"

"I fear we will soon find out, Inspector. Come, let us return to the temple."

They emerged from the door into the presence of the giant Buddha. Across the expanse of silent shadows, he saw his men framed in the brilliant doorway. He beckoned to them.

"Come!" They came in, walking carefully as though unsure of their footing. "Did you find anything?"

Sub-Inspector Aroon answered. "No, sir. We searched everywhere, and I reminded everyone we were looking for answers, sir. But we found nothing."

"All right. We are going down to the basement. Have your weapons ready. We do not know what we will find down here."

And he led the way down the steps into the basement. At the bottom of the steps, they came to an arch. Through the arch they found a rectangular room. At the far end, there was an opening that led to a long passage, and on either side of the passage there were doors. These doors were closed.

There were no keys to be found. So Superintendent Chakri Anchali walked to the first door and hammered on it.

"*Is there anybody in there?*" The reply was silence. "*Move back from the door! I am going to blow the lock. Stand back!*"

He stepped back, aimed his revolver at the lock, counted backward from three to one, and blew the lock. The noise was like an explosion in the confined space, echoing violently off the close walls. The lock erupted, hurling pieces of shattered steel and wooden splinters across the narrow passage. The door creaked a few inches.

He stepped back a pace and snapped, "Open it!"

Boonya turned to his men, pointed at the door, and snapped, "Open it!"

Sub-Inspector Aroon was the first to respond. He rushed to the door, and with the other officers close behind, he heaved at the door. Anchali frowned as he watched them. It was harder than he had expected, as though there were something obstructing the door. Inch by inch, the men forced the door back.

Anchali took his cell phone and switched on the flashlight. The men stood aside and allowed him to move in, where he played the light across the floor and the walls. There were ten of them in a space not more than nine or ten feet square. They were mainly bones, though some desiccated, leather-like tissues remained, holding most of the bones together. The big, hollow eyes and the grinning teeth stared at him, reproaching him, pointing at him with skeletal fingers, denouncing him for his failure to save them. Their rotting saffron robes elevated his failure to a spiritual crime. A dark, ugly voice inside his own mind told him again and again, "You are *guilty!*"

Guilty!

They blew the other doors systematically, one after another, and found a total of fifty monks, all dead, all rotting. They had all died at roughly the same time, evinced by the fact that they were all roughly at the same stage of decay.

In the last cell, there were just three corpses, and Anchali moved in among the bones, hunkered down with his flashlight. He had seen something and called to Inspector Boonya.

"What do you see, Boonya?"

Boonya scratched his head. "I see bones, Superintendent. And the robes of a monk, like all the rest."

"Look closer. What do you see on the robe?"

As he spoke, he pushed his finger through a singed hole in the cloth.

"Oh, a hole."

"A hole that is burned at the edges, and if we look behind the hole we see..." He carefully lifted to reveal the ribs behind it. "We see that the rib immediately behind the hole—the fifth rib—is shattered and also displays a hole. The ribs at the back, do you see?" He pointed, and Inspector Boonya drew closer. "The fifth and sixth ribs are ruptured. The slug entered with a great deal of force at point blank range."

He stood. "This monk was standing approximately where he fell. He was maybe five-ten, facing the door..." He leaned in toward the wall, running his finger over the stone. "The bullet struck here, and..." He hunkered down again, gently moving the skeleton, and picked up the mashed, twisted slug. "Here is the bullet, a 9 mm, perhaps a 45. Inspector, seal this site. It is now a crime scene. Make a thorough search of the entire complex. Do not touch any bodies you find. Simply secure them. I am going to return to the village to call HQ. I may have to return to Bangkok. If I do, you are in charge. We need more men, forensic teams, equipment— and weapons."

He stood and spoke with sudden savagery. "We are going to hunt these bastards down, and we are going to kill them!"

"Yes, sir."

As he left them to their task and made his way back up the winding track through the forest, he wondered at the irony of the situation. He, an embittered atheist, driven by a deep passion to avenge fifty Buddhists who would deeply disapprove of his feelings and his actions.

Revenge in the name of the Buddha.

He didn't care. The evil cancer that was the drug trade had to be stopped, and killing the perpetrators was one surefire way to do it.

FOURTEEN

"IT IS SOMETIMES necessary to be pragmatic about emotions."

The Bureau had lent us an office, and Nero now sat across from me behind the desk, watching me carefully.

"I am not a sentimental man, Alex. I could not hold the job that I do if I were. But I realize that you were very attached to Captain Gallin, and what has happened might have a profound emotional impact on your ability to continue with this job. I need you to be objective about this."

"You want me to be objective about my subjectivity." The words came out with more bitterness than I had expected. He arched an eyebrow at me and said, "Indeed."

"Well, my objective view, sir, is that only I can do the job. There are..." I paused to think of words that he would relate to. "There are subtle nuances to the case that it would take too long to acquaint a new officer with. The fact is Gallin and I both had the feeling we were working against the clock. If we take the time to get somebody else up to speed, we could lose precious hours. I need to get to Thailand. I should be there already."

"Are you sure about the Thailand connection? You have not been properly debriefed, and *I* have not been properly briefed."

"Gallin and I were both certain of the Thailand connection, sir. And if you'll forgive me for being pragmatic about my emotions, sir, what happened to Gallin suggests we were on the right track."

He grunted. "I have not spoken to Gabriel yet. The Mossad may want to send a replacement partner."

"No."

He arched both eyebrows, then lowered just one. "I beg your pardon."

"No. And sir, I would ask you a favor. Can we stop talking about Gallin in the past tense?"

He was well out of his comfort zone without a North Star to guide him back to safe ground.

"You heard what the surgeon said. Her condition is critical, and she has a less than fifty percent chance of pulling through. The bullet missed her heart, but it damaged her lung."

"She is still alive, and she is a fighter. She'll pull through. I don't want another partner, and I won't work with another partner. Besides—"

I knew he was about tell me I would obey orders and do as I was told. The 'besides' was strategically placed so he'd go for that instead of the rebuke.

"Besides what?"

"They were playing hardball. The reason Gabriel and Gallin were late for our meeting was because Tel Aviv called Gabriel to tell him not to share everything they knew. They don't know what to make of the current administration. One minute it is vociferously pro Israeli, next minute it's arming their enemies and handing out AI development contracts which could constitute a major threat to Israel. Gallin and I had"—I spread my hands and raised my shoulders—"an understanding. We have a kind of telepathy."

"Telepathy."

"Yes sir, we are able to communicate without using words."

"I know what telepathy is, Alex. Are you *in love*"—he said the words as though trying to lift moldy vegetables out of his fridge with his bare fingertips—"with Captain Gallin?"

"No!"

"I have to be able to rely on your objectivity, Alex. Forgive me, but I must be brutal. If you fly to Thailand today, the chances are that when you get there, you will be informed of her death. How will you cope? Will you go to pieces? Will you start killing, willy-nilly, those people you believe to be responsible? Will you go off the deep end and become temporarily—*or permanently*—insane?"

"No."

"Is there any particular reason why I should believe you?"

"Yes." I thought about it. "If Gallin dies, having been killed on this job, my first priority will be to honor her by finishing the job the way it is supposed to be done. She is a pro and a perfectionist. I'll do it for her."

He sighed, then grunted. "Sentimental. I assume you would do the job that way if she were alive, too. But I take your point; there is no time to read in a replacement. But Alex—" He studied me with penetrating eyes. "Be honest with yourself. If you feel you are losing your grip at any time, talk to me."

"I'll keep you in the loop, sir. I had better get to the airport." I stood but hesitated before leaving. "Is there anything on Dr. Epstein?"

"Only that that is not her name, and she is not with the Mossad. Aside from that, neither we nor the Israelis know anything about her. She has vanished without a trace."

I nodded and stepped to the door. His voice stopped me with my hand on the doorknob.

"Alex, don't make this about revenge. It will jeopardize the mission and could put many lives at risk."

I nodded and left.

I was flying with the company Gulfstream G800, taking off from the Moffett Airfield, Silicon Valley's own private airport on the shores of the bay. On the way, I passed by the hospital to look in on Gallin, aware it might be the last time I would see her. But she was in intensive care, could not be seen, and I was turned away.

San Francisco to Bangkok is about seven thousand miles, if you take the short route via Alaska and the Bering Sea. At a cruising speed of five hundred and sixty miles per hour, that made for a twelve and a half hour flight. It got me through a book on Gobekli Tepe, half of *The Big Sleep*, three movies, and a failed attempt to sleep and not think about what news I was going to receive when I got to Bangkok.

We touched down at four p.m. Bangkok time. The sky was blue, but humidity was high, and by the time I'd collected my baggage and climbed into my rental Jeep Wrangler, I had my jacket off, and my shirt was sticking to my back.

I was booked in at the Millennium Hilton, on the west bank of the Chao Phraya river. It had thirty-two floors and a flying saucer on the roof. I tossed my keys to the parking valet, checked in, had them send up my bags and a bottle of Bushmills, and called a number Nero had given me for the intelligence attaché at the US Embassy. As I sat in the chair by the window, listening to it ring and looking out at the perfect sky, I muttered to myself, "No news is good news. No news, so far."

A voice like nicotine-coated tectonic plates ground down the phone.

"This is Maurice Learner."

"Alex Mason, I think you're expecting my call."

"What can I do for you, Alex?"

"Why don't I explain over a few drinks before dinner? I have an aversion to telephones, even when they have secure lines."

"Sure. Where are you?"

"The Millennium."

"I'll see you there at six, in the three-sixty. How's the big guy? Still growing fat on oysters and Krug?"

"No, he's gone vegan and runs five miles every morning."

His laugh was like a slab of granite being dragged spasmodically over gravel. "I'll see you in a couple of hours. Vegan!" He started laughing again and hung up.

I showered and shaved and strapped my P226 under my arm. I took the elevator up to the three-sixty bar on the thirty-first floor and stood looking at the vast view of the city while the guy behind the bar mixed me a martini. A thin layer of smog lay over the seemingly interminable sprawl of suburbs and shanty towns that dwindled into the falling dusk. I let my mind drift over the vast landscape and wondered if Billy were out there, alive. Indeed, was Emon Chaiya out there? If so, with what name? Did she know where Billy was? Or had she simply killed him?

The potentials were vast, the facts very few. The waiter brought my drink to the table, and I sat to think and wait. I decided that on balance, I tended to agree with Gallin's view that if Squire was developing a weapon that could be a threat to Israel, the Mossad would not take him out. It would be especially stupid to kidnap him and *then* take him out. The Mossad was anything but stupid. If they had abducted him, they would keep him and use him. The last thing they would want to do was kill him. But then if not the Israelis, who?

That brought me back to Dr. Clara Belle Epstein, apparently not an Israeli. Who, then, did she represent? I picked up my drink and examined the olive for a moment, then sipped and set down the glass.

The obvious answer was one or all of the three powers who had in recent years united against an increasingly fractured West: Iran, China, and/or Russia. If that were the case, the same logic applied to them as to Israel. Why kill the creator of a potentially game-changing weapon? You do a Paperclip on him. You abduct him and use him.

So though I increasingly felt it was more likely than not that Dr. Billy Squire was still alive, I was also faced with what seemed to be an exponentially growing range of questions. Like, Why Thailand? Whether Iran, Russia, or China, why Thailand? All three countries had vast expanses of land where they could carry out both atrocities and experiments unobserved and undisturbed. So why bring Dr. Billy Squire here, of all places?

It hinted at some half-defined third party operating in the shadows. Some kind of Smersh or Spectre. An enemy of the West yet not the Eastern Block as we now knew it. Briefly, for a microsecond, I allowed myself to think of Gallin, how she would sit across the table from me and sip her drink and offer her thoughts, sometimes solid and grounded, sometimes insane, always brilliant and challenging. What would she say now, at this point in our conversation?

I was deprived of an answer because the elevator doors slid open, and a man who was six-four if he was an inch stepped out and stood scanning the terrace bar. He was not big as such. He was rangy and scrawny with long arms and legs and big hands and feet. His hair was dark and thick, his skin was sallow, and his eyes—sockets, eyelids, and pupils all—were deep and dark. He saw me and seemed to engage his whole body in getting his arms and legs moving to bring him across the terrace to my table.

He stood over me and gazed down without hurry, seeming to assimilate all the data available. Then he blinked slowly and said, "You're Mason, right?"

I smiled to show I wasn't being impolite. "And you are...?"

"I'm Maurice Learner, from the embassy."

"Take a seat, Maurice. What will you drink?"

He pulled out his chair and sat as the waiter approached. When he arrived, Learner looked up at him with eyes that seemed to be assessing the most painful way to exterminate him and said, "Bring me a cold beer, buddy."

He watched the waiter leave and then turned his slow, very dark eyes on me. "So I'm here. What can I do for you?"

I gave a one-sided smile and a small laugh. "I guess the honest answer is that I don't know. There are a couple of small things you can help me with, but I am not sure whether you can help with the big problem or not. I think the best way to approach this,

Maurice, is for me to explain the problem, and then you tell me if you have the resources to tackle it."

He closed his eyes, gave a slow nod, and folded his hands over his scrawny stomach.

"We are looking for a scientist who works for a defense contractor in San Jose. He specializes in artificial intelligence and alternative sources of energy. Three or four days ago, nobody knows exactly when, he disappeared. The last person who seems to have seen him alive was a prostitute from a club in San Jose called something unpronounceable." I closed my eyes and looked top right inside my head because somebody had told me that stimulated your visual memory. "The *Phû Hying Lew* Club. She was Thai. I believe the club is Thai. The name—"

"*Bad Girl*, it's Thai."

"Right, so the girl, who seems to go by several names, including Apsara and Emon Chaiya, disappeared at the same time as he did. We were told by one of her workmates that she had returned to Bangkok."

Maurice thrust out a thick, purple lower lip. "Did they elope?"

The waiter arrived and placed a frosted glass of beer on the table and left. I allowed the humor and good feeling to drain from my face. "You can take it we have explored and discarded that sort of question."

"Of course you have, but there are no bad ideas in a brainstorming session. It's like baseball. Did you ever play baseball?" I shook my head. "You move your shoulders, swing the bat a few times, scratch your balls, you're not hitting anything, but you're getting the feel." He grinned and rumbled.

"OK, they didn't elope. He loved—or loves—his job, and he had a team of guys who were close."

He shrugged. "OK, you opened sesame, you rubbed the lamp, you got the genie. Now what do you want him to do?"

I echoed his shrug. "The first and most obvious thing is to see if you can trace Emon Chaiya. Her background and where she is now might be very helpful."

"OK, we can certainly have a go at that. Odds are good that she has a police record."

"Also," I sighed. "This is a tricky one. The answer seems obvious until you start taking it apart."

"Try me."

"Why Thailand? If he's been taken by Iran, China, or Russia, why not take him there? Why bring him to Thailand?"

"It's a good question, and the answer is not as obvious as you might think. Iran, China, and Russia are among the most intensely scrutinized countries on the planet. Look what the Israelis did to Iran last June. The function of the whole Five Eyes setup is to scrutinize those three countries square inch by square inch and scour the messages that go in and out of them. This is one area where AI is coming into its own. So if—and it's still a big if—*if* one of those three has taken your man, shipping him to the Steppes, or the Gobi desert, or the deserts of southern Iran would actually be risky. Especially for Iran, who is also minutely scrutinized by Israel, who as we all know is an unofficial member of the Five Eyes. Who wouldn't want the Mossad's eyes in an environment where the most active, real threat is from jihad?"

I nodded. "Right."

"So a country like Thailand, or any of these neighboring countries—Cambodia, Malaysia, Myanmar, Indonesia—anywhere where corruption is an integral part of the system, where the governments and the police are quite openly for sale, is perfect. And into the bargain you have deep rainforests, and nobody pays much attention to what goes on there. Any place like that is kind of ideal for a covert operation, much more so than Russia, China, or Iran." He smiled, and it was a surprising sight on his sallow, saturnine face. "The billion dollar question you're asking is, has he been murdered or has he been abducted?"

I nodded. "That is the first of three major questions, and one Emon Chaiya could probably answer."

FIFTEEN

HE FISHED in his handkerchief pocket and pulled out a Romeo & Julieta cigar in a metal tube like a torpedo. He took his time extracting it and clamped it between his teeth.

"Don't worry. I don't aim to smoke it," he said. "I just like the taste, and I like to have it there in my mouth where I can chew on it."

"Sure."

He wagged a large finger at me. "Too many places, countries, and governments in this new millennium talk about freedom, but they don't believe in freedom. What they are really offering is the freedom to obey." He swiped his hand like he was brushing away all the bullshit. "I tell you, it's like living on a damned organic chicken farm. You can run around and eat seeds and potato peelings off the ground to your heart's content, but boy you better stay inside that fence and lay your damned eggs, or you are for the guillotine."

I offered him a distant smile. Not because I didn't agree with him but because his words had reminded me of Gallin. He looked at the tip of the cigar and sighed. "Don't get me started," he said, half to himself, then pointed at me. "Before we get back to your prostitute, you know what all these bans are? Cigarettes, cars that tell you to put your damned seatbelt on, recycling—it's not to protect our health or stimulate certain markets over others, no sir, nothing like that. What they are doing is *robbing us of our adulthood*. Adults are dangerous. Children are not. 'You are a chicken. You do not get to decide what is best for you. I am on the Hill, I get to decide. Not you. Trust and obey.'"

I felt my mind reach out for a thought. His words triggered something deep inside. I said, "Power" without really knowing why. He echoed the word.

"Power. It's a game as old as humanity, maybe older. The game is called, I Get to Decide."

He laughed suddenly, his grating nicotine laugh.

"Don't report me to the Thought Police, right? Anyhow, getting back to your Thai prostitute. You need to find this lady."

"I don't know how much pull you have with the authorities here. It would be useful to have a pretty comprehensive file on her." I gave a small shrug. "To know who she is, what her background is, who has she worked for. Did she marry? Has she got kids...?"

"I get it. We have good relations with the authorities, and we pull a lot of weight. The cops here are structured like an army. I have contacts right at the top. Whatever information they have on her, you'll have it by tonight."

I finished my drink and called for another.

"Now, Maurice, thinking ahead. I am increasingly convinced that this guy is still alive and being used by people hostile to us."

"I'd say that is ninety-nine percent certain."

"Right. If we accept that, then we are forced to take the next step, which is that he is being used to develop some kind of military device." I gave a small shrug and spread my hands. "It's what we were using him for. If he is snatched, it's not to use him to develop greener kinds of agriculture."

"Right."

"And that leads irresistibly to the next step, which is he has to be working somewhere. There is a physical structure housing him and all the equipment he needs to develop whatever it is he is developing. If we are talking energy sources and AI, we are not talking about somebody's garage. We are talking about a significant structure."

He closed his eyes, grunted, and sighed. "You don't know what he was working on. I'm having trouble getting my head around this. You said AI and alternative sources of energy, but you don't know what, exactly, he was working on. Have you asked the contractor that employed him?"

"They won't tell. And the director of intelligence and the Pentagon—the few people in the Pentagon who know—won't let us ask."

He grunted and sighed again. "It will be a joyful day, Mason, when we know who our friends are and who our enemies are."

"If that day ever comes, it will be a joyful day. So if he is in Thailand, by logical inference, there must be a place in Thailand where he's working, and he is *able* to work."

"You'd like me to find that place."

"No, but I'd be very grateful for a shortlist of probabilities, if that were possible. We are looking at fairly large, modern buildings situated in pretty dense rainforest with a good supply of power and probably a live-in staff. There can't be a lot of places like that. They must be on some kind of register, and I'm pretty sure there is at least one satellite keeping tabs on them."

He nodded. "At least one. I can do that for you." He drained his glass and went to stand. "I'm going to get on that. I'll be in touch later tonight."

I thanked him and watched his tall, angular body as he strode across the terrace to the elevator. The doors slid open, and he disappeared from view.

I looked at my watch. It was five past eight p.m. That made it five past six a.m. in San Francisco. I called the hospital. Nobody ever sleeps in a hospital—only the dead sleep in hospitals.

A bright female voice asked how she could help me.

"You have a special category patient by the name of Captain Aila Gallin. She was admitted with a gunshot wound—"

I hesitated a moment, trying to work out in my mind how much time had passed since then, but the voice cut me short.

"Yes, sir. May I ask your connection with the patient, sir? Access is restricted."

"Yeah, I am her partner. Alex Mason." I told her my access code, and I heard her rattle keys.

"Mr. Mason, the patient is still in a coma and in a critical condition, but she is stable."

"Thank you."

"I see an instruction here to communicate with a Mrs. Lovelock as soon as her condition changes. Would you like me to add your name to the instructions?"

I thought about it for a couple of seconds. "No, thanks. Mrs. Lovelock will contact me if her condition changes."

I hung up. I looked out at the million small lights floating on an ocean of smog far below. For some reason, a memory drifted into my mind of a man I had known in the south of Spain. He'd had an olive farm, and by day he would walk through the dry, caked soil tending to his olive trees, but by night, he told me, the entire farm swarmed with millions of woodlice that emerged from the dry soil as though the ground were boiling. So that if you walked out, you could hear them crunching underfoot, and before long, they were crawling into your boots and up your legs.

I shuddered. It was not a bad analogy. Here we were, living in our Western democracies, confident in our commitment to our Inalienable Human Rights, but invisible, just below the surface, enemies bent on our extermination swarmed. Enemies that looked and sounded just like us—who were us! Humans, just like us—but in our minds, we were different species.

I drained my glass and took the elevator down to the Oxbo on the third floor, where I was told I could have a good tenderloin and a Raven IPA from the Blindman's Brewery. I figured that had to be good news.

I took my time over dinner and, over a Bushmills and a double espresso, toyed with the idea of exploring the nearest red light districts to see if I could pick up a trace of Emon Chaiya (or Apsara). But logic suggested that she wasn't hanging out in red light districts anymore. I'd probably be more likely to find her at the Millennium Bangkok sipping a Bradford martini than hustling punters at the Patpong Night Market.

I signed the check and decided that the most useful thing I could do was to go up to my room and wait for either the report from Maurice or news from home. I took the elevator up and was closing my door when my cell rang. The screen told me it was an unknown number, but it was a Thai number.

"Yes, who is this?"

"You don't know me." It was a woman. Her accent was English, her voice warm and nice to listen to. "There is no point in telling you who I am."

I smiled as I dropped onto the sofa and sat gazing again at the vast expanse of lights beneath me.

"That is not a promising start to any kind of relationship. Do you know who *I* am? Or did you just throw a dart at the World Phone Book?"

"I was told you'd be facetious." That froze me in my tracks.

"Who told you that?"

"You're in Thailand."

"Am I?"

"Yes, you're in Bangkok."

"You're tracking this call. Let me save you time. I'm at the Hilton Millennium. What do you want? Do you look as good as you sound? Do you want to meet?"

"I was also told you were a misogynistic primate. So far my source has proved accurate on each score."

"Well done on choosing your sources. Again, what do you want?"

"You are looking for Dr. William Squire."

"OK, sweetheart, this is getting old. You have a really nice voice, and I could sit here and listen to you all night. The form is great, but the content is lacking. I sit here and listen, and you tell me about me. It's boring. Also, your source is not as good as you think he is. I am not here looking for your Dr. Squire."

There was silence. When she spoke again, there was a smile in her voice. "I must have been misinformed. I won't waste your time then."

I gave her a second. She didn't hang up. I said, "Wait."

"I thought you might say that."

"OK, so for the third time, what do you want?"

"It is not about what I want, Alex. It's about what you want."

"Well, kitten, you're telling me everything about me. You must know what I want. What I can't figure out yet is what the purpose of your phone call is, if you already know everything."

"To make you an offer."

"You want to make me an offer. Knock yourself out."

"I would like us to meet tonight. I have some important information to share with you about Dr. Squire."

I chortled loud enough for her to hear me. "When I was a kid at school, I guess I was about twelve, Nancy Fillmore—she was the girl all boys were in love with—she told me to go behind the bike sheds with her and she'd give me a kiss. When we got behind the bike sheds, her two brothers were there waiting to take my lunch money."

"But I don't want to meet behind the bike shed, Alex. We can meet in your room."

"Why can't you give me this information over the phone?"

"That is a silly question."

"OK, let's meet at the US Embassy."

She laughed long and loud. It was a very pretty sound.

"What are you so scared of, Alex? I had heard you were bold and heroic, everything a woman dreams about in a man. Are you afraid of me?"

"Your source missed one thing about me. But OK, come to my room. When should I expect you?"

"I have to make arrangements. I'll let you know."

The line went dead, and I called ODIN. I was put through voice recognition, and Lovelock's dark chocolate voice said, "Hi, stranger. I'm missing you around here."

"You playing darts with a photo of my face again? Aim more carefully with both eyes. Listen, this has to be quick. I need this number traced if you can. A woman just called me from it. Her accent was upper class English, but her usages were stilted, not natural British. She's going to call me back. I need my line monitored and her voice run through recognition. I want to know who she is."

"Gotcha."

She hung up, and I knew she was on it. Then I thought about it and called Maurice again. He sounded like he was gargling gravel until I realized he was laughing.

"You miss me already?"

"It's the emptiness. I can't take it. Listen, there has been a development."

"Tell me."

"Before that, a woman with a very sexy English accent. She sounds English, but she structures her sentences like..." I trailed off, thinking. "Grammatically correct but not like a native speaker. I'm trying to think of examples. She said, 'I would like us to meet tonight. I have some important information to share with you.' A native speaker, even an English native speaker, would say 'Meet me tonight,' or 'let's meet tonight,' but 'I would like us to meet tonight' has the ring of an educated foreigner who was taught English by a really good teacher who taught them the best English from last century."

He grunted. I went on. "I asked her something and she said, 'That is a silly question.' We wouldn't phrase it like that."

"That's a silly question, or just plain, that's stupid."

"Right. We'd contract 'that' with 'is.' It was small things, but I had that definite feeling I was talking to a well educated English-woman from the middle of last century."

"Did you see her?"

"No, she phoned about ten minutes ago. Does it suggest anyone to you?"

"Not off the top of my head. What did she want?"

"She wanted to come and see me tonight."

"Oh, man, you are straight out of a movie. What did you tell her?"

"I asked her if she looked as good as she sounded."

He sighed. "Sweet. I'd lose my job for saying something like that."

"Well, she called me a misogynistic primate, so you're not missing much. She's going to call me back to arrange a time. I just have one reservation, Maurice. I think she's going to try to kill me."

"Based on what? You have a misogynistic belief that women tend to overreact, and she wants to kill you for what you said?"

He had a good laugh at that one, like he was grating granite over his concrete pasta. I waited till he was done and said, "No. I guess you'd call it a hunch. You know what unsettled me most, Maurice? She wasn't asking for anything. She was offering."

"Offering what?"

"Information on the scientist I am looking for. She knew his name. I haven't even told *you* his name."

"I'd noticed."

"Which means either she's part of the group who have him, or she is one of us working for them, whoever they are."

"That about covers it, but like you said, she's not asking you for anything. She is offering."

"Yeah. What it boils down to is this: She is using our scientist to lure me into a meeting from which she hopes to gain nothing. That doesn't make sense. Who does that?"

He said it, simple and clear: "Nobody. She's using him as bait. She's a hunter, and you're the prey."

SIXTEEN

IT WAS past eleven and headed for midnight when she called. I was sitting on my terrace with my feet on the balustrade sipping a twenty-one-year-old Irish single malt under a late moon.

"Yeah."

"Where are you?"

"Under the moon, sipping an old Irish single malt."

"That sounds like fun."

"It is. You want to join me and explain why you want to help me?"

"That sounds like even more fun. It also sounds as though you are suspicious."

"When the midwife pulled me screaming from my mother's womb, she held me upside down, smacked me on my butt, and told me, "Remember, there are no free lunches, and anyone who helps you is really helping themselves."

"That's pretty harsh."

"She also told me, as she handed me over to my mother, 'What they don't tell you about the good Samaritan is that when he left the guy at the inn, he sent a message to the guy's wife, saying, 'If you want to see your husband alive…'"

"That's dreadful. I don't believe it."

I shrugged though she couldn't see me. "I told the midwife, 'Why are you telling me this? What's in it for you?' So I'm pretty clear that if somebody offers me help, they want something in return. While we're at it, if you are going to drink old whiskey with me under the moon, I might at lest have a name. Even a false one."

"How about Jane Smith?"

"Unoriginal, but it will do. Come on up."

She must have been just outside because it was just a few moments later that there was a tap at the door. I wasn't all that surprised when I opened it to see that she wasn't alone. There were two guys with her, each about six foot, and that was just across the shoulders. They had dark eyes, dark hair, olive skin, and lumps under the left armpits of their badly cut sky-blue suits.

She was Dr. Clara Belle Epstein.

"Dr. Gizmo," I said. "I see you brought your friends from the bike shed. I'd like to say it's a pleasant surprise, but it's not pleasant and it's not a surprise."

Her smile had all the warmth of an industrial deep freeze. "May we come in, or do we need to kneecap you first?"

"No, come in, make yourselves at home, have a drink, all five of you. Do your gorillas drink, or should I call down for some bananas?"

She stepped in and stopped to look up into my face while they squeezed past her. I was surprised to see how easy it would be to believe she had a heart and soul. She was beautiful.

"It won't help," she said. "This wiseass act. It won't help at all."

"It's not an act," I said and smiled sweetly. "I am actually a wiseass."

"Then you are going to suffer a great deal of pain over the next few days before you die. I can at least tell you that you will be grateful for your death, when it eventually comes."

"That's nice. Thanks."

The big guys went into the sitting room, and she reached out with her left hand and closed the door. She was very close, so her body was touching mine, and her face was just a couple of inches away. Her breath smelt sweet, and her lips were soft and pink.

"Let's sit down and have a drink and a chat," she said.

One of her gorillas stood by the sliding doors onto the terrace; the other blocked the passage to the suite door. She made her way to the credenza where I had a couple of bottles and poured a martini and a generous shot of whiskey. She pointed to one of the chairs. I sat, and she handed me the whiskey. She sat perched on the sofa with her elbows on her knees, holding her drink in front of her mouth.

"You're obviously not Israeli," I said, "but you're not Iranian, either."

She arched her eyebrows. "Am I not?"

"No." I shook my head. "You're Persian."

Her eyebrows went higher, and she threw back her head and laughed. "Persian? Interesting."

I pointed at the gorillas. "They're Iranian. You? The educated English accent, the Mediterranean looks, the elegant style, the air of having been to a Swiss finishing school last century. I'm going to go out on a limb and say that your parents escaped from Persia when the Shah was deposed and the ayatollahs took over."

"Well, you might be right, but then again, you might not. You'll never know."

Her mouth said that, but her eyes said I'd scored a bull's-eye. I smiled. "So how does the beautiful daughter of a Persian minor aristocrat become an agent for Tehran?"

"If you don't mind," she said, "I'll do the asking, and you do the answering."

I shrugged and spread my hands. "Shoot."

"We will, Mr. Mason, but not just yet. You've already seen I'm a pretty good shot." She waited for a reaction. She didn't get one. I told myself she didn't need to know that I gave a damn about Gallin.

"Clearly you are not FBI, but you have access to authentic FBI documents, and the Bureau will cover for you if need be. So who do you work for? Central Intelligence? Maybe, though I don't think the FBI and the CIA are that cozy.

"And Captain Aila Gallin, seconded I am guessing from the Mossad. To the CIA?" She looked skeptical. "Unlikely. Especially in the current uncertain climate over Gaza. So question number one, Mr. Alex Mason, for whom do you work?"

I was pretty sure I had a lot of pain coming my way, and I tried to brace myself for it before answering. I pursed my lips and blew out.

"You say CIA like it was a single thing. It's like saying I work for the Pentagon. What, are you advising the president on security? Are you in the artillery, the Air Force? In the CIA there are many mansions."

She glanced at the guy by the terrace door and gave a microscopic shake of her head.

"You have done that once," she said to me. "You get to do it three times. You have two left. Now I am going to ask you again, and please remember I am not stupid." She smiled, and it was a really nice smile. "If you think back a little, in my last incarnation as Dr. Epstein, the robotics genius, my IQ was well over one hundred and fifty. I know you are obfuscating and playing for time. You know I know. And you know we have a countdown. The fourth time you do it, I will hurt you a lot."

"Will you do it personally, or will you get them to do it?" I jerked my head at the gorilla. Her smile became more amused but less nice.

"You *will* find out. Now, Alex, for the second time. For whom do you work?"

"I love your syntax. It's beautiful, a pleasure to listen to. And you have such a lovely voice. I work for the Pentagon. More precisely, so you won't put anything under my fingernails, the Office of the Director of Intelligence."

She frowned a little, like she hadn't been expecting that

answer. "Not the Office of the Director of National Intelligence? ODNI?"

"No. Not that one. They don't have guys like me, and they don't hang out with the Mossad. They use the CIA's Special Activities guys for that kind of thing."

She was still frowning. "ODI? The Oh Dee Eye? I have never heard of that department."

"No, you won't have. Aside from the fact that it is ultra secret, it is not called ODI or the Oh Dee Eye. But it exists, and I will tell you what it is called once I am certain you will die before you can tell anybody."

She gave a little giggle. "You are a cool customer, Alex Mason."

"You know? That is exactly what the midwife told my mother. She said, 'Be careful with this one, he's a cool customer.'"

She cocked her head on one side. "Is that two or three? You are more subtle than you seem. So you work for a department of the Pentagon called the Office of the Director of Intelligence, though for now we have no acronym."

"Nicely summed up."

"Now, and please be aware that as far as I am concerned, you have used up all of your evasive answers. Now I want clear answers, or there will be a lot of pain. So for one point—that is one point on the Numeric Pain Rating Scale—where is Billy?"

If I had been prepared for the question, I would have looked smug. If your opponent thinks you have information they need, it gives you an edge, however small. But I was not prepared for the question, and she saw the surprise on my face.

"If I knew that, I would not be sitting here with you."

The pain was excruciating. It was not one on the NPRS. It was way up in triple figures. It went through my head like knitting needles, flipped the room upside down, and made me feel sick.

When the room stopped spinning and rocking, I found myself staring into the carpet. Every part of my being ached, and my stomach was threatening to crawl out of my mouth. I pushed myself up onto one knee and croaked, "That was not necessary."

Her voice was sweet and gentle. "You see, Alex, that we have moved into a new phase. I warned you that it would hurt."

"I told you the truth. For Christ's sake! The very reason I am *in* Thailand is to look for Dr. Squire."

"That may be true." She gave a small shrug and sipped her drink. As she smacked her lips, she said, "And it may not."

The gorilla picked me up by my hair and punched me with skill in the liver. A punch to the liver is dangerous. It can kill you. Delivered with skill, it is one of the most painful blows a person can receive. He dropped me, and I curled up, swearing to myself I would not let her see my pain, unaware that the noises I was making were nothing short of a pathetic exhibition. It really hurts.

They watched for about a minute. Then she said, "If he does that another couple of times, he will rupture your liver. From what I have seen—and I have seen it a lot—that is one of the most painful ways to die. Poor liver, it is a very sensitive organ. Now let's try again. Where is Billy?"

I justify it by telling myself it was a judgment call. To this day, I am not sure if I was playing for time so I could kill the bastards and find Billy or whether I knew I could not take another punch to the liver from that gorilla. The fact was, another blow like that one would have crippled me, another two would have killed me, and I would have been no damn use to anybody.

"We are not sure—*wait!*" I held out my hand to stop Apeman. "We are investigating the possibility of a lab in the rainforest, possibly run by a third party." I gradually pulled myself up against the sofa. "Not Russia, clearly not Iran"—I gestured at her—"and not China."

She turned her face away to stare at the black glass in the terrace door. The lights that winked in the distance looked very red.

She said something quietly in what sounded like Persian, and the two thugs dragged me to my feet. I was pretty sure they were going to kill me, and I quietly promised Odin, and Gallin, I would take at least one of them with me.

Instead she came close to me again. "Please make no mistake, Alex. I know that under your debonair exterior, you are little more than an animal. But if you give us trouble, we are quite willing to kill you in the lobby, in the street, or in the car. In this country we are above the law."

I played up, though I didn't have to try very hard. "You think after what this son of a bitch did to my head and my liver, I'm about to cause trouble?"

Her lip curled. "Maybe you're not as tough as I thought." She gave a small shrug. "Or maybe you're tougher than you look."

They dragged me out the door, and as they closed it behind me, Apeman 1 grinned and showed me a fifty cal short-barreled Smith and Wesson 500. He shoved it in my kidneys and breathed in my ear, "Dis gun blow you in haff." Then he laughed, like he'd been really funny.

I nodded and chuckled. "That's witty, subtle. You got the family neuron this week?"

We sank fast down toward the lobby. Then slowed and stopped, and the doors hissed open. The lobby was quiet, almost empty. Dr. Gizmo linked her arm through mine, and Apeman 1 and 2 stayed close behind us as we crossed the large, marbled open space toward the glass doors.

I smiled down at her like we were on a date. "You mind telling me where we are going?"

"Yes."

"Yes, you mind, or yes you'll tell me?"

She laughed and leaned into me, with her head on my shoulder. As Apeman 1 opened the door for us, she said, "I am going to take you to a house where first you will be waterboarded, then, after that, one of two things will happen. One, you will be dismembered bit by bit until we have all the information you can give us, or you'll be turned and used as a double agent. That decision is not mine." We had stopped beside a Mercedes SUV. She laughed gaily, stood on tip-toes, and kissed me on the mouth. "Personally, I would love to dismember you with a very sharp scalpel. There is really nothing like it. The pain is excruciating and comes in three parts: physical, mental, and emotional. The bitter *sadness* that takes hold of the victim is something to behold. Believe me."

I held her chin in my hand, and her eyes filled with hate. "You know what they say, kitten," I told her. "You get more of what you focus on. Be careful what you focus on."

Apeman 2 gave me a hard shove on the shoulder, and I climbed in the back of the wagon. He clambered in behind the wheel. Dr. Gizmo got in the passenger seat up front, and Apeman 2, with his snub-nosed artillery cannon, climbed in beside me. He had a smile on his face like the gatekeeper to hell welcoming the damned.

"I shoot you in heed," he said, "and *puff!* No face."

"You worked that out all on your own, huh?" I turned to Dr. Gizmo up front. "I tell you, this outfit of yours is slick. No expense spared on personnel, huh? The stuff this guy knows about the Smith and Wesson 500 is impressive. I bet he even learned to watch YouTube to get that stuff, at the very least."

"Shut up, Mason, or I'll tell him to blow your leg off at the knee."

I smiled at Apeman. He smiled back, and we pulled out into the traffic.

SEVENTEEN

WE DROVE north and east through the city for a little over an hour. Apeman 2 did a lot of fancy maneuvers along the way. He backtracked and did figures of eight, looped back on himself, and kept one of his small, beady eyes on his mirror the whole while.

Even at that time of night, the traffic was heavy and chaotic. Bangkok is truly a city that never sleeps, and everywhere you looked, there were people in Bermuda shorts and plastic flip-flops spilling off sidewalks and dodging between cars, trucks, and three-wheeler vans. Many of the sidewalks were festooned with makeshift stores cobbled together from awnings, gate leg tables, crates, and steel clothes racks. Tailing anyone in that environment would have been hard to near impossible. Apeman 2 knew that and did his level best to elevate the task to impossible.

After an hour, we came to the outskirts of the city. The road-side shanty-markets and milling crowds fell away, and we were suddenly out in the darkness, speeding among a flat expanse of fields and farms that stretched away to either side. After maybe five minutes, he began to slow. A dense hedgerow rose up on our left, and he slowed to a crawl before turning left into a narrow opening. We followed a track for another minute or so, lurching and bumping over ruts and potholes and came at last to a steel gate set in a tumbledown wall. The gate folded back at the press of a button, and we entered a big yard with gabled, red stone buildings on three sides. Motion-sensitive floodlights came on. We all climbed out of the SUV, and Apeman 1 shoved me toward the farthest of the three buildings. Dr. Gizmo fell into step beside me and smiled up into my face.

"How does it feel?" She asked it like I had just become a father for the first time or had a book published. I didn't answer, so she went on. "Knowing you'll be dead in ten or fifteen minutes, and it's going to really hurt."

"It'll be worth it," I told her, "just to have become this intimate with you."

She sighed and rolled her eyes. "You are such an arsehole. I am going to really enjoy doing this."

We came to a portico over a small porch. There were windows on either side. The one on the right was a bow. But there were no lights. The Apemen stood on either side of me, and Dr. Gizmo unlocked the door and stepped through. A light snapped on, and I was shoved through into a small hallway. She opened a door on my right, and we went through to a warmly lit living room that ran the length of the house. Heavy drapes were drawn over the bow window at the front and the windows at the back. There was a ragged carpet on the floor, a red sofa under the window, and a couple of mismatched armchairs. At the far end of the room there was a melamine table with four chairs.

In front of an open fireplace between the two sections of the room, there was a man in his early sixties, standing watching me. He had dark eyes and thick dark hair turning to gray at the temples. His right hand covered his mouth and his chin, and his left hand was thrust deep in his jeans pocket. He glanced at Dr. Gizmo and took his hand away from his chin long enough to point at me briefly and raise his eyebrows in a question.

Gizmo said, "This is Alex Mason."

To me, he said, "You impersonated a federal agent." His

accent was like hers, English from England but over-precise. "The CIA can't do that. Nobody can do that. It's like a golden rule. If they allow that to happen, all trust in the badge, in the ID, will be lost."

"Is this leading up to a question, or are you just telling me off?"

"I am asking you, what department of the intelligence community in the US can swing something like that?"

I gave a small laugh. "Oh, I would say most of them, if not all. The trick isn't pulling off the stunt. The trick is getting away with it."

He took a step toward me. He still had his hand over his mouth, like he was shocked. "The Federal Bureau of Investigation was contacted, and they confirmed your identities. Special Agents Alex Mason and Captain Aila Gallin, a Jew."

"Is that what they said, Captain Aila Gallin, a Jew?"

"Who do you work for, Mr. Mason?"

"I already told Dr. Gizmo here that I work for the Pentagon's Office of the Director of Intelligence."

"It doesn't exist."

"Oh, it does. I know. I work there. But we are very, very good at keeping secrets. Even the Feds dance to our tune."

He did a sudden, theatrical turn away and ran his fingers through his hair. Then he turned back to me. "You are looking for Dr. William Squire."

"Oh, am I?"

"What do you know about the Thai whore? Did you plant her? Was she your agent? Where is she now? Where are they both?"

"Huh, I was going to ask you the same questions. How about that?"

He spread his hands like he still couldn't fathom people's stupidity. "You know, you must understand, there are forms of torture that nobody can resist. You *will* tell us what we want to know."

"Yeah, you're probably right, but there's a problem with your reasoning. Like you said at the beginning, *we* are looking for Billy Squire. So you know, it usually follows that if you're looking for somebody, it's because you *don't know where they are*."

I narrowed my eyes, smiled, and nodded to emphasize the sarcasm. Before they could answer, I pointed at him with an upturned palm and added, "Dr. Gizmo tells me you're Iranian."

She gaped and looked alarmed, and he scowled at her. They were automatic reactions, and there was nothing they could have done to avoid them. She started to say, "I never..." and they both stopped because I was grinning.

"Hey, a little give and take. No harm done."

"We are going to kill him anyway," Gizmo told the guy. He looked mad and snapped, "Have you told anybody else?"

"I haven't told *anybody!* He's lying!"

"Come on!" I laughed. "What were the options? It was obvious pretty much from the start that she was not Israeli, especially after she shot Captain Gallin. So what options were left? Who, from that region, with those looks, is going to get involved in international espionage? She could have been Russian, but the Russians operate differently. So you're Iranian. What do you want?" I looked around the room and pointed at one of the armchairs. "May I sit down? It seems to me we have a lot to talk about."

It came as a surprise, and it hurt. It was either a back-hander or an open slap across the back of my head. It hurt like hell and sent me sprawling across the floor with the room rocking and spinning around me.

I dragged myself slowly out of the haze of pain and saw Dr. Gizmo laughing. Her mouth looked real red. The guy, whose name I still didn't know, was staring at me with that same expression of not understanding a damned thing that was going on.

I fought back the impulse to throw up and said, "That was really not necessary. I am trying to cooperate with you."

"Cooperate by *prying?*" He said it savagely, like I had really let him down. I was struggling to retain consciousness and not vomit on their filthy carpet, but I played along and snarled, "Cooperate by *understanding!* We might have a major situation here." I managed to get up on one knee and studied his face a moment, like despite everything, we were intelligent men who shared an understanding of the world. "Do we know to what extent the Russians are involved? Do *you* know? Do we *know* if the Chinese are involved? How hard would it be for the Chinese to operate here in Thailand?"

He made a contemptuous "*Pah!*" noise. "And what about the Americans? How hard for the Americans to operate in Thailand?"

I heaved my ass up onto the red armchair and felt my stomach reach fat fingers up toward my throat. I again fought back the impulse and groaned. Knitting needles throbbed in my head. "We, the Americans," I said, "have extremely close security and military ties with Thailand. If we had brought Dr. Squire here, my department would know about it, and *I would not be searching for him!*"

"Bullshit."

It was Dr. Gizmo, but she didn't sound very convinced of her own analysis. I glowered at her. "Sweetheart, you need to make up your mind. One minute you tell me that I know where he is, and the next that I don't. Which is it?" I turned to the guy, like he was the smart one, and you couldn't expect sense from a woman. "We had him, he was doing classified work for *us!* Then he was snatched." I gestured with an open palm at Dr. Gizmo. "She *knows* that. She was there."

She went to speak, but I cut her off by raising a finger. "Dr. William Squire worked for a defense contractor. That means the work he was doing belongs to the Pentagon. That means he was snatched, A"—I held up one finger—"by Iran, B"—I held up another finger—"by Russia, or C by China. Option D is that it was a collaborative effort, but your presence here argues against that, so all that is left option E, a private operator working for interests within a military industrial complex." I paused, looking at him and pointedly ignoring her. "Those were the possibilities we were working on."

His hand was covering his mouth again, and he had his left hand on his hip. He spoke as though to the floor.

"And what had you learned? How far had you got?"

"Not far at all. I had just managed to liaise with local law enforcement. A courtesy on our part to say that we were here, and a courtesy on their part to help us out. Like I said, we have a very good relationship with Thailand. Then your sadist for hire came storming in with her two simian protomen and blew everything to hell."

"Being offensive will not help your situation, Mr. Mason."

"Screw you, Hussein. How damned stupid do you think I am? What do you think was the first thing I did after Mata Hari here called me telling me she had important information for me?" I looked from one to the other. Neither of them answered. "First I called my office in DC, and then I called the CIA at the embassy in Bangkok. If you think I am bluffing, ask yourselves, why *wouldn't* I do that?"

I laughed out loud. Neither of them moved. I pointed at Dr. Gizmo. "*You knew the name of the scientist we were looking for!*" I paused, staring at her. "How many people in the world do you think know he is missing *and* that we are searching for him in Thailand? But you had to show off, didn't you?"

She swallowed, and the guy arched an eyebrow at her.

I shook my head in disbelief. "Who trained you? The Russians? Because believe me you have all the arrogance and all the stupidity and lack of skill of the Russian secret services. I thought you guys at the MOIS were supposed to be the business. Or are you the IRGC Intelligence Office? Either way, you stink of amateurism."

He nodded. I could see the anger mounting in his face. "Keep it up, Mason. See where this gets you."

"You're missing the point, Hussein."

"Stop calling me that!"

"That's your name till I hear otherwise. You're named after a great American benefactor of the Islamic nuclear cause. Or do you prefer Salami? That was the name of your dead boss, right? Stop griping. The point, I was telling you, is that this stupid trap you laid is not getting me anywhere." I pointed at him. "It's getting *you* somewhere."

"What are you talking about?"

"Listen carefully, Hussein Salami. There were three, exactly three, women in the world who could have known that we were in Bangkok looking for Dr. William Squire." I counted them out on my fingers. "My partner"—I glanced at Dr. Gizmo—"whom you killed, and I will kill you for that." I turned back to the guy. "A prostitute in San José, and Dr. Clara Belle Epstein, AKA Dr Gizmo, AKA something Persian. Do you *seriously* think I would have fallen for that stupid, sexy femme fatal approach of hers without taking out suitable insurance?"

Dr. Gizmo stood suddenly. "He is bluffing! If he was being tracked, they would not have let him get this far."

He looked at me. "So? Where is your insurance? You have shown us you know nothing useful. You are going to die in a couple of minutes. Where is your insurance?"

I smiled. "I know nothing useful? Who told you that? I told you we were talking to the CIA and local law enforcement. Think about it. If you are going to set up a lab for a guy like Dr. Squire, you need either a cave or a rainforest to hide him in, and then you need very corrupt local authorities and local law enforcement who will allow the infrastructure to be set up and maintained—and look the other way when required. The CIA and the Royal Thai police have a very good, long-standing understanding on that score. They tell the CIA everything they need to know, they get paid a lot of money, and the CIA doesn't take them out and shoot them in the wee hours of the morning. So by tomorrow morning, while I am having my coffee and croissants on my terrace, I will start receiving intelligence about where Dr. Squire is most probably held."

The guy I had down as Hussein put both hands over his eyes and swore in Persian. "What a *mess! What an ungodly mess!*" He whirled on Dr. Gizmo. "This is your fault! This is your incompetence!"

The apemen were beginning to look worried. Like they might have to decide soon which one of the two to back. That would require thinking. Which, judging by their faces, was more painful than severe constipation.

I said, "Yes, it is her fault. But stay cold, Hussein Salami."

"*Don't call me that!*"

"Like I said, stay cold, Hussein Salami, because the only thing this woman got right tonight was to say that you might decide to turn me and use me as a double agent. You make the right kind of transfer to my account in Panama, lend me Dr. Gizmo for a couple of nights of robotic fun, and she will leave my suite at the Hilton carrying all the information you need about Dr. William Squire's whereabouts in the Thai rainforest."

She swallowed hard. "It's a trap."

I laughed like I despaired of her stupidity. "A trap? What kind of trap? Show me. Tell me how I trapped you, and into what?" I laughed again, more amused this time than despairing. I pointed at her. "You are just scared of what might happen during those two night when you pose as my wife. Well, don't worry, kitten. You don't need to enjoy it. You only have to obey and pretend. And you walk away with something that will make your ayatollahs very happy indeed."

He said, "How much?"

I didn't flinch. "Two hundred million dollars."

"You are out of your mind!"

I jerked my chin at Dr. Gizmo. "Ask her if it's worth it. She knows what he was working on. Ask her what the ayatollahs would be willing to pay. It's worth twice that and more."

He glanced at her. She returned the stare, but her rigid silence gave him all the answer he needed. He turned to me.

"How?"

"You take *us* back to my hotel. She stays with me and makes sure I behave. I will introduce her to my contacts here as my partner, replacing Captain Gallin. When I have gathered the relevant intelligence, you make the transfer, and I hand over the material to Dr. Gizmo."

"OK, it's a deal."

"But I have two stipulations, and they are deal breakers. One, she"—I pointed at Gizmo—"is my wife. She killed my partner, whom I really cared about, and she pays for that as my wife. We understand each other?"

He nodded impatiently. "Yes."

"Now wait a minute!" Gizmo was on her feet again. The Hussein guy yelled at her, "*Yes!*" He pointed at her. "*Shut up! Sit down!*"

She went pale and sat slowly and silently.

"Two, I want to know who the hell I am working for."

EIGHTEEN

"WAIT!" He held up both hands. "What...where...who is this insurance you say you have? You talk you talk, you talk. But let's analyze. What is this insurance?"

I placed my ankle on my knee and raised my right index finger. From the heel of the right shoe, which Maurice had sent me by embassy messenger after our telephone conversation, I removed a small microchip. I held it up for them to see.

"The CIA knows where I am. They have a black chopper two miles away. I send them an emergency message, and they will be here in a matter of seconds, and they will tear you apart so not even your dentists will recognize you." I put the chip back and leaned forward with my elbows on my knees. "You can execute a CIA informant in Tehran and those bad boys at Langley Virginia don't even blink. But a man trained by the Pentagon? Do you know how much I cost? In aeronautical fuel alone used during my training, I could buy your house and your car ten times over, buddy. In man hours, specialist coaches, wrecked vehicles, hospital hours, and insurance coverage, I cost as much as an F16, pal. They are not going to let you hurt me."

All four of them now looked confused and worried. Hussein Salami put their thoughts into words.

"What about our deal?"

"They are not listening to us, Hussein. Central Intelligence does not get to listen in on the Office of the Director of Intelligence without permission. Our conversations, as you are seeing, are far too sensitive. I don't send a signal, I go home, everything is cool. I send a signal, and they come in and chew you up and spit you in the river. Now who am I working for?"

"How do you send your message?"

"Who am I working for?"

They were quiet for a long time. Then he said, "I am Colonel Arash Ghasemi of the IRGC-IO of Iran. She is Captain Daria Karimi. You are now working for the Ayatolla Ali Khamenei, personally."

I nodded. "Good, now as a gesture of good will..." I put my right foot down and pointed at my left foot as I raised it and laid it on my right knee. I held up my hands like they were holding a gun on me, then pointed at the heel, pressed a button, and drew out an oblong metal container, two inches in length, one inch in depth and a couple of inches across. I held it up for them to see, then said to Apeman 1, "Take this over to the colonel so that he can inspect it."

Apeman looked at the colonel for confirmation, received a nod, and came over. I handed him the box, which weighed a few ounces, and spoke as he took it to his boss. "You'll see it has a small button on the surface. If I stamp, or that button gets pressed hard, they know they have to move in."

The three of them leaned in, Dr. Gizmo, the colonel, and Apeman, peering at the surface, looking for a button that wasn't there. I laughed, they looked at me, I said, "Hey, Siri, call Boom-Boom!"

What happened next was ugly, but I can say that Gallin was fully avenged. Compressed within the small box which I had removed from my heel was close to eight ounces of C4. It wasn't exactly what Q might have given James Bond back in the sixties, but it was a pretty good effort by Maurice's guys. When Siri called the number the nerds had listed on my cell as Boom-Boom, it ignited the C4 and exploded with enough force to pretty much vaporize Dr. Gizmo's head, along with Colonel Arash Ghasemi's and Apeman 1's. The three bodies were torn to shreds, the heads were spread across the ceiling, and Apeman 2 was thrown against the wall and now lay groaning.

I had known what was coming, so I had had a bare second to throw myself on the floor with my eyes squeezed shut and my hands over my ears. Even so, my head was reeling and my ears were ringing. Apeman 2 must have been in a bad way. I got to my feet, staggered over to the mess, and fished a Glock 19 out of Apeman 1's jacket. Then I walked over and shot Apeman 2 in the head and put him out of his misery.

After that, I stepped out of the house and went to sit on the tumbledown wall at the side of the gate. I had been prepared for what had happened. Hell, I had planned it with Maurice's help, but even so, the shock had been powerful. I now felt a chill creeping through my body, and I began to shiver. If I'd had a Camel right then, I would have smoked it.

It had been an act of revenge, plain and simple. I had tried to dress it up as part of the investigation, and ultimately an act of self defense, but I knew in my bones that I had taken their lives because they had taken Gallin's.

And that was another thing that had shocked me. The last I had heard was that Gallin was critical but alive. Yet at some point, on seeing Dr. Gizmo as her true self, I had accepted Gallin's death and lured Dr. Gizmo—Captain Daria Karimi of the Islamic Revolutionary Guard Corps—into a trap where I would be able to kill her in revenge for Gallin's murder.

It had been a shock. Partly because I am an out and out empiricist. I believe in what I can weigh and measure. Yet I was aware that somehow, by what Einstein had called 'spooky action at a distance,' I had connected with Gallin in the moment of her death. I had, somehow, been with her.

More even than that. I had lost close friends before. It's a business where people get killed, where life is cheap and trust is priceless, but I had never before been driven to buck the rules and seek out-and-out revenge. Gallin had meant more to me than even I had known. Without her, life was an empty room with a lingering, fading presence.

Away in the distance, a yellow light appeared, glowing brightly. After a moment, it split like an amoeba into two headlamps. A little after that, another set of lamps appeared behind that one, and the sound of powerful engines reached me across the dark early hours of the pre-dawn. A minute later, the gate and the tumbledown wall were bathed in the warm light of the headlamps of a Land Rover and a Jeep.

I heard the gravel crunch under their wheels as they came to a halt. Doors slammed, and Maurice Learner approached me as a deformed silhouette through the glow of the lamps and stood before me. He didn't look happy. He looked worried. He pulled a pack of Camels from his pocket, shook out a couple, and offered me one.

I shook my head, then took one and poked it in my mouth. He pulled a battered, brass Zippo from the same pocket, flipped the lid, and thumbed the flint. I leaned into the flame and inhaled deeply and gratefully. He lit his own and squinted at me through the smoke.

"We listened and recorded like you asked us to. We sent you the files. There's not much on it, except proof that you're out of your mind."

I smiled. "A reporter once asked Thomas Edison how it felt to have failed to create a successful light bulb over two thousand times. Edison replied that he had not failed over two thousand times. He had succeeded more than two thousand times in proving that that was not the way to do it."

"Cute. What's your point?"

"That sometimes a negative can be more informative than a positive. Iran was aware of Dr. Squire. So much so they planted

Dr. Gizmo on him and had her monitor his work. But when he was taken, neither she nor her superiors knew how or where."

He grunted and released billows of smoke from his nose that glowed luminous in the haze of light from the trucks.

"It raises a question about how closely Russia and Chine are cooperating with Iran. We know Iran and China are close allies strategically and economically. Were they a party to Captain Karimi's insertion as the Jewish Dr. Gizmo? Or was Iran acting independently? Either way, it looks like they don't know where Dr. Squire is. The same goes for Russia."

He grunted again and took a deep drag on his cigarette. "I suspect Putin has a big pain in his wallet right now. Zelensky's drones have turned Ukraine into a seven billion dollar financial nightmare for him, and after the twelfth June raids on Iran, I wouldn't be surprised to see Russia pulling back a little from the Three Dystopian Musketeers club for a while."

"Maybe." I took another drag and felt my muscles relax a little. "I guess that depends to some extent on what Squire was working on that got somebody so excited. Gizmo didn't seem to know much, which was odd. Either way, we can say that if Russia and/or China were working with Iran, they don't know what has happened to Squire any more than the Iranians do. If they were working independently"—I spread my hands—"where are their operatives? Where are their Dr. Gizmos?"

Maurice shrugged. "I don't know. We weren't read in to this operation."

It was my turn to grunt. "Well, I can tell you there was no Russian or Chinese presence echoing Iran's. Iran's plant was clever, though ultimately detectable after Squire disappeared. But I'd put my hand in the fire that there was no Russian on the team and no Chinese."

"It would have been useful to interview the colonel."

I allowed a twisted smile to crawl up the side of my face. "Well, if you step inside the house, you can read his mind. It's spread all over the walls and the ceiling."

He didn't laugh. "Not funny. I'm sorry about your partner, Al."

"She was one in a million. I'll miss her."

He dropped his cigarette and stepped on it. Then he eyed me a moment through the dark, with the headlights bathing the side of his face. He drew breath, and I knew he was going to tell me something about the dangers of revenge, but he obviously thought better of it, and instead he sighed and nodded.

"I'll take you back to town. The boys will stay and clean up."

"You got any whiskey in the car?"

"Of course. Come on. Let's get you the hell out of here."

We walked to the Jeep, and I climbed in the passenger side while he got behind the wheel. He fired up the engine, then reached behind him to the back seat. He dropped a manila file on my lap, then spun the wheel and started back toward the road.

"Emon Chaiya," he said. "Thirty-five years old. Got into prostitution aged twelve with the help of her mother who used to tout her to Western sex tourists. She got pregnant at thirteen and kept the child. Apparently she had a good business head on her and started making money and investing it."

I frowned at him in the dark cab. His face had a ghostly green tinge from the dash.

"Investing it?"

"She bought a small bar when she was eighteen years old. She allowed some of her ex-colleagues to look for customers there and pitched the bar to foreign tourists with plenty of money. By the time the kid had turned ten, she had a chain of four nightclubs, catering to very rich foreign tourists and the Bangkok elite. Word is she was blackmailing a number of her clients, and that is how she made so much money so fast."

"She's rich?"

"She was until she disappeared. But don't get ahead of things. When her boy turned sixteen, she pulled strings and tried to get him into college. The kid wasn't interested. His mom could afford to buy him an Audi sports car, and he could make a packet on his own anyway selling coke and heroine. So who the hell needs college, right? Things got tense and, so the story goes, they had a few bust-ups, and he threatened to go his own way. Which wasn't something her backers—or her blackmail victims—were very happy about. Her they knew; she was reliable and predictable and, in her own sweet way, trustworthy. In the sense that, if you behaved and paid up, you were OK. But him? He was a loose cannon. If they let him off the chain, they didn't know what he might do. Did he have access to her files? Was he going to start doubling up on the blackmail?"

I gazed ahead though the windshield, trying to make sense of what I was hearing. Bangkok was a prairie of lights on the far side of what was a black gulf. I knew they were fields blanketed by darkness, but in my exhausted, hurting mind, it was an impenetrable gulf. "So what happened?" I asked in a voice that sounded mechanical in my own ears.

"It didn't take long. He wound up dead in a back alley, shot by the cops. Probably a contract. Cops can be guns for hire here. She went crazy for a few days and then disappeared."

"Disappeared?"

He nodded. "They lost all trace of her. This was about five years ago." He pointed. "In the glove compartment. There's a pint of Bells Scotch Whisky in there. I think we could both use a drink."

I thought for a moment, reached in the glove compartment, and pulled out a brown paper bag with a pint of Scotch in it and an unopened packet of paper cups. I smiled, and he gave a rasping laugh. "When you told me your plan, I thought I'd better come prepared."

I poured a couple of measures and handed him one.

"Do we have anything yet on planning permission for builds in the rainforest, institutes, facilities, labs...?"

"Yes and no. As you can imagine, it's a sensitive issue. It's a foregone conclusion that that kind of project is going to involve a lot of greased palms, especially if it's a foreign concern. So any inquiries have to be very sensitive, very diplomatic, and..."

"Involve a lot of greased palms."

"Right, my bill is in the post. But my contact did mention something that might be of interest to you. He said there was a cop, a Superintendent Chakri Anchali, who has been looking into the same thing—"

"What do you mean, looking into the same thing?"

He took his right hand off the wheel and waved it in circles for a moment. "Not your scientist's disappearance, obviously, but institutes, academies, laboratories et cetera, built discreetly in the rain forests."

I frowned hard. "That is one hell of a coincidence. How long has he been looking into it?"

He laughed. "That was what I thought at first, but it's not as much of a coincidence as you might think. This country has one of the biggest drug and prostitution problems anywhere in the world. It's part of the Golden Triangle, and massive amounts of heroin are manufactured here and shipped out to the West. So there are two kinds of politicians and two kinds of cops here. Those who fight it, and those who grow rich on it. It seems Superintendent Chakri Anchali is one of the good guys. He has devoted his career to fighting the drugs trade, and he developed the theory that foreign cartels were investing in so-called institutes, academies and laboratories to legitimize on paper what were in practice processing plants." He glanced at me. "Instead of setting up bivouacs in the jungle which can be spotted from the sky."

"Can I talk to this guy?"

"Yeah, but apparently he's been up at the northern border looking at some mass graves. He's on his way home for some meetings, though. I said we'd like to have ten minutes of his time. They said they'd get back to me tomorrow."

I could feel my mind reaching and stretching into darkness. I knew there was something there, I could feel it, but I couldn't see it.

"Labs," I said. "When is a laboratory not a lab?"

He glanced at me and snorted. "You better have another drink, pal. You sound like you need it."

NINETEEN

AT FOUR A.M. THAT MORNING, Superintendent Chakri Anchali disembarked from the police helicopter that had flown him the three hundred and sixty miles from Chiang Mai, in the north of the country. He had felt an unsettling burn in his stomach most of the way from the village to Chiang Mai and all of the way during the flight.

His anxiety had at first been about persuading his superiors that the bodies in the rain forest represented a serious problem and a threat and warranted serious forensic study and armed troops. He was not naïve, and he had been in the force long enough to know that there was endemic corruption at all levels. He had been warned off in the past. He knew that his life was at risk, but he also knew that there was a growing body, both politically and in law enforcement, committed to tackling that corruption, and above all eliminating the cancer of human trafficking and drug trafficking.

So the phone call he had received as he was boarding the aircraft at Chiang Mai had worried him and deepened his anxiety. It had been a call direct from Police Chief General Arthit Bannarasee himself, ordering him to go directly to the Royal Thai Police Headquarters on Ram I Road. He had faltered and informed the general that he would not arrive until at least four in the morning. The general had not so mach barked as snarled, "I don't care what time you arrive, Superintendent Anchali, you come straight to Headquarters, and to my office!"

There was a car waiting for him, a dark Audi with a uniformed chauffeur who saluted smartly and held the back door for him.

It was a fairly direct drive along Route 7, which should have taken half an hour, but at that hour of the morning, in an official Royal Thai Police car, after barely twenty minutes they were turning through the red, iron gates of Police HQ and pulling up at the three gabled arches of the palatial façade to the monolithic tower that was the Headquarters itself.

The driver held the door for him, and the superintendent climbed out, clutching his attaché case, and pushed inside.

There was that kind of silence in the lobby which you get in large, official buildings a couple of hours before the dawn, as though dreams are walking abroad through the empty, echoing corridors, seeking minds to occupy and pull down into darkness, held back only by frail electric lights.

A uniformed sub-inspector checked his ID and told him, "Nineteenth floor, sir. Turn left out of the elevator and the general's office is at the end, on the right. He is expecting you, sir."

He rode the large, empty elevator to the top of the building. In the large plate-glass mirror, he looked drawn and afraid. The last time they had found mass graves from human and drug trafficking, General Somyot Poompanmoung had intervened personally in the investigation, pressured by the United States. Was that what this summons was about? The hollow in his gut told him that the answer was both yes and no. There was more to it that than that. All his career he had been fighting the corruption he knew existed at the highest levels, which allowed the trafficking to go on. So was the new police chief, General Arthit Bannarasee, his guardian angel or his nemesis?

The elevator hissed to a stop, and the doors slid open. He

turned left as instructed and marched to the office at the end of the corridor. A guard stood outside. He checked the superintendent's ID, saluted, and tapped on the door. After a moment, he opened it and said, "Superintendent Chakri Anchali, sir."

Then he stood back, saluted again, and allowed Anchali to enter.

The office was large, as large as a small apartment. Two of the walls were glass affording a vast view over the city, now dark but twinkling. The other two walls were taken up largely with floor-to-ceiling bookcases in dark wood, with hollows allowed for doors, presumably leading to a private bathroom and perhaps a bedroom.

There was a vast, ancient oak desk to the left with a huge, black leather chair behind it. Persian rugs and bull skins lay on the floor. At the far end of the room, beside the vast glass wall, there was a coffee table in heavy, red wood and a nest of deep, leather armchairs in a similar burgundy.

General Arthit Bannarasee stood by one of those chairs. Superintendent Anchali was relieved to see that the expression on his face was not hostile. Still sitting, watching him, was a large, swarthy man in his forties. His face, once handsome, was becoming jowly and his eyes piggy. Anchali thought, absently, that this man's greedy soul was shaping his face and his body, making them ugly.

The general came forward, extending both hands. "Superintendent, thank you for coming at such short notice, and at such an antisocial hour. I am afraid the matter that concerns us is a most serious one."

He extended a hand toward the seated man, who watched the superintendent with the unwavering focus of an owl.

"Let me introduce our good friend Mr. Moschid Robles, one of the leading economic and scientific minds of our times. Mr. Robles, this is Superintendent Chakri Anchali, one of our leading detectives and a tireless, relentless champion of justice. He has done more than any policeman I know of to fight against the drugs and human trafficking trade that plagues our country."

Robles blinked. Anchali was surprised when he spoke that his voice was a little high and nasal, and his accent was American. He said simply, "And how is that working for you?"

Anchali went cold inside. Something about the tone of the man's voice, something insolent hidden behind his eyes, drained the blood from the superintendent's face. He hid it behind an inscrutable smile and gave a small nod of the head.

"The enemy is very rich and very powerful, and they are not constrained by the law as to what they can and cannot do. These are their strengths, and they make the battle difficult for us. But their weakness is that they are lazy and self-indulgent and driven by greed. Whereas we are driven by justice and a passion to see our country free of this sickness. We will win."

An unpleasant smile twitched the corner of Robles' mouth. "Admirable sentiments, Superintendent, and beautifully expressed."

The general gestured to a chair. "Please, Chakri, sit. Will you have a drink? Some coffee and a brandy?"

The last thing he felt like was a brandy, but he noted the use of his first name and saw that they were both drinking cognac. It would be ungracious, even insulting, to refuse. So he nodded and smiled.

"Thank you, General. That would be very welcome."

The general moved to a sideboard and spoke with his back to them while pouring coffee from a silver pot and brandy from a crystal decanter.

"I have read your recent reports with great interest, Chakri. A potential mass grave in the Mae Hong Son area, near the northern border?"

"Yes, sir, we initially found three bodies that had been badly mutilated. We extended our search over a thousand square meters, and we have uncovered ten bodies so far, many of them young women—girls."

The general set the cup and the glass before him and sat. "And you say you believe this is a route from Thailand into Myanmar?"

The superintendent glanced at Mr. Robles, wondering what entitled this American billionaire to be privy to this confidential investigation. The American was watching him with his owl-eyes, waiting.

"There is a track through the rainforest that leads north to the border and south to the River Pai. Where it meets the river, we found the Pain Nam Jai, a large Buddhist monastery. We found it open, and all the monks herded into cells and shot. The bodies were largely skeletal, so this must have happened some time ago. There is a possibility the..."—he paused and took a deep breath, searching for an appropriate word—"the *merchandise*, which may be heroin, opium, and/or girls, might be ferried down the river by night, passing through the town of Pai itself, and stored at the monastery before being taken on foot or by donkey and mule to the border crossing at Loi Tai Leng, where it can be moved on to Poland and the West by road."

The general nodded and sipped his coffee. "Admirable work in very difficult conditions, Superintendent. Admirable." He turned to Robles. "You can see, Moschid, the quality of the man. Unstoppable and incorruptible. A real credit to the force."

Anchali felt his face flush and reached for the cognac. He glanced at the American as he sipped.

"I am particularly interested—" He paused, then started again. "Your research is both penetrating and wide reaching. You are hunting dangerous traffickers in the rainforests around the Mae Hong Son region, building files on known traffickers in Bangkok, and also compiling files on planning applications for buildings such as institutes, research facilities, and laboratories in the rainforests. To keep all of that in your head at the same time is impressive."

Anchali nodded and smiled. "You are too kind, sir. It is not as impressive as it may seem. To memorize all the features of a face, as a list, would be an extremely difficult task, but when those features fit together as an image—as a coherent unit—the task becomes easy. All those different elements, the traffickers, the routes, the so-called institutes, they begin to fit together and form a coherent unit." He smiled and spread his hands. "A face."

Robles arched an eyebrow. "Any particular face?"

Anchali gave a small, self-deprecating bow. "A metaphorical face, Mr. Robles. I have not identified the heads of our drugs trade yet." The 'yet' was quiet but definite.

"But you foresee that you will."

"It is as inevitable as the rising of the sun."

"That inevitable, huh? That's very impressive indeed. So talk me through this. What is the significance of the facilities in the rainforests?"

The superintendent turned to the general. "Sir? I am not sure what the situation is here. Am I being ordered to brief a foreign national?"

The general nodded several times. "Yes," he said simply.

He took a deep breath. "Improvised jungle labs using tarpaulins and bivouacs and manned by peasants—often peasants who don't appear in any official birth or marriage registry and so are not missed if they disappear—are expedient but very vulnerable. They can be detected by plane, drone, or by satellite, and they can be ambushed comparatively easily. It occurred to me that with the vast and growing wealth of the international drug cartels, it would be expedient for them to use local, official agents to apply for planning permission and build one or a number of facilities. They might be registered as institutes, academies, research centers..."—he spread his hands and shook his head—"...even laboratories. In this way, hostile official attention would be diverted, money could be whitewashed in their construction, and drugs could be manufactured in large quantities away from the prying eyes of satellites, helicopters, planes, and drones."

His face became serious, and he glanced apologetically at the general.

"It is deeply painful to me, but it is a fact that there are still pockets of corruption within government, local and national, within the military, and within the police. For those who run drug trafficking here in Thailand, such a plan would not be difficult to execute. They will have all the necessary contacts. I am certain there are several such facilities in Thailand already, right now."

Robles looked down at his thumbs and arched an eyebrow, like he was mad at them but would talk to them later. "Indeed," he said. It wasn't clear if he was agreeing or simply taking the information onboard. "So, Superintendent Anchali, what is your plan? What is it you plan to do?"

The superintendent frowned and turned to his chief for guidance. The general watched him with dark, expressionless eyes and nodded once. Anchali swallowed hard and turned back to Robles. Every instinct in his body told him this was wrong. You do not divulge classified police operations to foreign billionaire entrepreneurs, especially when they invest heavily in your country. But he must obey his general and so become a party to whatever this was.

"I—" He fought against the constriction in his throat. "I plan to make recommendations," he said.

"What recommendations, Superintendent?"

"To seek out, ambush, and destroy the gang that is using the monastery on the river Pai. We would need satellite imagery, spy drones, and several detachments of heavily armed men..."

He trailed off. Robles nodded with no expression in his dark eyes. After a moment, he said, "And the installations?"

"We are in the process of identifying the ones we think most likely to be fronts for processing heroin and related drugs. It would be useful to coordinate the elimination of the trafficking gang with the storming of the suspects' facilities."

He turned to the general. "Sir, I have not discussed this with anyone yet. These are just my thoughts on arriving back from Hmŭbān p̄ā. The utmost secrecy..."

The general closed his eyes and raised a hand.

"Chakri, my friend, do not worry. Mr. Robles is a great friend of Thailand, more than you can know. You talk to him, and it is as though you talk to me. I like your plan. We will discuss it in more detail tomorrow, after you have rested. You may assume that it will get the green light and all the funding you need."

Robles raised his index finger and leaned his head forward, as though he were counting the number of legs he could see, and he could only see one.

"But I need you now to listen carefully to something I need to tell you."

Anchali frowned, feeling a strange sense of nausea inside, as though a dark destiny he had always feared had now at last appeared suddenly on the horizon and was coming for him.

"Yes, sir. Of course."

"Some of those facilities you have been researching, and putting in your file, some of them are mine."

"I see, Mr. Robles. I am sure they are used for legitimate purposes. If you—"

"I use them," Robles said, cutting the superintendent dead, "for exactly what you suspected they are used for. You are a very smart cookie, Superintendent Anchali, and I would love to see you prosper in your career and reach significant heights where you can truly benefit your country. Your country needs men like you."

Anchali was staring at the floor. He felt cold and pasty. "Sir, I must have misunderstood you."

"You didn't misunderstand a damn thing, Anchali. You understood exactly what I said to you. I own about six of those facilities, and we use them to produce heroin, which we sell all over the Western world. I have no moral qualms about it, Superintendent. It's simply Darwin's law of the survival of the fittest. If those people are stupid enough to buy heroin and kill themselves with it, I figure the human race doesn't need them in order to evolve to the next level. Am I wrong?"

Superintendent Anchali was fighting hard to control his trembling. He wanted to ask Robles if the human race needed murdering bastards like him, who instead of helping and supporting their fellow humans, instead of making better, more wholesome societies, drove the young, the foolish, and the vulnerable into servitude and ultimately into hell. He wanted to ask him too about the twelve-year-old girls forced into prostitution and drug addiction, if they fit also into Darwin's theory of evolution. But he had been long enough in the service to know when to keep his mouth shut. He filed the general and Robles away in his mind for eventual extermination, nodded, and listened.

Robles plowed on. "Let me make something clear, Anchali. I am totally opposed to drugs. I think drug dealers and drug users are the lowest the human race can reach—"

"There is one lower level," Anchari said, unable to stop himself.

"Oh? What's that?"

"Those who take young girls, as young as eleven and twelve, force them into prostitution by getting them addicted to heroin, and then sell them into the slave market in Poland. It is part of the same trade that flows from the laboratories."

Robles nodded ponderously. "OK, Superintendent, I hear you." He shook his head. "I hear you, and you are absolutely right. But now I want you to consider something. What if I were to tell you that all of these people, all of this suffering and sacrifice, was for a higher purpose?"

Anchali turned to look at the general. "A higher purpose? What higher purpose than the safety and well-being of our people, our nation?"

The general didn't answer. He just watched him. It was Robles who said, "That is exactly the higher purpose I am talking about, Superintendent. The safety of your nation, the safety of your people, the safety of your family."

TWENTY

SHE WATCHED HIM, not face to face but through a glass, darkly. He sat with his back to her on a chair made of steel tubing and blue padded panels. He was staring at a bank of computer monitors and electronic machinery that meant nothing to her. It was a large room, and dotted here and there, she could see electronic equipment, freestanding and on desks and tables. None of it meant anything. It barely registered. What she was aware of was the strange love she felt for that strange man.

What registered was a numb, hollow pain that stretched from her heart down to her belly. It made her arms and legs weak. It made her face contract and tears well behind her eyes.

She showed none of this. Her entire emotional world was contained within steel walls, and not a glimmer of feeling was expressed. She moved to the door a few feet to her left and opened it. He remained unaware, consumed by his own thoughts. Consumed by his own mind, she thought.

"Hello, Yack-yack," she said.

He jumped, like a spring out of the chair, turning in mid-jump to land facing her. His jaw hung open. His eyes were wide. She laughed in spite of herself.

"You surprise to see Apsara! I surprise to see you, too!"

"Oh, my God..." He breathed the words as he came around the chair toward her on hesitant steps. "I thought you were dead."

"I thought you dead too, Yack-yack." And then, after years of arid desolation in her emotions, tears flowed from her eyes. Something happened in her chest, in her heart, and love and grieving flowed in ways she could not control. He came to her and held her, and she clung to him with her grief catching in her throat. She wanted to tell him. She wanted him to know her feelings. But no words came, only keening sounds and noises that were more eloquent than words. And he clung to her and swayed and whispered over and over, "Apsara, Apsara..."

Mr. Smith stood beyond the dark glass and watched them. His wet smile hung somewhere between a smirk and a leer. At the end of the corridor, a door opened, and a large man came through in an elegantly tailored linen jacket and chinos. He was swarthy, in his mid forties. His face, which should have been handsome, was becoming jowly through excess, and his eyes were pouchy and piggy. Smith smiled as he watched the man approach.

"Mr. Oakland," he said. "You are just in time to see the emotional reunion." He gestured at the glass, where Emon Chaiya and Billy Squire were still clinging to each other as though they would never let go. "If I had a soul, I'd be weeping with happiness."

Moschid Robles, known to Mr. Smith as Moschid Oakland, or Mr. O, watched the couple a moment as they slowly let go of each other and began to wipe the tears from each other's faces as they laughed.

"Perhaps now he will start to work. This should balance his levels of neurotransmitters, and she will be able to focus his attention where it is supposed to be focused." He went silent, and after a moment, his lip curled in disgust. "This is what it means to be human? His intellect clouded by biology! Today he is essential. By the time he finishes his work, he will be obsolete!"

Mr. Smith laughed. "You wanna make babies? Get a damned

test tube!" He turned chuckling to Robles. "How'd it go in Bangkok?"

"Superintendent Chakri Anchali has agreed to curb his investigations in light of our contribution to Thailand." Moschid Robles turned away from the glass panel, beyond which Emon Chaiya had sat on a chair, and Dr. Squire was kneeling at her feet, talking earnestly to her. He studied Smith's face a moment, then added, "Superintendent Chakri Anchali has a mother. Did you know that?"

"No..."

"She's the only family he has. She has the beginnings of dementia and resides in a home just outside the city. I made him realize that his investigations could put such a vulnerable woman seriously at risk."

Mr. Smith's smile faltered. "We should have picked that up earlier, huh? I'm sorry, Mr. O. I don't know how we missed it."

"He had gone to some lengths to conceal the fact. Your work is adequate. You have no reason to worry. But you can do better, Mr. Smith. You can always do better."

"I will."

"I know." Moschid Robles turned back to watch Dr. Billy Squire and Emon Chaiya. "Superintendent Chakri Anchali will come to visit us in a couple of days."

Mr. Smith's eyebrows shot up. "Seriously?"

"Yes, of course seriously. I promised he could see what all that drug revenue pays for. I will introduce him to Emon Chaiya, our Apsara. She will be excited to meet him."

He turned and moved to the door through which Emon Chaiya had gone a few minutes earlier. Mr. Smith watched him, frowning, feeling unsettled.

As the door closed behind him, Moschid Robles smiled down at Billy Squire, where he sat at Emon Chaiya's feet, holding her hands.

"Are you happy, Billy?"

Billy turned, excited, and half rose. "She's alive!" he said. "I really thought she was dead. And she thought I was dead!"

"So you see? I have proved you both wrong. You should know I always reward those who help me, those who are loyal and my true friends."

He moved over to Billy and hunkered down in front of him.

"Now we have been talking these past days, haven't we, Billy, about your work." Bill nodded and looked at the gray, woven carpet on the floor. "And I have been telling you how important it is— for *all* of us—that you continue your work."

"Yes, I was—"

"I *know* what you were, Billy. It's my job to know. You were desolate and alone. That's why I went out and found your Apsara for you. So that you can be happy again and focus on your work." He waited. Billy nodded, but he nodded staring at the floor. "Are you grateful, Billy?"

"Yes! Oh yes!" Now he looked up into Robles' eyes. "I am really grateful."

"And how are you going to show that gratitude, Billy?"

"By working really hard and finishing the C-14 project. I think we can have a working model very soon."

"There." Robles spread his hands and smiled. "Now you have made me happy. There was an upheaval there for a few days, but now we all have everything we want, and we can settle down to a good, creative, productive routine. What do you say?"

"Yeah, I want to do that."

Robles' legs seemed to fold, and he sank effortlessly into a half-lotus position. His face became radiant with a smile that was both ecstatic and deeply peaceful.

"C-14, Billy. Truvidium C-14. You and me, we reach out and touch the lives of billions of people. Our minds, right? We have been blessed by some..."—he spread his hands and looked up, seeing not the ceiling but the infinite cosmos beyond—"...by some Cosmic Consciousness. Our minds are not like other men's minds, right? We see and understand where others are blind. And we—" He looked into Billy's eyes and seemed to bathe him in the radiance of his gaze. "You and I, blessed by the cosmic mind, can reach out and touch billions upon billions of men, women, and children and change their lives. Do you want to do that, Billy?"

"Yes," said Billy quietly. "I do, I want to do that."

Robles reached out and touched Apsara on her leg. There was nothing sexual or animal about the touch. He smiled at her briefly, then returned his gaze to Billy.

"Apsara will support you. She will give you anything you need. She will listen to your thoughts, talk to you if you need her to. She is your muse, your consolation, your love. She is my gift to you. Use her. But, Billy, give me that power source. Give humanity that power source. Make that miracle happen, and make it happen *now*."

He seemed to uncoil from the floor to rise to a standing position. They watched him turn and leave. When the door had closed, Apsara said to him, "What power source, Yack-yack?"

He smiled at her. "I guess I can tell you now. It's something Mr. Robles and I have been working on for a few years, since he got me out of Harvard and moved me to Princeton. It was a big secret. Even back at San Jose, we couldn't let the others know in case they stole the idea and used it for nefarious purposes."

"Nefer..."

"Nefarious. It means really bad. Because we are talking about energy like the world has never seen before."

She frowned. "Energy?"

"Energy released by a modified diamond, Apsara. Diamonds are made of intensely compressed carbon. It is the hardest naturally made material on the planet. It's compressed so tight it actually changes its atomic structure. Now in its radioactive decay, it releases the isotope carbon-14. That isotope can be captured to generate low levels of energy. That much was proved by the University of Bristol and the United Kingdom Atomic Energy Authority back in 2024. Such a battery would have a useful life of over five thousand years. Can you imagine?

"To increase the energy output, you'd have to accelerate the rate of decay. But that's impossible. You can't accelerate the rate of decay. Carbon-14 decays by a natural process where a neutron transforms into a proton and emits an electron and an antineutrino. The decay rate is fundamental and determined by the weak force, which is a fundamental force of nature. So on the face of it, the diamond C-14 battery would last thousands of years but generate enough energy to run your watch or your pacemaker. No more."

She stared at him, understanding only a fraction of what he was saying but aware intuitively of its transcendent importance. He went on.

"But Moschid and I got to thinking. It's not the rate of decay that is important. It's the volume. What if we could generate a volume of decay that would give us gigajoules of energy? We could run entire cities, *nations, for millennia* on pure, clean energy."

"How...?"

He gave a small sigh. "It is really hard to explain, and it involves using two synthetic elements which have extreme nuclear weights. One is called element 115 and has a half life of only two hundred and twenty milliseconds. The other is called oganesson, element 118, which is the heaviest element known to man and is highly radioactive. So we had reason to believe that if element 115 could be stabilized in crystalline form with carbon-14 and then bombarded under pressure with element 118..." He stopped, sighed, and then laughed. "OK, I know this is making no sense to you at all, but Apsara, trust me, the effect is massive. The release of energy is orders of magnitude above what is released by atomic fusion."

"Atomic...?"

"Yes, far superior. The problem we have had until now has been the stabilization of element 115. Not so long ago, we didn't even believe it existed! But in the last year, we managed to find it and stabilize it. Meanwhile, deep underground, under this very facility, Apsara, we have created a modified diamond that is six feet across and almost four feet deep. I'm going to get Moschid to let me show you. The next stage is to bring the diamond together with the oganesson in a compression chamber where the particles cannot escape. The energetic release when that happens will be unimaginable."

"It will explode, like bomb?"

He stared at her blankly for a long moment, then smiled and gave a small laugh. "No, the energy will be harnessed to produce electricity. The energy is comparatively easy to control and harness. Small batteries, just a few inches long can be developed to drive cars and even airplanes. This will change the world as we know it, Apsara. Fossil fuels will have to be used to make the first ones. But once we have a couple of power plants up and running —say one in Europe and one in the States—we can close the mines and the oil wells, even the nuclear reactors, and there will be free energy for everyone for the next five thousand years. It's utopia come true. Moschid Robles is a truly great man. I am telling you, he will go down in history as the man who saved humanity."

IN HIS OFFICE on the top floor, with views across the canopy of the rainforest, Moschid Robles, the future savior of humanity, pressed a button on his large, steel desk. "Send Jacob in."

He didn't wait for the reply. He released the button and pressed another. A steel hatch slid back, and a computer monitor emerged from the desk, along with a keyboard and a trackball. A further panel slid back, displaying a flat monitor integrated into the desk surface.

After a time, there was a tap at the door. It opened, and a clean-shaven man in his thirties with a crew cut and a white lab coat stepped in. He stopped and let the door close behind him. "Mr. Moschid, what can I do for you?"

Moschid Robles smiled and intoned, as though quoting Shakespeare, "Where would you like to go today?" He pointed at the surface of his desk, now a computer screen, and said, "Come, sit. We are moving forward."

The man called Jacob approached the desk and sat, looking down at the screen. His voice when he spoke was hushed, as though in awe. "What is it?"

"It's the E-115 diamond, Jacob. Dr. Squire has emerged at last from his depression and is eager to get to work. Soon, perhaps within days, we will have a working prototype capable of generating gigajoules of energy."

"That is fantastic news, sir."

"It will be if we don't blow Thailand off the map."

Jacob was about to laugh but saw that Robles' face showed no sign of amusement. So he blinked instead. Robles went on.

"In the next days, we will be moving the diamond and the element 118 into their housing and start measuring output. However, and this is where you and your team come in, we have developed a handful of small E-115 diamonds, and I want you to start adapting the theoretical designs you have to practical weapons applications. I want everything from handguns to space-based lasers and EMP generators." He pointed at Jacob. "I want to send a burst of laser from this location up to a satellite and have the satellite redirect that pulse to a target."

Jacob was smiling. "Sir, we've had all of these at theoretical level for some time. I knew you would want them, and we have brought them to a point where practical application will be very fast. Um..." He paused, trying to read Moschid Robles' face, then pressed on. "In our brainstorming sessions, sir, it has occurred to us that though it is very unlikely that the Russians or the Chinese are developing anything similar, you can never be one hundred percent sure, and we would need to have an application that would effectively eliminate any hostile use, rapidly and decisively."

"Correct."

"So I assigned a team of our brightest brains to developing such an application. They have come up with a range of three practical options so far. Meanwhile we have also been developing other standard applications, as you instructed us."

"Give me a quick, thumbnail sketch. What are your three"—he smiled, and it was like the smile of a Komodo dragon—"Final Solutions?"

Jacob swallowed, and the corners of his mouth twitched in a failed attempt to return the smile.

"The first, which we call Odin's Spear, is a network of six satellites, so small they would be virtually undetectable, loaded with a laser cannon capable of taking out entire buildings and even cities. The very energy source itself could provide the satellite with high-speed mobility to avoid detection and extremely high precision in targeting."

"I like that, Jacob."

"The second is what you yourself suggested a moment ago. A cannon based on Earth which fires a beam to a satellite, which then redirects the beam. We call that Thor's Hammer. The advantage of such a weapon is that the beam can be that much more powerful and destructive. The disadvantage is that the cannon has no mobility and if detected could become vulnerable. The hardware for that already exists. We—that is ZPE—have the satellites. All we need to do is repurpose what we have.

"Our third option is to develop a variation on the atom bomb. We call it Ragnarok because it would take time to develop, and the destructive force could be such that we'd annihilate all life on the planet."

"We don't want to do that, not yet at least. Get to work on Odin's Spear and especially Thor's Hammer. Find a satellite and start repurposing it now. I want those projects ready to go as soon as the battery is functional. Make it happen, Jacob."

"Yes, sir. Thor's Hammer and Odin's Spear."

TWENTY-ONE

I WAS ON A TITANIUM DISK. At least that's what I told myself it was. It was slightly luminous and very big, maybe six hundred feet across. It was not floating. It did not feel as though it was floating. It was more like it was suspended, very high above the clouds, almost, but not quite, in the stratosphere. When I looked down, I could see the sprawling mass of the world's continents splayed out beneath me with here and there areas hazed out by misty clouds.

When I looked up, I was surrounded by people in robes who were frowning at me. The frowns were not angry but quizzical. At first the voice in my head told me that these were the gods of Olympus. "The Olympian gods," I heard my mind say, but then I began to recognize them.

This was not Zeus. It was Bill Gates. That was not Hermes but Mark Zuckerberg. And that guy was not Ares (Mars to the Romans) but Elon Musk. Not Athena but Georgia Meloni, not Aphrodite, but Gal Gadot.

It was the last observation that made me open my eyes and realize I had been dreaming. The likeness between that actress and Gallin had never struck me before, but it was remarkable.

I rubbed my face and stared at the window. The bright glare told me morning was well behind me.

"Mourning is behind you," I told myself and realized I was still half asleep.

I stood under a cold shower, listening to the telephone ring. I made several observations to myself about what the telephone, and the caller, could go and do with themselves, then dried myself off and called down for coffee, rye toast, and fresh figs.

After I had shaved and dressed, I found and called back the number that had called earlier.

"Superintendent Chakri Anchali."

"Superintendent, this is Alex Mason. I'm sorry. You caught me in the shower."

"Mr. Mason, this is more than anything a courtesy call. Mr. Learner asked me to call and talk to you. I do not really see how I can help you."

I frowned and scratched my head, but before I could answer, he went on.

"However, if you insist so much, perhaps we can meet at your hotel."

"That would be fine. I am just about to have breakfast—"

"It is almost two p.m."

"Yeah, I had a long night."

"I know, Mr. Mason, but I am afraid my time is very limited. I have many commitments. If you cannot make it now, we shall have to postpone it indefinitely. Perhaps I can send my Inspector."

"Superintendent, you must have misunderstood me—"

"You know, Bangkok is a very beautiful, ancient city. Why not go visit a Buddhist temple? I know many Americans are very interested in Buddhism. Why not go to Wat Prayurawongsawas Worawihan Buddhist temple, not far from you? Get a taxi. Ten minutes you are there."

"No, but Superintendent, I would really like us to meet—"

"Have your breakfast, take a day of leisure, ten minutes to the temple, good place for reflection and finding the truth. You can be there in three quarters of an hour. I will contact you later. Maybe next week. Go to temple. Nice garden with fountain and turtles."

He hung up.

I sat on the terrace and had my breakfast. It was clear that Superintendent Chakri Anchali was either crazy or being about as subtle as an elephant in a china shop with a Carolina reaper up its ass about meeting discreetly.

I opted for the elephant and the Carolina reaper, finished my breakfast, and called for a cab.

My driver was, I am pretty sure, the reincarnation of Bruce Lee, with all his martial genius reapplied to driving a cab in Bangkok. He even made little cat noises as he ducked, dove, and skittered through the milling, manic traffic.

They drive on the left in Thailand—in theory at least—but, like Mr. Lee, my guy discarded all rules and regulations that got in the way of where he was going. He drove on the right, the left, in the middle, and even skipped over a couple sidewalks along the way.

When I finally disembarked at the Wat Prayurawongsawas Worawihan temple and paid him, he took the money, winked at me from behind his aviators, and said, "Intawesting wide, huh? Be water, my fwend. Be water."

At least, I am pretty sure that's what he said.

The temple of Wat Prayurawongsawas Worawihan is an extraordinary thing to behold. If somebody took Gandalf's hat and turned it into a temple, it might look something like that. It is a gleaming white disk with a huge, gleaming cone rising from the center, very high into a tiny peak.

I made my way in, with the uncomfortable, lingering thought that Gallin would have been fascinated to see that place. I eventually found the garden with the pond and the fountain and stood looking down at the small turtles, glistening wet, waddling on and off slippery rocks and wooden planks, in and out of the water.

Was it Professor Roger Penrose of Oxford who said nobody ever dies in their own experience? All we do is die out of other people's experience. Our own experience goes on forever, into eternity. Like the turtle sliding, wet and glistening, below the water, out of my experience. But *his* experience goes on, in a new, different environment.

Was that what had happened to Gallin? She had opened her eyes, emerged from her coma, sat up in bed, and greeted her grandmother and her great grandmother who stood waiting for her, and walked away, leaving her lifeless body behind, in the hospital bed?

"It's a beautiful place. A place of peace."

I turned and saw a man of indeterminate age gazing down at the turtles. His English was good, but the Thai accent was unmistakable. He glanced at me and smiled.

"Why do we fear death so much? Our own death, other people's death, our loved ones who are killed, or other people's loved ones who we killed? Always death is that big deal. The big door at the end of life."

I gave a small smile on the ironic side of my face. "Do you read minds professionally or only in your spare time?"

He chuckled, like he'd performed a simple trick and still managed to fool me.

"Maybe," he said, "the thought does not come from your mind but from the pond, the temple, and the turtles. Maybe they design it to make us think about death. I come here often to think about this."

I couldn't think of a reply. So instead I said, "Are you Superintendent Chakri Anchali?"

"I am," he said, "and you are Alex Mason. I am glad to meet you, Mr. Mason. I cannot stay very long. I do not want to be seen speaking with you."

"Why?"

"Your question is too wide. I will not answer it. You are interested in my research about facilities built in recent years in the rainforests to conduct research or development."

"Yes."

"I will send Mr. Learner a file with the results of my research. It will show nothing of interest. You and Mr. Learner will exchange messages about how the research is useless, and you will file reports with the CIA that the research is useless. Do you understand?"

"Yes, perfectly."

"Tonight I see you at Craft, Sukhumvit 23, you understand? You go with Maurice, like you are looking for girls. Near Soi Cowboy. I find you." He nodded and smiled. "Nice talking to you." He made to move away but hesitated. "Every time I come here I tell myself, there is no death. But never it brings me consolation. It is the great emptiness, the great mystery. Goodbye."

He turned and walked away into the milling crowd.

I found a bench and sat. I pulled my cell from my pocket and stared at it for a long moment. Finally I called Maurice.

"Good morning," he said like he was gargling gravel. "You just woke up?"

"I've been up since five a.m. I went for a ten-mile run, then worked out in the gym for a couple of hours before having a breakfast of whole-grain rice cakes and green tea."

"...really?"

"No. But I am at an unpronounceable temple that looks like a wizard's hat, watching the turtles dip in and out of the water. Maurice, I feel I am wasting my time in Bangkok. I feel after my partner's death I need to hand over to somebody better equipped than I am to handle this investigation. But before I go, I feel I need to savor some of Bangkok's legendary nightlife. So tonight, pal, you and me are going to Soi Cowboy, or at least to a place near there called Craft, on Sukhumvit 23. Any objections?"

"None whatsoever. Pick you up around eight?"

"Good."

"See you then."

I hung up and again sat staring at my phone. I don't know how long I sat there, but the quality of the light had changed when I finally dialed. I reached ODIN and was put through voice recognition, and Lovelock came on. "Hey handsome, you want to talk to the man?"

"No, I want to talk to you."

"I told you I'm married, lover boy, and I am faithful to my man."

"And a very lucky man he is. But that is not what I am calling about."

She must have detected the tone of my voice because her own changed, and she became more serious.

"What is it, Alex?"

"I don't want to put you on the spot, but I think, or *feel* might be more accurate, that Nero may be holding back information for fear it might affect my ability to perform my job."

She grunted and managed to make it sound not just sexy but elegant. "What information, Alex?"

"Gallin. She died yesterday, didn't she?"

"How could you possibly have known that?"

I felt that strange pressure inside my nostrils, a constriction in my throat that threatened to distort my words if I spoke. I managed to say, "We..." then took a deep breath. "We had a deep connection." I had to pause again. "One of those things you can't explain scientifically. I felt it when she went."

"Boy, you're pretty serious about her, huh? What time was that, Alex?"

"I don't know, the small hours over here. Mid afternoon in Cali, I guess. So it's true. She's gone."

"Two-thirty in the afternoon, she went into cardiac arrest and stopped breathing. She was brain dead for about three minutes, but the resuscitation team managed to get her heart beating again, and after an hour, she opened her eyes. She's been in and out of consciousness since. That is some heavy shit, Alex. How come you didn't pick up when she came back?"

I didn't hear the question. I was too busy smiling. "So she's OK? She's out of danger?"

"She is very weak, but the latest is that she is now out of

danger. Man, I knew you liked her, but that's heavy. Do I need to be getting jealous?"

I laughed, more from relief than because of her joke. "Never," I said, and then added, "Well, maybe a little. Has she got guards?"

"She has two Mossad boys who look as though they might eat your vital organs raw if you get too close to her door. One of them is called I-Eat-Bullets-and-Spit-Them-out-with-Deadly-Accuracy. The other is called Welcome-to-the-Gates-of-Hell. They're cute."

"Thanks, Lovelock. You're the best."

"I know, lover boy. Come back soon."

I stood and went back to the pond to gaze at the turtles. They looked back at me with their beady eyes, like they knew something I didn't.

"You're turtles," I told them. "You have brains the size of a grape. I'm human, at the top of the food chain. What could you know that I don't?"

There was a woman next to me with permed, fluffy white hair and a pink cardigan. She was staring at me like I was insane. I smiled at her.

"My partner is alive," I explained. "You wouldn't understand. The turtle didn't either." I gave a small shrug. "Probably for the same reason."

I left, and as I exited the garden, she was still frowning, trying to work it out.

I made it back to the hotel in time to shower and shave and spend a considerable time going through my limited wardrobe looking for an outfit that said I was a sub-human on holiday in Bangkok seeking to get laid. I decided I had no clothes that expressed that idea but substituted my tailored suit for a pair of Wranglers, a linen shirt, a linen jacket, and a pair of handmade Spanish riding boots.

Learner arrived punctually at eight, and we took the embassy's hybrid identikit car with embassy plates across the river, past the Lumphini Park on the Rama IV Road and turned north along the Ratchadaphisek Road until we came to the Sukhumvit overpass and Soi Cowboy. There we parked illegally outside Craft and went inside for the first of a number of beers.

After an hour and approximately six attempted pickups by twelve of the most beautiful girls I had ever seen, Superintendent Chakri Anchali walked in. There was nothing about him that said he was a cop, yet somehow you looked at him and you just knew what he was. Perhaps it was an accumulation of small things like the way he scanned the joint when he went in, the mildly contemptuous expression on his face that said *everyone* was guilty, or the way he walked as though he had a handgun strapped to his hip. Whatever it was, you just knew.

I noticed it, but nobody else seemed to. He came to our table and nodded to us before sitting down. A waitress appeared immediately, wiped our table, and smiled at him.

"Hello, Chakri, beer?"

"Three beers."

She went away with the order, and we watched him as he stared at the center of the round, wooden table.

"We have very little time," he said. "In two or three days they will kill me. I don't care if they kill me, but when I am dead, they will systematically destroy Thailand. Already they have men in power who will make Thailand a land of sin and corruption so much more than it is now. If I die, there will be nobody to continue my investigation or my fight."

Maurice scowled. His voice was a rasp.

"Who, Chakri? Who is going to do this?"

"The enemies of humanity, my dear friend. They will kill my mother, they will take me to visit their main facility in the Thap Lan National Park. There they will kill me. We have met already, but in case we are being watched, introduce me to your friend."

Maurice looked surprised. "Oh! Sure, Chakri, this is my good friend Alex Mason."

Superintendent Chakri Anchali held out his hand. "Shake hands, Mr. Mason." I shook and felt the flash drive slip into my hand. "That is all you need in order to identify the heroin labs and the routes to the border crossings. But the lab in Thap Lan National Park is not making heroin. It is making something else."

I said, "What?"

"I don't know, but they invited me to go and visit in a couple of days. They will tell me when. And when they do, I know they are going to kill me. This lab is not run by drug cartel boss."

"Who runs it?" I asked quietly.

"You won't believe me when I tell you. This lab is run by American billionaire, Moschid Robles."

TWENTY-TWO

WE WERE AT THE LONG, dark night of the soul, where it was always three o'clock in the morning, sitting in a corner of hell called the Climax Club. The air was red and throbbed, so it was almost impossible to hear each other talk. The advantage was it was actually impossible for anybody else to hear us talk. Because what we said would, according to Superintendent Chakri Anchali, get the three of us killed without a shadow of a doubt.

He leaned across the small, round table where our tall drinks stood virtually untouched, and we leaned in to hear him. "These people," he said. "You have to understand, these people are more powerful now than governments."

Maurice winced, like he was embarrassed. "Chakri, is this some conspiracy theory shit? You're not going to start talking about unidentified anomalous phenomena and the military industrial complex, are you?"

The superintendent's face contracted with irritation.

"Come on, Maurice! You know me! I deal in realities and facts. And you know perfectly well that Moschid Robles has the wealth and the power to hold Thailand to ransom!" He pointed a savage finger across the table. "And if he wanted to, he could cause

USA a lot of pain—and more to the point, powerful people in the administration. *Don't* patronize me with your bullshit!"

Learner raised both hands like the superintendent's finger was a gun.

"OK! OK! But how do you know this actually *was* Moschid Robles? Moschid Robles is a close friend of the president's, for Christ's sake. He is one of the pillars of American society and one of the richest men in the world. You're telling us he arranged a personal meeting with you?"

"Yes!" He nodded vigorously and spoke angrily. "At four o'clock yesterday morning, with me and General Arthit Bannarasee, the chief of the Royal Thailand Police. I had to go straight off the helicopter. There was a car waiting for me. I had just arrived back from a mass grave, a killing field near the border. I wanted to ask for weapons and resources to pursue this finding and connect it with the research I was doing on the jungle facilities. You know what they told me? They told me, 'Stop your investigation.' And he, Robles, tells me if I go to his special facility in Thap Lan National Park, he will show me how the money from those heroin factories I want to close down is being invested for the good of Thailand, and for the good of the whole world." He paused, staring at Maurice with furious eyes. "Then he told me they will torture and kill my mother if I betray them."

Maurice leaned back in his chair. "Sweet Jesus!" he said and stared at me. "He's serious!"

I sighed heavily. "I wish I was surprised."

Maurice scowled at me. "What?"

I leaned forward. "*I said, I wish I was surprised! But I'm not!*"

He looked at me sidelong and shook his head. "This is nuts."

"The Third Reich was nuts, Maurice. Operation Paperclip was nuts, the Manhattan Project, Hiroshima and Nagasaki, MK Ultra, the Cold War and the arms race, Vietnam, Ukraine, October 7th..." I shrugged and spread my hands wide. "The list goes on and on, Maurice. Jesus! You're in the CIA, for crying out loud. You know how crazy things can get! Give one man two hundred billion dollars and an unlimited supply of cocaine, see how crazy things can really get!"

"OK! OK!" He rubbed his face with his big, bony hands, let them fall to his lap, and sagged back in his chair. I leaned forward and shouted above the music.

"Maurice, the twelve richest men in the world, of whom ten are Americans, own between them over two thousand, three hundred and six billion dollars." I shrugged. "Give or take a billion. Two thirds of them control nine tenths of the world's IT, and two of them control ninety-nine percent of social media. How much impact do you think that small group of visionaries has on world affairs? How much of what is discussed and decided at Bilderberg and the World Economic Forum each year comes down from that small group of twelve? Just how much potential for crazy do you think lies in those two *thousand* three hundred and six *billion* dollars?"

I went silent and wondered for a moment if I had been channeling Gallin in her absence. Maurice was looking at me like I was crazy. I raised a finger. "Tell me one thing I have stated as fact that is not a fact."

"The potential for crazy."

"That was a question, Maurice, which you didn't answer. Think about it."

Superintendent Chakri Anchali leaned forward. "Twelve men," he said, "with that much wealth and power. Look around you. Where is the benefit? Everywhere you look, what do you see? The decay of the nation state, the accumulation every year of more power in fewer hands, war, corruption, *evil!* Can these twelve men, with two thousand three hundred *billion* dollars do *nothing* to stop the heroin trade that spreads from Thailand to Mexico and Colombia? Can they do *nothing*, with so much wealth, *nothing* to stop human trafficking? *Nothing?*"

We fell silent, and I looked out at the club bathed in pulsing red light. It was packed with young humans jumping and bouncing mindlessly to the throb of what passed for music. It was a fair bet that they were all drunk and high, at the very least on marijuana, probably on other synthetic drugs too. I could sense Gallin. I could almost hear her intelligent voice in my head. "All those minds," she would have said. "All those minds being destroyed."

The cash registers, the dataphones, the debit cards and credit cards, the bank accounts upon which they drew, the banks that housed those accounts—hell! even the music being streamed through the amplifiers and speakers, all of it was controlled by algorithms controlled by just eight men.

I turned to Maurice. "You going to stay for the end of the conversation? Or do you want to go home and forget we had this discussion?"

He shook his head. "I'll stay for the end."

"Let's go get some bacon and eggs. I can't take much more of this noise."

We rose and made our way out to the street. I allowed the superintendent to pull ahead slightly and took Maurice's arm to stop him.

"Listen," I said. "Don't take this the wrong way, Maurice. I like you, and I think you're one of the good guys. But I know the system well, and I know what the system can do to good guys. Make no mistake, I don't want the superintendent turning up washed up on some beach or river bank or getting dug up in some killing field. You turn the other way if you have to. But if he or his mother get hurt and I trace it to you, I'm coming for you, pal. And I *will* have the backing of my department."

He scowled. "Back off, Mason."

I shook my head. "No. I never do. You got a good friend in me. Let's keep it that way. Are we good, or do you want to go?"

He sighed. "I'm not going to take offense—this time. I already told you we're good."

I nodded and held out my hand. We shook and went to join Anchali, who was waiting, watching us.

I asked him, "You got some place where we can talk quietly?"

He nodded and turned to Maurice. "You know Bang Bo District?"

"Sure."

"Khlong Dan, Samut Prakan, Paa Tong Koo Restaurant. We can have breakfast there. You two go one way. I go another way. We meet there by accident. OK?"

We agreed and watched him walk away toward the Craft Bar, where he had left his car. I checked my watch and saw it was just after six a.m.

"How long will it take us to get there?"

Maurice shrugged. "Roundabout route to make sure we're not tailed, forty-five minutes. The sun will be rising by the time we arrive."

In the end, it took the better part of fifty minutes. Though we had the diplomatic plates, we didn't want the plates or the car to get noticed. So we took it easy and made lots of loops and figure eights along the way. By the time we arrived at the tiny costal village, we were pretty certain we had not been followed.

We pulled into a large parking lot of beaten earth, located behind a small banana plantation off the main coastal road. The eastern horizon was starting to turn gray over the sea, but the sun was not up yet. We found three cars parked there already, and warm light was spilling from the windows of a large, timber café by the water's edge. The light bathed a terrace full of unoccupied chairs and tables. There was a strong smell of freshly brewed coffee and sweet, freshly made Thai donuts.

One of the cars was Anchali's. We pulled up next to it, and Maurice killed the engine and the lights. I watched Anchali climb out from the driver's seat, and we got out too.

"Before we go any further," I said, "we all check for wires."

Maurice sighed. "Sure, but I can tell you that if the Company wanted to record this meeting, they have devices you would not find with the naked eye. If I am not wearing one, it's because I didn't know till we got here that the conversation would get this interesting."

We checked anyhow, found we were clean, and pushed our way into the café. We found a couple of fishermen up at the bar and a smiling woman behind it. Behind her, there was a door to a brightly lit kitchen where a man who was probably her husband was sweating profusely and making Thai donuts, the Paa Tong Koo that gave the place its name.

We ordered coffee and three rations of donuts and found a table in a corner where we could have some privacy.

I drew breath, but Anchali spoke first.

"I want to make a deal with you. I cannot enforce it. It will depend on your honor and your integrity. I ask you, if you believe you cannot fulfill the deal, tell me now. Do not tell me yes and then betray me. You can, both of you, you can go now."

Learner answered. "You better tell us what the deal is first, Chakri. I can tell you we both want to help you. Hell, we can both see this is something important for us as well as for you. But before we commit to anything, we need to know what we're committing to."

The superintendent nodded. The smiling woman came with our coffee and plates of donuts. She said something in Thai which Anchali answered. She smiled harder and hurried away. When she was gone, he said, "I am going to die. Tomorrow, maybe the day after. I am alive now because they want to know how much I have investigated and who knows what I have investigated." He looked at me, and there was a strange mix of steel and pleading in his eyes. "I have given you everything I have investigated. Everything I know is on the flash drive I have handed to you. Everything is now in your hands. They will take me to their facility tomorrow or the day after. They will torture me. I will resist as long as I can. When they know what I have investigated, and when they think they know who has my research, they will kill me."

Maurice was frowning. He looked distressed. "So don't go," he said.

Anchali shook his head. "I have to go. This is the deal I will make with you. I will wear a wire—"

I cut him short. "They'll find it. You'll wear a bug instead. I can have one here in a few hours. It won't be detectable, and it will transmit on a varying frequency, so it will be untraceable."

He nodded and shrugged. "OK, good. I will play their game as long as I can, giving them information which will be mixed with fact and lies, about what I have learned, and where that information is stored. You—" He looked at me. "If my intuition is correct, you are a good man. Do what you can, make some campaign back in America, put an end to this traffic of drugs and girls. It *must stop!*" He turned to Maurice. "You are an old friend, Maurice. I know you are a good man. Collect my mother from her home where I have put her, take her somewhere safe in the United States, where she can finish her life in peace."

"Jesus, Chakri, are you sure we have to be this extreme? Let's talk about this."

"We can talk, old friend. What I want to know is this: If we find no other solution, will you do these two things for me?"

I nodded because I knew he was probably right. I said, "Yes. I'll do that. But let's see if there is some way you don't have to make that sacrifice."

Maurice nodded too. "Agreed. I'll get your mother to safety, but let's review the plan because right now it sucks."

The superintendent shrugged. "Review it how, Maurice? They will come for me. I don't know when or how. And when they do, it will be a matter of time only before they begin the interrogation."

I said, "Where?" He frowned at me. I said, "Where are they going to take you, exactly?"

He puffed his cheeks and blew. "On the 304, in Thap Lan National Park, how can I explain—?"

"Is it on your list?"

He nodded. "Yes."

"With details of its exact location?"

"Yes."

"Then give me the reference, the document, and I'll find it

later this morning." I turned to Maurice. "You have a Special Activities team here?"

"What do you think?"

"I'll need some of their equipment for tonight. I'll talk to my boss. He or she will talk to your boss. I have to be there within eight hours, and I need to be as silent and deadly as the bubonic plague." I turned back to Superintendent Anchali. "You have my word, Chakri, I am going to do everything in my power to make sure you continue to be a prime pain in the ass for another fifty years at least, and I am going to uncover this project and kill it stone dead."

He smiled at me for a long moment. "I wish I was not an atheist, Mr. Mason. I would call on God to bless you and give you strength. I hope I am wrong, and if He exists, let Him hear my prayer."

I laughed quietly. "A very dear friend of mine told me once that it makes no difference anymore whether God exists or not. It is time for mankind to come of age and take responsibility for its own actions. That is what we are going to do."

He snorted and sipped his coffee.

"You sound like a bloody Buddhist," he said.

TWENTY-THREE

IT WAS nine-thirty in the morning when Superintendent Chakri Anchali pulled up outside his apartment block. There were two dark Audis there, waiting. As he killed the engine and opened the door, all eight doors of the two Audis opened, and eight men in dark blue suits wearing dark aviator sunglasses approached him and surrounded his car. None of them, he noticed, were Thai. They all looked American to him, or at least Western.

One of them, six foot two with fair hair and pale skin, stood in front of him and smiled. The smile was insolent.

"Superintendent Chakri Anchali?"

"Yes."

"I am Chad Moseley. I work for Mr. Moschid Robles. He asked us to collect you and deliver you to the facility."

"You need eight men to deliver me to a facility a hundred miles away?"

"Mr. Robles was very insistent that we protect you, sir. He believes organized crime might be after you." He gestured at the two vehicles. "The cars are bulletproof, and we are all experienced special operatives, sir."

Superintendent Anchali made to move toward his apartment block. Chad Moseley stopped him dead with his quiet, agreeable voice.

"Oh, Mr. Robles has everything you'll need at the facility, sir. Clothes, shoes, toiletries... You name it."

Anchali drew breath to speak, then seemed to realize the futility of it, and his shoulders sagged. Mosley opened the front passenger door of the rear car, but as Anchali went to climb in, he said, "Are you carrying a weapon, sir?"

"Yes, of course."

"May I have it?"

A sudden bitterness rose up in the superintendent's belly. "What if we are attacked by organized crime, Mr. Moseley?"

"We'll take care of you, sir. It's just routine. The facility has very strict rules on the possession of weapons."

Anchali handed over his Glock. Moseley smiled and thanked him. "It will of course be returned to you once we arrive at the facility."

He climbed in the car, and they took off at speed, headed north.

———

FOR APSARA IT WAS A FIRST. She had never loaded, programmed, or in any other way used a washing machine. Now she had loaded one, programmed it, and started it, full of Billy Squire's clothes. That was not all: the clothes he was now wearing, upstairs in his lab, she had ironed the day before, and in ten minutes or so, she would start to make their lunch.

It made her smile. It made her smile only because she knew there was a time limit on it. She would ease Billy back into working, they would wean him off her once he was absorbed by his work again, she would be paid in full, and then she would be gone, freed from her obligations and protected by her insurance.

She moved from the laundry room into their small kitchen

with its view over the canopy of the forest. It was pleasant and peaceful and quiet. The triple glazing was essential, they had told her, to keep out the multitude of insects. But it made for a graceful, tossing, silent world with sudden, silent explosions of birds over the treetops.

The loud rapping of knuckles made her jump. She crossed their sitting room and opened the door. There was a small woman with round, rimless spectacles, pale blond hair, and pale skin. She wore no makeup but held a red plastic clipboard.

"Are you alone?"

"No. I have big gangbang in bedroom. Stupid question, stupid answer."

"Mr. Robles asked me to make sure you are alone."

"I alone. What you want?"

"Mr. Robles would like you to come and see him, now."

She rolled her eyes. "You come now! You come now! Mr. O think he God. One day God tell him, you no me."

She followed the girl down a passage and then up in an elevator to the top floor. From there they went down another passage to a large set of doors, where the girl knocked, waited a second, and allowed Apsara through.

He was sitting on the corner of his very large, very ancient oak desk, looking out of the large, square glass section of wall. He turned and looked at her.

"Emon Chaiya, Apsara, Angel. It's good to meet you at last. You are a very demanding, powerful, obstinate woman. I have grown to admire you."

"Mr. O, Mr. Robles, God. I am whore. And all the years I am working, I am hearing men telling me I am special, I am different, they gonna save me. I tell them all the same thing. You fulla shit. You want something. You pay price for it. Now you fuck off. You know what Buddha say? See things"—she put her finger to her eye, then pointed around her—"as they are. See things as they really are." She wagged her finger at him in the negative. "Nobody gonna save me except me. What you want?"

"You have helped us a lot over the last couple of years. We are very grateful. You had a price you have insisted on for your services, and I confess I have been slow to deliver."

"You no gonna pay me?"

"I am going to pay you, Apsara. I am finally going to pay you."

Tears sprang into Apsara's eyes. She blinked, squeezed them shut, and opened them, then wiped her eyes and her nose with the back of her wrist.

"True?"

"True. Come, sit down." He gestured her to a large, suede armchair beside a suede sofa. "You want a drink?"

"Gin tonic. Bombay Sapphire and Schweppes. Don't give me no Nordic shit!"

She sat on the suede chair while he mixed a couple of drinks. He stood over her and handed her the tall, frosted glass.

"Bombay Sapphire and Schweppes, plenty of ice and a squeeze of lemon. Just as you like it." He sat on the sofa, sipped his drink, and set it down on the low table in front of him. "Your son," he said at last. "Sanun. He was a bit wild. Enterprising, brave, reckless, refusing to accept the limitations placed on him by the world around him. He reminds me of someone." His smile was not patronizing. She was surprised to find it was an honest smile. "He reminds me not just of you. He reminds me also of me. Unfortunately instead of choosing you as an ally, he chose to include you in all those things he was rebelling against. You tried to help him, you tried to guide him, but Thai law regarding drug trafficking is strict."

She sat in silence, listening to him, simply reliving the dark days—the darkening days—that led up to her son's death.

"You talked to him. You tried to talk to him. But teenagers of that age know everything. You can't tell them anything. They already know everything. They know so much their ears get clogged up so they can't hear anything except their own, righteous voices.

"So he went out that night, oh, about five years ago now. He had an order, and he was going to deliver. He arrived at the house on his 125 Suzuki motorbike. It was a shabby, dirty place covered in graffiti with a filthy staircase where everybody peed and shit. His client was on the top floor. He climbed the stairs, stepping over the junkies who were sleeping there in their own feces, and found the door of the apartment open. When he went inside, he had his first experience of, as you say, seeing things as they really are. Because his client was lying across the sofa with the top of his head blown off and what little brains he had splattered across the wall. There was a man there waiting for him. A man who hates drug dealers so much that he has devoted his entire professional life to hunting them down and killing them. Back then he was just a promising inspector. Now he is an even more promising superintendent.

"Your son, it seems, turned and ran. The inspector gave chase. He clattered down the stairs in pursuit. It seems your son tripped over one of the junkies and fell. As the inspector took aim, he himself tripped and fell, and your son managed to exit into the street. The inspector was close behind him.

"Sanun had no time to grab his bike and make his escape. The inspector was too close behind him. So he ran, desperately, and ducked into an alley. Tragically, the alley was a dead end. Your son tried to surrender. But the inspector was not interested in surrender. What he was after was *extermination*. It is what he is still after today."

Her voice was barely a whisper.

"What his name?"

"His name is Superintendent Chakri Anchali."

She shuddered. She had waited so long, lost so many hours of sleep, fought so hard, the name had become the Holy Grail. It had become everything she lived for and aspired to. And now she had it. She said it to herself several times, slowly and quietly, as though afraid she might carelessly drop it and lose it.

"*Superintendent Chakri Anchali. Superintendent Chakri Anchali. Where can I find him?*"

He threw back his head and laughed. "Didn't I tell you we were grateful? Believe me, when Moschid Robles is grateful, he is very generously grateful, my dear Apsara. You don't have to *find* him. He is on his way here right now."

TWENTY-FOUR

IT WAS nine-thirty in the morning, and I was standing, dithering, between the shower and the bed, when my phone pinged. I indulged in a brief outburst of Norse and Anglo-Saxon farming terminology before checking my messages and saw one from Superintendent Anchali which said simply *They here already*.

I sat on the bed and called Maurice.

He answered on the first ring and said, "I know. What do you want to do?"

"I want to have a shower and sleep for twelve hours. What I am going to do is drive to Thap Lan National Park and find their facility. You need to get my stuff sorted yesterday. Don't let me down, Maurice."

"I'm not going to let anybody down, Mason. Relax. You want to give me some idea what this is about? Just to, you know, like motivate me a bit?"

I hesitated a moment. Then, without really knowing why, I said, "There was a thousand years between the fall of the Roman Empire and the Renaissance. They were the Dark Ages, when all power was concentrated into the hands of maybe a dozen supremely powerful families. Human beings were reduced to the level of animals, exploited, tortured, and massacred for the glory and benefit of their masters. But above all, Maurice, the freedom of their minds and souls was crushed under the heels of those dark religions emerging from the Middle East. Religions that said, 'Thou shalt serve. Thou shalt not think. Thou shalt not speak. Thou shalt not be free.' To be good was to be subjugated."

"You OK, pal? You're getting a bit heavy on me there."

"Maurice," I said, feeling Gallin's spirit invading my head again, "you listen to me. Listen to me good. We came close to democracy in this world after the Second World War, in the middle of last century. For ten thousand years before that, mankind was subjugated by those who were able to inflict the most violence. Our Western, democratic glory lasted maybe fifty years before we started declining toward totalitarianism again. Now, tonight, we are about to plunge into the Dark Ages again. Now maybe you think I am crazy. But what if I am not? What if the only things standing between humanity and that event are the Office of the Director of Intelligence, me and you? You want to take that chance?"

"You're out of your mind, Mason." He sighed loudly. "But no, I don't want to take that chance."

"Make whatever excuses you need to make, but get me the team, and for Christ's sake don't let me down."

"You had better be right about this."

He hung up.

I called Nero and spoke to him for maybe fifteen minutes, during which I sent him the contents of Superintendent Anchali's flashdrive. After that, I called room service and had them bring up a gallon of black coffee. I also told them to have the Wrangler ready for me in half an hour. Then I stood under the shower for fifteen minutes, turning it from hot to cold and back again every thirty seconds. That managed to make me even more sleepy, but by the time I had dressed and had consumed the coffee, I had gotten my second wind.

I collected my car but didn't drive north. I drove south through the teaming, morning city, and eventually along Route 3, back toward the place where we had had breakfast earlier at sunrise. I passed the place after about forty minutes and kept going, following the Sukumvit Road until, shortly before arriving at the broad expanse of the Bang Pakong estuary, I came to what looked like a collection of shacks a short distance back from the side of the road. They were covered in corrugated metal roofing and contained everything from sacks of animal feed, flower pots, potted plants, a fruit and vegetable stall, and a bar. The bar was a large refrigerator on wheels with a parasol and a makeshift awning over three tables and twelve chairs.

I pulled in and parked beside an unremarkable identikit car which stood in the shade of some banana trees. I went to the makeshift bar and asked for a beer. He cracked it for me. I paid him and made my way over to where Maurice was sitting with his back to the road.

As I sat, he said, "You guys at the Office of the Director of Intelligence always this unprofessional?"

I shook my head. "No, sometimes we try to invade Cuba or plan coups *d'état* in allied nations like the UK. When we're not doing that, we conduct experiments in consciousness on unsuspecting citizens without their consent using hallucinogenic drugs."

"That was a long time ago. We don't do that kind of thing anymore."

"Well, that's a relief. We don't usually run around recruiting nefarious agencies of the military industrial complex to conduct illegal military assaults on remote laboratories either. But, hey, needs must when the devil drives, right?"

"I don't like you when you are sleep deprived."

"That makes two of us. Have you got anything for me?"

He nodded and looked at the beer bottle he held in both hands on his lap.

"Yeah, your boss spoke to my boss, who spoke to the president, no less, who said he had already spoken to your boss and the hell with international law."

I smiled. "America is great again."

"Right? About time, too."

We finished our beers, and I followed him over to the unremarkable identikit car. He paused and made mindless small talk for thirty seconds while we both scanned every inch of the horizon. Then he said, "Open your trunk."

As I did so, he pulled a large camouflage rucksack from his back seat and slung it in the Jeep. I slammed the trunk shut, and we shook hands. Before letting go, he contracted his brow.

"Explain something to me. Why the hell would a guy abduct his own employee?"

I smiled. "Because he wasn't Robles' employee. He was ZPE's employee. And whatever Squire had developed would belong either to ZPE or, contractually, to the Pentagon. If it's what it seems to be, I'm guessing Robles wants to keep it for himself."

He nodded.

"See you on the other side, pal."

"I'll be there."

I climbed into the Jeep and pulled out onto the road. In my rearview, I could see him, shrinking, watching me as I pulled away. I didn't cross the Bang Pakong. I headed north and a little east for fifty miles until at Chachoengsao I turned east and picked up the 304, which carried me the next seventy miles into the dense woodlands of the Thap Lan National Park.

It happened suddenly. One minute I was driving through cultivated farmland and cute villages, and then the rainforest closed in around me. The road was broad—three lanes and well maintained—but either side of the road, aside from the occasional wood and straw shack, there was nothing but miles of deep, apparently impenetrable forest.

I kept my eye on the GPS, closing in on the location Anchali had provided on his flash drive. Pretty soon I came to a gap in the central reservation barrier. My SanNav told me to turn around and head back the way I had come, and after five minutes, ahead, I saw a collection of shacks, bivouacs, and tarps supported on stakes driven into the ground. Like so many of those improvised marketplaces, it sold just about anything you might need if you lived in the rain forest.

Among the stalls I now noticed a broad, dirt track half hidden among trees. I turned in, slowed, and began to roll gently into the dense, dappled-green light of the woodland.

Finding somewhere to leave the Jeep wasn't so easy. Jeeps are big, even the Wranglers, and in a rainforest, space is at a premium. I let the car roll gently for five minutes doing four or five miles per hour until I found a small clearing on my right. I pulled into it and managed to nose my way through a few saplings until I was pretty much hidden from view. A few branches pulled off trees deeper in the forest and laid strategically across the hood and the soft top finished the job.

After that, I hoisted the rucksack on my back and started picking my way through the trees. It was not as easy as it might sound. This was not a pine forest in the Adirondacks or the Wind River Mountains. It wasn't quite the Brazilian jungle, either, but the trees were inches apart instead of feet, the branches intertwined with each other and creepers swarming over any gaps left between. A machete would have been useful; it would also have made a lot of noise. So with one eye on a compass, I picked my way through what gaps the forest gave me, sometimes climbing over fallen trees, sometimes crawling through verdant tunnels, always headed steadily east.

It was a one and a quarter mile walk, and it took me close to two and a half hours to reach the broad stream that lay across my path, just two hundred yards from the facility. There was a bridge, and I congratulated myself on a half-decent job of moving through the forest because I arrived just fifty yards from the bridge. In fact, as I lay in the dense undergrowth, I could see the drive up to the main entrance, several cars, including two dark Audi saloons, and several guys in Secret Service suits with the regulation aviator shades.

To use the bridge was impossible. In broad daylight I would be spotted immediately. Even at night I had no doubt there were sensors strategically placed to alert security of anyone crossing that line.

Any approach had to be from the forest. The abundant wildlife meant that movement and heat sensors could not be used because they would be going off constantly. Security would be limited to patrols and cameras. Which meant that my ideal approach would be from the rear at night. But the urgency of the situation meant that my approach had to be by day, and from wherever I could make it.

Very slowly, and with great care, I slid down the bank and lowered myself into the murky water. At this point, the river was some fifteen or twenty feet across but a good five feet deep. I kept low and moved toward the densely overgrown bank on the far side. The current wasn't strong, and I made it across with a minimum of effort and noise. Once there, I grabbed a handful of creepers and branches and hauled myself up through the mud and the slime. I stayed on my belly and crawled very slowly through the undergrowth until I had a clear view of the front of the facility.

Now I could see the two Audis parked outside the large, plate-glass doors. There were two guys in suits sitting with their asses against the trunks. They seemed to be smoking and talking. A little to their right, there was a Range Rover, but there was no driver taking part in the conversation. I eased back into the under-growth, turned left, and began to crawl very slowly, and as silently as I was able, toward the back of the building.

There I found a big, broad lawn, maybe a hundred feet deep and a similar width. There were four guys there in camouflage fatigues strolling back and forth with a couple of Rottweilers. I sighed as silently as I could. Do you shoot the guys or the

Rottweilers first? Shoot the dogs and the guys spray the area with automatic fire. Shoot the guys, and by the time they hit the ground, the dogs will be licking their lips and belching as they digest your liver.

A full circuit of the building took me over an hour and left me practically back where I'd started, a few yards from the bridge and with absolutely no means of access. Waiting till dark would not help and would waste too much time.

So I did the only thing I could do. I buried the rucksack, marked the spot, and stepped out from the trees.

The two guys in suits turned their heads to look at me but didn't seem very surprised. Perhaps it was more common than I thought to have a bewildered Westerner wander out of the rainforest at random locations in Thailand. I put a pleasant though serious expression on my face and started walking in their direction. One of them got his ass off the trunk and embarked on a steady but not confrontational intercept course. When he was six or seven feet from me, he said, "Mr. Mason?"

I couldn't think of a wiseass reply that would carry any credibility, and 'who wants to know,' under the circumstances, would seem a bit stupid. So I smiled pleasantly and said, "Yes, is Mr. Robles in?"

He nodded and said, "Yeah, he's waiting for you upstairs."

Sometimes I guess you just have to accept you've been outclassed. He frisked me like he didn't expect to find anything. He didn't, because what I'd had was buried under the trees. When he was done, he said, "OK, you're good. Follow me."

I followed him across a broad, marble lobby to a bank of elevators. We boarded one and rode it to the top floor, where I followed him down a broad corridor to double doors, which he rapped on and opened without waiting for a reply.

"Mr. Mason, sir. He's just arrived."

He stepped back and jerked his head for me to go in. I gave him an anorexic smile and went inside.

The room was broad, light and airy. The view from the

windows was over the green canopy of the forest. His desk was sideways on to the window, so he could see the room as well as the vast wilderness of trees. He was sitting at the desk reading a thick file when I went in. He looked up as the door closed behind me. He observed me without expression for a moment, like he was absorbing data and making no secret of it.

"Alex Mason," he said.

"Moschid Robles."

He gave his head a little sideways jerk like he only half agreed with me. "I use several names. Mr. Oakland, Mr. O, some even call me the Druid. But you are right, of course, I am most widely known as Moschid Robles. Have you come to kill me?"

"I don't think so. Is there any reason I should? My department is more about intelligence gathering, Mr. Robles."

"Oh, good to know. What is the intelligence you are gathering?"

"I am a little confused, as is my department, as to why you appear to have abducted your own employee, from your own company headquarters in Silicon Valley, and brought him out here to Thailand."

He gazed into the middle distance for a moment, frowned, and gave his head a little shake. It was a gesture that said he would never really understand the stupidity of human beings. He closed the file and turned his frown on me as he placed it on the desk in front of him.

"You are an intelligent man. You have an IQ of one hundred and thirty-five. You got a first class degree from Stanford, and you have consistently excelled professionally. I would employ you right now if you were available. I know Nero personally, and I know that he considers you one of his best—not to say his best—operative." For a moment, I thought he was fishing, but he didn't bother to assess my reaction. He just plowed right on. "And yet, your conditioning is such that you are unable to make that simple intellectual leap. I'll tell you why. Because you have the habit of asking open questions. I shall illustrate, and you yourself will see how the right question will tend to answer itself." He held up a finger. "Question one: Why did you abduct your own employee, from your own company headquarters in Silicon Valley, and bring him to Thailand? The emphasis here is on the absurdity of abducting somebody who already belongs to you. Question two: What advantage do you get from secretly bringing your leading scientist from Silicon Valley to the Thai rainforest?"

I stared at him for a long moment. He remained expressionless. I said, "If this is to be the extent of our interaction, I consider the journey to have been worthwhile."

"The human needs to learn to focus his mind, Mr. Mason. The holy trinity—" He raised a finger with each item. "Attention, concentration, observation. These are the three facets of focus. When man learns to focus his mind, many doors are opened to him. So what benefit do I derive from secretly bringing my best scientist to the rainforest of Thailand? Sit."

He pointed to a chair across from his desk. I sat. He went on.

"Of course you could focus on the legal ownership of what he produces. But on a much more practical level, here there are simply far fewer restrictions upon how I can use him. And what restrictions there are, I can pay to have removed. We had reached a point in our research and development where I needed to use him freely."

He gave another brief shake of the head. "Imagine if you had focused on the question in the right way hours ago, how far you might have reached by now, taking into account all the factors, like his specialization—energy—and all the factors relating to that subject today."

My mind groped. I smiled. "You feel like catching me up?"

"Yes, Mr. Mason, I do. I feel strongly motivated today because we are almost ready, thanks to our immensely useful Apsara."

He leaned forward, and for the first time I saw an expression on his face. He stood and turned to look at the window. He opened his mouth and started to laugh. It was a strange, mechanical laugh, with his eyes wide open, as though even in the midst of his hilarity, he never for a moment lost his hold on his awareness.

"In the coming days," he said to his reflection in the glass, "we save the world."

TWENTY-FIVE

"YOU HAVEN'T SLEPT," he said suddenly and turned to face me. He pointed to a drinks tray on a dresser by the wall. "Get a drink. Do you want some breakfast? Eggs and bacon?"

"No." I shook my head. "Coffee. I could use some coffee."

"Bring us some coffee," he said, as though invoking it from thin air. To me he said, "Bring the whiskey decanter. We'll have a *carajillo* while we talk."

I sighed and went to get the whiskey decanter. I placed it on the desk, and as I sat I asked, "Why are we talking?"

He raised a finger. "What benefit do I get from talking to you?" He sat and poured. "Nero is a man for whom I have a great deal of respect. You would be surprised how much power he wields. We have had many fascinating conversations over the years. But in recent years, he has avoided me."

He raised a hand to stop me in case I was going to ask.

"What advantage does he believe he has he gained by avoiding contact with me? Quite simply that he has increasingly found my view of the world disturbing and unpleasant."

He sipped. "He is, for all his clinical intellectualism, a deeply emotional man. I am not. I have no emotions. I have risen above my emotions. I have seen them for what they are, and I have detached my ego from them. I am the Observer, dispassionate, clear-seeing, and unfolding the full potential of my mind. That is quite frightening for many people."

"You sound like the blurb on a self-help book."

He nodded. "Yes. I want Nero. I want him onside. You I don't care about. You are well above average intelligence, but average intelligence—100 on the IQ scale—is just two points above a cretin. But Nero, if he could be made to see things as they truly are, would be a great asset to the world."

"And you want me to take a message to him."

"Yes. The benefit for you is that I don't have you killed. You get to leave and fly home."

The door opened, and a man came in. He was wearing a white jacket and white gloves, and he was carrying a silver tray of coffee. He set it on the desk, bowed, and withdrew.

"OK. I'm sold. What's the message, and how and from whom are you going to save the world?"

"I will answer your questions in reverse order. Because you will not be able adequately to transmit the message unless you understand what we are doing here."

He took his time pouring the coffee, then laced it with a generous slug of whiskey. He slid one cup across the desk and picked up the other to sip it. As he set it down again, he said, "In 1979, Margaret Thatcher, the British Prime Minister at the time, commissioned Professor James Lamoureux, the eminent, independent natural scientist, to prepare a report, an analysis of the impact of industrialization on the environment. This was long before concerns about global warming, climate change, and the melting of the icecaps. But she was a far-sighted woman.

"His report, when he delivered it in 1981, was immediately classified as top secret, and sight of it was limited to a handful of people, including the president of the United States at the time, Ronald Reagan. This was because the contents were so explosive the general public could not be allowed to know about them. Nero is aware of this."

He sipped again and sighed, drawing his lips back over his teeth.

"In synthesis, he said that the steady development of industrial society would lead to massive overpopulation, increasing lifespans, spiraling demands on limited resources, and the spiraling generation of rubbish and human excrement, amid an increasingly unstable climatic environment, until the planet became uninhabitable for humans."

I sipped my own *carajillo* and said, "That was forty-five years ago. How wrong was he?"

"Not. Not in the least. He wasn't wrong at all. Of course, wind of the report spread, though very few got to see it, and people started making all sorts of wild predictions. But Lamoureux himself had said from the start that it would be very difficult, if not impossible, to predict any kind of timeframe. He said it was inevitable, and so far the development of society and industry has followed his predictions to the letter. And for all the net zero bullshit, wind farms and green sustainable energy they fantasize about, we are headed *irrevocably* towards the shit-caked dystopia that Lamoureux predicted."

"So why didn't they do something about it?"

"Because there was a second part to the report. Any solution to the problem—*any solution to the problem which humanity attempted to implement*—would be more damaging and more catastrophic than the problem itself.

"The report was presented to a small group of people, twelve in total, at one of the earlier Bilderberg meetings. We discussed it behind closed doors in the strictest confidence. Agreement could not be reached, and no universally acceptable solution was ever proposed."

I cleared my throat. "I would imagine that an insurmountable problem would be that any attempt to reduce industrial output and waste and the human population would shift the balance of power violently in favor of China and Russia—or the Soviet Union as it was then."

"Indeed. That was one of the key issues. Another was that the size of the population back then was four and a half billion people. How do you feed, house, and clothe four and a half billion people without mass production and mass distribution? There would be world famine, deaths in the millions, and of course, as you said, China and Russia would step right in. Look what is happening now with those stupid lithium batteries and the pursuit of net zero. China is growing more powerful by the day! Look how they crippled Spain, Portugal, and part of France for twenty-four hours."

"But you have found a solution. Or rather, Dr. William Squire has found a solution."

He didn't answer for a moment, but for the first time I saw an expression of pleasure on his face.

"Billy has developed an extraordinary energy source, the like of which nobody has ever seen before. *I* have found a solution to the world's problem."

"His energy source is not the solution? What's the solution?"

"Wrong question again, Mr. Mason. The correct question is, what, exactly, is the *problem?*"

I frowned. "OK, what exactly is the problem?"

He leaned forward, and his face was radiant. "People like—so many people like you—believe the problem is insufficient energy for all those insect-like humans scurrying around in their hive. 'Let's give them *more* energy, so they can make *more* people, until we are all piled on top of each other, defecating on each other and eating each other!' The problem, Mr. Mason, the exact problem, *is* humanity."

I took a deep breath. "Oh, shit."

"And *that* is what you produce too much of, both literally and metaphorically."

"What *we* produce too much of? Are you not human?"

"I am evolved."

"*What?*"

"I am evolved, Mr. Mason. Look at me. I have an intellect

which is off the chart. I have a global vision which will carry this world, and our species, into our next phase of evolution."

"Christ, why do the crazies always have all the power?"

"Because if it were left in the hands of what you would call normal, sane people, we would never evolve."

I had no answer for him. So I said, "I dread to ask this, but what is your solution?"

He nodded several times, looking at the silver coffeepot, like I had at last asked a sensible question.

"A small group of us began to tackle this question toward the end of last century. It was impossible to get agreement among the twelve, so five of us decided that we would take it upon ourselves to engineer it."

"Engineer what?"

"I was fortunate to find Billy and his E-115 carbon-14 energy source. This will allow us to address the problem and apply the solution."

"What solution, Mr. Robles?"

"The extermination of approximately ninety-nine point five percent of the human race."

I threw my head back and roared with laughter. The laughter subsided into a mild chuckle. He watched me with no expression on his face at all.

"It is of no use to me if you return to Nero and make him believe I am delusional and believe I can do something I cannot. What is it in fact that you find absurd and laughable?"

"Come on, Robles! You seriously expect me to believe you plan to wipe out eight billion people? You expect *anyone* to believe you have the ability to wipe out the human race? Get real. You think Nero is going to believe that bullshit?"

"Yes."

I snorted, then shrugged. "OK, send me back, and I'll deliver your message. Just one thing: can I see Dr. Squire before I go? You had the whole of NATO kind of worried when you took him away. You, a defense contractor, kidnapping your own employee like that. Didn't it occur to you it would attract attention?"

"Yes."

"Yes?"

"Have you finished with your questions and your coffee?" I nodded slowly. He stood. "Then come with me."

He crossed the room toward the door. I drained my whiskey and followed him. As we exited into the corridor, he turned to me, all kinds of conversational, and said, "You heard about the C-14 diamond batteries that the British came up with a couple of years ago, with a half life of almost six thousand years."

"Of course."

He stopped at the elevators. He didn't touch anything, but the doors hissed and opened. He stepped in, and I followed.

"Their lifespan is enormous by our standards. Nanoseconds by cosmic standards, and their energy output is minute."

The numbers on the screen began to descend, though there was no sense of movement in the car. I watched as we went below the first floor to a third basement below ground level.

"What Billy has done," he was saying, "is to find a way to stabilize element 115, which you have probably never heard of, and fuse it with the carbon in the diamond. Then, and by creating a radioactive reaction between these elements and oganesson, which is far too complex for you to begin to grasp, he has vastly increased the output of the diamonds."

The doors opened, and we stepped into a long, white corridor that stretched out to right and left. He turned left.

"We have not been wasting our time, mind you. While Billy was busy with his research in San Jose, we have been busy here in Thailand, in what they used to call the Tiger Economies, building much of the hardware."

"And in the noble endeavor of smuggling heroin into the West." I put a heavy sneer into my voice, but he didn't seem to notice.

"Yes," he said. "That brought in much needed cash. In the

West, I would have had to launder it, and there would have been some tax burden to shoulder as well. Here I was able to plow ninety percent of it into the labs and the development, and we were able to construct this."

We had come to a set of heavy double doors. He pushed them open, and we entered a large room with a very high ceiling. At the far end was a large, metal chamber with several tubes running in and out of it. It was connected to several banks of monitors, and there were men in jeans and sweatshirts fiddling around it.

At the near end of the room there was what appeared to be a huge cylinder some twenty feet across and twelve to fifteen feet high. There was a gangway running around the rim with four steep stairways leading down to floor level. He gestured at it.

"This we call the well. Believe it or not, it is two miles deep. There is a chamber at the bottom made of lonsdaleite. Ever heard if it?" He laughed and didn't wait for an answer. "Then there is what you would think of as an hydraulic press, though it is far more complex and powerful than that. The press itself is also lonsdaleite, and the whole thing produces pressures in excess of seven hundred and fifty thousand pounds per square inch at temperatures of approximately one thousand one hundred degrees centigrade. That would be two thousand F to you. These are conditions which will rearrange the atomic structure of the carbon into extremely hard diamonds, almost akin to oganesson."

"If you're trying to blind me with science, you're doing a great job."

He ignored me and walked over to the well. He placed both hands on its steel surface and gazed up at it, like Primal Man worshipping a mountain.

"What we have done is to create an entirely new type of diamond." He turned to look at me. "Come."

He led me across the large room, among machines and monitors that meant nothing to me, until we came to the chamber I had seen when we first entered. I now saw that it had a large glass panel in it which allowed you to look inside. I felt myself go cold as I looked. Somehow, on some visceral level, I knew I was in the presence of something new and terrible. Something humanity had never faced before.

It was a gem. It was transparent, but it radiated light of varying colors. It was as though the aurora borealis had been trapped inside a diamond. But this diamond was at least six feet long and four feet across.

"What is that?"

"It is a completely new kind of diamond, Mr. Mason. You are one of a few dozen humans who have seen it. I have named it truvidium."

I stared at him. "Truvidium?"

"A word with roots that go back to proto-Indo-European. To the Tower of Babel. The Druids were named by a play on words. In ancient Celtic, they were of course *druí*, or magician. But it was actually much older than that. *Dóru* was a tree, more precisely the oak. A sacred tree to the Druids. And *weid* meaning wise, seeing or knowing. So they had the wisdom of the oak, but also were *true-vids*, true seers. They saw reality as it truly is."

"You actually believe all this shit, don't you?"

Nothing changed in his expression as he gestured at the extraordinary gem inside the chamber.

"That crystal which Billy and I have created will generate energy for half the planet for the next five or six thousand years." He turned to face me. "You tell me that you see the truth and I am insane, believing in bullshit. Yet I ask you, which of us has created this?"

I had no answer. He knew that and turned away from me to call out, "Billy! Billy, come here!"

A small man in a white lab coat ducked under a large, sage green tube that fed into the chamber. He had a pleasant face and smiled at me.

"Billy, this man is Alex Mason. He has been around the world searching for you. He thought maybe you were dead. Are you dead?"

Dr. Squire laughed. "Not as far as I know. How you doing?"

He reached out, and we shook. Robles said, "Mr. Mason does not believe that our truvidium has the power to run cities, Billy."

Billy looked vaguely surprised. "Oh, it sure has. Not just cities, continents. This baby is *powerful!*" He laughed. "We are about to run our first major tests." He turned to Robles. "OK if he watches?"

"Oh, yes. By all means. But Billy, first of all, tell Mr. Mason what would happen if this gem fell into the hypothetical wrong hands."

Billy Squire blinked and shook his head. "This is orders of magnitude more powerful than the most powerful nuclear weapon. It could cause immeasurable destruction to entire cities. In one blast." He smiled. "You want to watch?"

"Of course he does," said Robles. "He needs to take a well informed message back to Nero before Nero watches Rome burn."

TWENTY-SIX

WE WERE IN A SMALL ROOM, maybe fifteen or twenty feet square. There were no windows because we were a full forty feet or more underground. There was a steel desk in the middle of the floor on which a panel had slid back, turning the desktop itself into a large, flat computer screen. At the moment, it showed a satellite image of the Earth. Robles spoke absently without looking at me.

"We have a couple of satellites. We'll be launching more in the next weeks." He moved around the far side of the desk so that he was facing me and stared hard at me like I had asked a stupid question. "Only I have the full picture. Nobody—*nobody*—has the *full picture* but me. You understand?"

"I understand."

There was a tap at the door. Robles said, "Enter," gazing down at the globe. He didn't look up when the door opened and Superintendent Chakri Anchali walked in. He and I stood staring at each other for a long moment. Robles spoke as though to the screen.

"You two know each other, of course." Now he looked up. "Alex, Chakri, you both still believe in the myth of loyalty and trust. You do not have the true vision. Let me tell you, there is no loyalty, no bond of love or friendship. There is, in the end, only self-interest. Maurice," he said, "and several of his colleagues were kind enough to provide quite detailed electronic surveillance and accounts of your meetings. *Wake up!*" he said. "Trust no one!"

He looked back at the screen, and it closed in on the UK and the East Coast of the United States.

"The two largest mosques in the United Kingdom are the Al-Jamia Suffa-Tul-Islam Grand Mosque in the city of Bradford in West Yorkshire and the Baitful Futuh Mosque in London. The Bradford mosque can accommodate a full eight thousand worshippers, all crammed together for the greater glory of God. The one in London can accommodate thirteen thousand. When they are at prayer on a Friday there are, concentrated there, some twenty-one thousand Muslims." He looked at his watch. "That would be about now. Show them."

Two red dots appeared at Bradford and London. Then he turned his attention to the East Coast of the States.

"The Islamic Cultural Center of New York," he said it, and it glowed. "And the Islamic Center of Washington, DC. Ah."

This last he said as he looked past me and the door opened again. A small, rather attractive Thai woman came in.

He reached out his hand to her. "My dear Apsara. This American man is Mr. Alex Mason. He is nobody to you. But this other man is Superintendent Chakri Anchali. You remember I told you about him. He murdered your son. Here."

He handed her a Glock 17. In infinite slow motion, I saw her take it.

He looked at Anchari and laughed. "What? Did you think I had some other use for you? Did you think I needed to know about your investigations and findings? No, my dear superintendent. You are simply payment for services rendered."

I watched as he stared at her. I watched her face twist into a grotesque mask of hatred and loathing. I heard shouts, mine and

Anchari's as she aimed the gun, and then the gun was bucking and exploding again and again. Seventeen times it kicked and spat. Until the man I had known and liked lay in the corner, torn to shreds, a mess of blood and gore.

There was an echoing, ringing silence that seemed to go on forever. Then the semi-automatic clattered to the floor where dense blood was oozing from the corpse. Robles' voice startled me, though she seemed not to hear it.

"You have been paid," he said. "We don't need you anymore. Go and pack and leave."

She began to sob convulsively, making a terrible, visceral wailing noise. He came to her, put an arm around her, and ushered her to the door. "Go," he said as he opened it. "You are not needed anymore. Go."

He closed the door after her and returned to the desk.

"Do you begin to understand who I am?" he asked. I shook my head. The room seemed to rock for a moment. He ignored me. "Mr. Mason," he said, pointing at me. "Take your phone and call Nero. Tell him that in a matter of a few minutes these four centers will be annihilated."

"*What?*"

He spoke loudly and deliberately, as though trying to get through to a cretin.

"We are about to trigger the first phase of World War Three. I need you to tell him."

I was shaking my head. "Don't do it. You don't need to prove this. I believe you. Don't do it."

"So now you believe me. Your phone, Mr. Mason. Now or I will have Apsara brought in here and beheaded right in front of you. Call Nero. Now."

I pulled my phone from my pocket, and I confess my hands were shaking. I dialed, and after voice recognition, I snapped, "No time for jokes. Put me through to Nero immediately. It's urgent!"

Four immensely dilated seconds passed, and Nero came on.

"I am with Moschid Robles. We are at a lab in the rainforest, about forty or fifty feet underground. Dr. Squire is here. He is safe and well. They have developed some kind of Star Trek Carbon-14 battery that has incalculable power, and Robles is about to run an initial test. He claims he is going to destroy the Al-Jamia Suffa-Tul-Islam Grand Mosque in Bradford, UK, and the Baitful Futuh Mosque in London, killing some twenty-one thousand people. At the same time, he is going to take out the Islamic Cultural Center of New York and the Islamic Center of Washington, DC. I don't know how he is going to do it, but he says it is a matter of minutes, and I believe—"

Robles cut me short, rising his voice to be heard in DC.

"You were wrong to avoid me, Nero! I am traveling to Kuwait and London in the next hours. I'll call you on the way. This is happening, Nero, and it is too late to stop it. Get onboard while you can. I want you onboard. Watch the skies!"

The desktop screen changed suddenly. It split into four, and each section displayed a street view of each of the mosques. Robles sighed.

"Keep watching, this is real time," he said. "I have cameras at each of the sites. I can't stay and watch. I have a plane to catch. But you watch. It should be exciting to see such an historic event live." He paused with his hand on the handle. "I need hardly say, Mason, that this place is dark, magnetically shielded, extreme stealth."

I watched the door close behind him. I had a feeling of utter desolation, as though the entire universe had gone insane and reality was slipping through my fingers. I stared in mounting horror at the bloody mess on the floor, and then there were shouts from the desk. I turned, transfixed, as I saw, in rapid succession, one blinding flash after another as the four mosques were blasted out of existence.

Long seconds passed, and I was in total paralysis. Then I was listening to Nero's voice shouting, roaring my name. I put my cell to my ear. "Sir—"

"What the hell is going on?"

I staggered for the door and wrenched it open. "This is too elaborate to be a hoax. Sir, I think he's blown the mosques. I think he's killed twenty-one thousand Muslims, and he is going to blame it on us or on the Israelis or both."

"In the name of all that's—"

I interrupted him, shouting as I ran. "This facility is electronically cloaked by an energy source you can't imagine. I sent you the approximate coordinates. You are going to need bunker busters, sir. This energy source is made of oganesson and carbon compressed at seven hundred and fifty thousand pounds per square inch at two thousand degrees. Does that mean anything to you?"

"Jesus Christ!"

"I'm going. Watch for my smoke signal!"

I hung up and burst into the lab where I had seen the truvidium crystal earlier. I stopped dead. Billy was holding Apsara, who was sobbing and shrieking convulsively. Near him there was a small cluster of men in suits. They weren't holding guns, but they looked as though pretty soon they might be.

One of them was saying, "You need to come with us, now. Both of you need to come with us, sir."

I didn't think. I charged. I skidded and stumbled to a halt beside them, wrapping one arm around Billy and the other around Apsara.

"Come on, guys," I said, nodding meaningfully at the guys in suits. "Car's waiting outside. Time to move in a hurry."

It was completely unexpected. If they had had any idea what was going to happen, I would never have gotten away with it. As I stroked Apsara's hair and eased her toward the exit, I smashed my instep into the nearest suit's crotch. I knew speed and fluidity were of the essence. So as he wheezed and bent forward, I stepped in and took his Glock from under his arm. It was close range, and I couldn't miss. I blew the nearest guy's head into the next guy's face. While he was screaming and wiping glia and neurons from his eyes, I pumped two rounds into the fourth guy's chest, then turned and put a slug through the Glia-Goo's forehead. For good measure I shot the guy whose balls I'd busted in the back of the neck.

All the scientists were now screaming along with Apsara and stampeding toward the elevators. I bellowed at Billy Squire, "Get her the hell out of here!" He began to run, but then I yelled, "Wait!"

I reached in the suit's pocket and pulled out a fob for one of the Audis. I threw it to him. "Go to the US Embassy. Ask for Maurice Learner. Understood?"

He nodded dumbly, then half screeched, "But *why?* What's happening?"

I took a fistful of his collar and pulled his face close to mine. "You just destroyed four mosques, killed twenty-one thousand Muslims, and started World War Three. *That's* why! Now get the hell out of here!" To the panicking scientists headed for the elevators, I bellowed, "*Robles has gone! This place has been sabotaged! It's going to blow!*"

While they were all cramming into the elevators, I made use of the dead suits' weapons to do as much damage as I could to the electronic machinery that was keeping the truvidium crystal working. I had no idea what I was doing or if it would cause critical damage to the system, but I had to try.

By the time I was done, the scientists had all stampeded upstairs, and I followed. When I emerged from the elevators, there was a handful of guys in camouflage with dogs trying to impose some order among the panicking crowd. I slipped past them and crossed the parking lot to the trees and undergrowth where I had left my rucksack. I retrieved it and loped back to the milling crowd. I saw Billy and Apsara climbing into an Audi and a guy in military fatigues arguing with them. I went over and barked at the soldier, "Leave him alone. That's Dr. Squire. You need to get downstairs with your men *now!* There is some crazy Thai cop down there going nuts with a fire axe. If he does significant damage, this whole place could blow. *Move!*"

I read once that soldiers and policemen are among the easiest people to hypnotize because their brains are trained to take orders and instructions. This guy turned, barked at his men, ordered everybody outside, and the six of them got in the elevator and went down. I gave them ten seconds, then forced the doors open, took a grenade from the rucksack, and dropped it down. I did the same for the other elevator shaft. The floor shook twice, and I shook my head. "Never take orders from strange men," I said.

When I got outside again, Billy and Apsara had gone. The Range Rover had gone, and so had the other Audi. The crowd had thinned, and a very earnest nerd grabbed my arm. "They say it's going to blow! We're headed for the employees' parking lot. You want to ride with us?"

I shook my head. "Go," I said. "You do not want to be here. Go!"

He went.

I went back inside and climbed the stairs to the top floor. I found an office I figured was roughly center of the building, piled as much furniture I thought might be flammable into the center of the floor, and set about forty-five pounds of C4 on top of it, hoping the down-blast would ignite it. Otherwise I'd have to come back with a gas can, and I didn't want to do that.

I set the detonator and clattered down the stairs, then ran the mile and a quarter along the track in the mottled shade of the trees to where I had left the Wrangler. I dialed nine on my cell, and a second later, there was a massive detonation that shook the ground and sent the birds exploding out of the trees.

I fired up the Wrangler, spun the wheel, and raced back toward the main road, telling myself something was badly wrong.

I was emerging from the forest, hurtling back toward Bangkok when the jets screamed overhead. I pulled off the road and stared up at the sky to watch them. They were black and triangular, with no markings. Their speed was incredible. There were four of them, and each released a barrage of missiles that plunged into the forest. The detonations were muted, like distant thunder, but they made the ground shake. When they were done, the jets streaked off at a speed that would break a pilot's neck. So they were drones.

A tall, black column of smoke rose churning and unfolding toward the sky, and seconds later, a shriek that was so loud it made me cover my ears and duck literally filled the air, making it physically vibrate. There was a blinding flash where the column of smoke had been, and hot wind bowed the trees a couple of miles away and then washed over me and rocked the Wrangler where it stood. On the road, cars swerved and screeched. A couple collided and crashed.

I had covered my eyes with my arm. When I looked again, the whole of the Thap Lan National forest seemed to be in flames. They had sown the wind. Now they were reaping the whirlwind.

I climbed back in the Jeep and continued on my way toward the capital. Soon, on the far side of the road, sirens began to wail, police and fire trucks hurtling past toward the blazing forest.

When I reached Chachoengsao, I called ODIN. I went through the routine and Nero said, "You're alive."

"Are you sure?"

"This is not the time to get emotional, Alex."

"Are you sure?"

He decided to ignore me, which was probably a good decision. "Did you see the strike?"

"I managed to leave a good smoke signal. Three jets I could not identify showed up and unloaded maybe fifty bunker busters into the facility. Then I heard a missile arrive. It was invisible, but it tore the air apart and struck home. I think it was a tactical nuclear device. I'm hoping I am not radioactive. Billy—sorry, Dr. William Squire and his girl took off in an Audi for the American Embassy."

"What about Maurice Learner?"

"I don't know. Robles claims he was using Learner. He says

Learner gave him information about our meeting with Superintendent Anchali, but he didn't know I had a backpack full of explosives and a vehicle hidden in the forest. Learner knew that but didn't tell him. I think he was playing a double-cross, but he's on our side."

"Where is Robles?"

"I only know what he told you. He's flying Kuwait London. He's going to call you. How hard is the damage control going to be after the destruction of the mosques?"

"I don't know. Practically impossible, I should think."

"So have agents waiting for him at Kuwait and London and pull him in."

"Thank you, Alex, I'd never have thought of that."

"There's just one thing, sir."

"What?"

"It was all far too easy. The brains that devised that technology were that easy to fool?"

"I know. I agree. Get to the airport. The company plane will be waiting."

"Yes, sir."

"Oh, and Alex?"

"Yeah."

"Captain Gallin—"

I went cold inside and felt suddenly nauseous. "What about her?"

"She has been transferred to London. I will send you the address of the private hospital. She is out of danger and recovering well."

I sighed. "Thanks."

"Take care."

And he hung up. I drove on toward the city, toward the airport, running through the whole thing in my mind. We had destroyed the facility. We had destroyed the truvidium-C-14 generator. We had taken Dr. Squire. The damage we had done Robles was severe—wasn't it? So why had it been so easy? Or as he would have put it, what benefit did he get from making it so easy?

The only possible benefit to him would be that we would believe we had pulled it off.

And we hadn't.

TWENTY-SEVEN

WE TOUCHED down at London's City Airport at eleven
p.m. after a brief stop at Kuwait. I'd had a couple of very dry
martinis, a steak, and a bottle of wine and slept like the dead for
eight hours while we soared at forty thousand feet above the
planet.

When we touched down, there was a Royal Air Force captain
there to meet me. He saluted smartly, told me his name was
Captain Fletcher, fast-tracked me through security, slung my bags
in the back of a Royal Air Force Range Rover, and sped me, faster
than you'd think possible in a crowded city, to a house on the
corner of Mount Row, a short distance from Grosvenor Square.

He looked at me in the mirror and said, "They're waiting for
you inside, sir. I'll deliver your baggage to Captain Gallin's house
in Holland Park."

I thanked him, climbed out, and stood looking at the tall,
redbrick building with the Jacobean gables and the tall chimneys.
I climbed the six steps to the large, black doors and pulled the
chain that must have rung the bell deep inside the house.

Nothing happened for a while. I rang again, and nothing
happened again. I was about to ring a third time when the door
opened very quietly. Unless you were paying attention, you would

not have noticed. A man who looked as though he had recently been dehydrated and shrunk by a remote Amazonian tribe looked up at me. He was wearing black tails, black and gray striped trousers, and a wing collar.

I smiled at him even though neither of us wanted me to. "I believe I am expected. My name is Alex Mason."

He stepped back to let me in and closed the door behind me. He led me into a place of tall, narrow shadows, burgundy Persian carpets, and leather chairs that had been slept in by generations of men who smoked cigars and drank too much port and brandy. I followed him through passages and under archways and came eventually to a large, mahogany door, where he knocked softly before going inside.

"Mr. Mason," I heard him say. Then he stepped out and gestured me in.

I don't know what I had expected. I had not expected to be met by an Air Force captain. I had not expected to be driven to this strange house in Mayfair. And I sure as hell did not expect to find what I found when I entered that large, ancient library.

The morning light leaned in through leaded windows that overlooked a very green lawn. It made distorted patterns on the dark hardwood floor and the Persian rugs that covered it. Tall, mahogany bookcases reached up to the ceiling and seemed to lean in over my head. There was a large marble fireplace with brass firedogs. Only cold ashes lay in it. Around it were arranged a red sofa and three chesterfield chairs. All but one were occupied.

Gallin was on the sofa, looking pale but alive. She didn't smile when she saw me. Beside her was her father, Gabriel. He was watching me, expressionless. Opposite him, in the winged chesterfield, was Nero. He had his head tilted forward and was watching me from under his brows. Beside him in another chesterfield was Moschid Robles. Robles was the one who spoke.

"Sit down, Mason. We need to talk."

I stared at Nero. "What is this?"

His voice was cold. "Do not make judgments on what you do not understand."

Robles said again, "Sit down, Mason."

I glanced at Gallin. Her voice was barely above a whisper. "Sit down. You need to hear what they have to say."

The remaining chair was positioned facing the fireplace so that when I sat I was facing all of them, like I was on trial. I looked at Robles.

"You made it too easy."

"I enabled you to have the facility destroyed, yes."

"It benefited you because that was not the real generator."

"You are learning to ask the right questions, Mason. Well done. I see why Nero has such faith in you."

"You use satellites. You don't want to be in a rainforest. The humidity, the moisture would interfere with the transmission too often. You would want to be based on a mountain. The Himalayas or the Andes."

He nodded. "Soon the weapons will be satellite-based, and we are already preparing a moon-based weapon."

I screwed up my face and shook my head. "*Why?*"

"That mindless question again."

But it was Nero who answered. "Alex, I understand your confusion, and in many ways I share your view—and if not your view anymore, certainly your feelings. But as I said to you before, we have to rise above emotions. We have to face reality. Reality is not bound by emotions.

"Alex, in 1841 the USS William Brown sank on its way to Philadelphia from Liverpool. A small group of survivors managed to board a couple of lifeboats. One, a longboat, was overloaded with forty-one passengers and crewmen.

"After twenty-four hours adrift, a high wind rose, sending waves over the longboat's gunwales. Soon it began to rain heavily. The first mate in charge of the lifeboat had an impossible choice to make. Either they all perished, men, women, and children, or he and this crewmembers must throw the excess passengers overboard, to drown in the freezing water.

"And that was what they did. They sacrificed all of the male passengers, save two married men and a boy, fourteen in total, in order to save the rest. The boat was picked up the next day. That is, in a microcosm, what we face today."

"You can't be serious, sir."

He shook his huge head. "You have no idea, Alex, how close we are to the brink. Why do you think Russia, China, and Iran are fencing and feinting as they are? Why do you think the desperate race is on for AI weaponry? Why do you think Iran is so desperate to achieve nuclear weapons? Desperate is the word. Because we have reached the tipping point. Because what comes next is alternating drought and deluge as the world's atmosphere becomes overcharged with a lethal mixture of CO_2 and massive volumes of moisture from the melting ice.

"You know as well as I do that wars are invariably caused by the need for land—land that can be used to generate wealth. Well, Alex, the problem does not lie with the land being submerged under rising sea levels, as it was twelve thousand years ago. The problem lies in the spreading desertification and the relentless rise in populations. Our planet, Alex, is becoming *uninhabitable!* And this is happening for one reason, and one reason alone. Because humanity has become a plague that is killing its host."

Gabriel spoke suddenly. "Let me ask you, Alex, if you saw a man about to kill Aila, what would you do?" I didn't answer. He insisted. "Please, tell me. What would you do?"

I glanced at her. "I'd kill him."

Now she spoke. "If we had a family, Mason—just go with me —if we had a family and our home was under siege by armed men seeking to kill us and our children. What would you do?"

"You know what I'd do."

"Tell me."

"I'd kill them."

Robles said, "So when we have a small minority of civilized, humane human beings under siege by over eight billion parasitical zombies filling the world with rubbish, with crap, with toxic gases, what should we do? When in a couple of generations we could have a beautiful, green, thriving planet with ample resources for everyone. Preserve Harvard, Yale, Oxford, Cambridge, a few human, manageable cities, foster culture, education, and a harmonious relationship with our home planet."

I said, "Start again from scratch."

Nero added, "But with the wisdom we have gained from reaching the brink and stepping back."

"You are talking about murdering eight billion people."

"Have you seen the news, Alex? We are on the brink of nuclear Armageddon! If we do not act within hours, the planet will become uninhabitable, not because of the changing climate but because it will be radioactive. We have the chance to use truvidium C-14 to destroy the plague and generate vast amounts of energy for millennia to come. But we have to act now!"

I looked at each of them in turn. "So what's stopping you?" I gestured at Nero and Robles. "You two alone have the power to make this happen. What are you talking to me for?"

Moschid Robles took a deep breath, puffed out his cheeks, and blew. "We, the group who have developed truvidium C-14, are a very small group. You saw that even Billy, the chief scientific architect, was not aware of the use the cell was going to be put to. We are a small group; we have relied on secrecy and manipulation to get as far as we have. For years, I have been after Nero to join me because his organization has the one thing that mine lacks: access to the Pentagon, the power to use violence.

"I have now the power to strike, as you have seen. But what then? How then do we stop the survivors from descending into tribal anarchy and ignorance? We need somebody with the intelligence, the power, the infrastructure, and the organization of Nero to bring order out of catastrophe."

I shrugged. "You have him." I pointed at him. "He's right

there, and you have seduced him. You also have Gabriel and Captain Gallin, as far as I can tell."

Nero nodded. "But I have made one thing clear, Alex. There is a red line. I will not be a party to this, though I see its necessity, unless you are onboard."

I was just shaking my head and drawing breath to tell him to go to hell, but he cut me dead.

"Nobody knows this, Alex, but a small handful of people. Not even you know it. When we were young, your father was a close friend of mine, but your mother and I were lovers. She conceived, and I asked her to leave your father and marry me. She refused, and our relationship ended. You are the product of that union. You are my son. If we are to do this, then I need you by my side."

I was aware that my jaw dropped. I looked at Gallin and narrowed my eyes, asking her telepathically either to pinch me or kick me hard in the ass. Finally I turned back to him and said, "*What?*"

"I have had the DNA tests carried out. There is no doubt."

Before I could answer, Gabriel leaned forward and tossed a bound report in front of me.

"Russia and China are mobilizing. They are sending troops to Iran. The Israeli air strikes in June seriously damaged their nuclear capability, but we have strong evidence that medium range nuclear missiles are being sent from Russia."

Nero said, "I spoke with the NSA this morning, and British GCHQ confirms their findings. Both Russia and China are mounting a massive assault on NATO and American defense computer networks using very advanced artificial intelligence. It could be an attempt to disable our defenses prior to a nuclear strike."

I covered my eyes with my palms. "Jesus Christ! What have you *done?*"

"Join us." It was Nero. I dropped my hands into my lap and stared at him. He held my eye. "It's an impossible choice, Alex.

But it is the choice which has to be made, between certain annihilation and survival."

I looked at Robles. "You did all this just to force Nero's hand?"

"I need him onboard, and he needs you onboard. You see me as the villain, but I am the man—the *only* man—saving humanity."

Nero said, "Are you in, or do we unleash nuclear war with Russia and China?"

I sighed deeply and closed my eyes. I felt nauseous. "I'm in," I said.

I opened my eyes and watched Nero and Robles look at each other and nod. They rose to their feet, and Robles said, "Let us go downstairs."

He led us to a short passage which in turn led to a large kitchen and butler's pantry. Before getting there, on the left, we came to an elevator. We boarded it, and it carried us down into a deep basement. When we emerged, it was into a large cellar with a large, steel table much like the one I had seen in Thailand. Against the far wall, there was a bank of computers, and standing on either side of the door there were four men in jeans and leather jackets. They had that unmistakable special ops look, which was reinforced by the automatic weapons they had hanging from their shoulders. Nero glanced at them and asked, "You don't trust us?"

"Once this is done, you will be irrevocably committed. There will be no turning back. Until then, I need my insurance."

"Once what is done? What is this?"

He approached the table, and we gathered around. There was the same large, detailed map of the globe.

"The strikes you witnessed in Thailand, Mr. Mason, were designed to trigger the first stages of global conflict. That was achieved, and with it, I was able to secure the support of Nero. This now allows me to take the next step and, ironically, *avert* that global nuclear conflict."

"By killing billions of people."

"Millions, Mr. Mason. We will take out the major cities and markets, we will cripple industry and shipping, and aviation. Millions will die, but for every man, woman, or child who dies in the strikes, hundreds will die from famine, disease, and anarchy in the ensuing collapse of civilization."

I jerked my head at the armed guards. "What's with the gorillas?"

"For about a couple of minutes, the location of the weapon will be visible, on the northwestern slopes of Mount Aconcagua, in the Mendoza region of Argentina, just a couple of miles from the border with Chile. Though I am sure you have become completely committed to the cause of saving humanity, those few minutes could be enough for people of your skill and intelligence..." He shrugged and let the words hang. "It is always best to play it safe when one can."

The four guys stepped forward and, while three of them covered us, the fourth frisked us. He removed my Sig but found Nero, Gabriel, and Gallin unarmed. As they withdrew, Gallin looked at me. She was pale and drawn.

"Mason, please don't do anything stupid. This is about survival."

Nero said, "I second that. Let us please get this over and done with."

Robles began to work on the huge touch screen and closed in on the Andes in Argentina. He spoke as he worked.

"We will take out London—don't worry, this bunker is blast proof—New York, Brussels, and Berlin in the first wave. In the second wave, we shall take out San Francisco, Los Angeles, no great loss to anyone, Paris and Madrid, Rome—"

"Ah, there!" It was Nero, pointing at a glowing red spot in the Argentine Andes. "I have the coordinates."

I shook my head and said, "How did you manage to build a huge, complex lab at such an altitude?"

As I said it, I pressed the toe of my left boot against heel of my right. The flash-bang popped out, and I hunkered down, saying,

"What's this?" I tossed it at the guys by the door saying, "I think this is yours, guys," then closed my eyes and covered my ears.

The report was massive in the enclosed place. When I opened my eyes, Robles was staggering backward with his hands over his ears. The four guards were in a similar condition. I saw Gallin. She looked untroubled and was moving toward Robles while with her head she indicated the guards. I made for them while she rammed her instep into Robles' balls and smashed her elbow into his jaw. He went down.

I reached the nearest guard and ripped the automatic from his shoulder. He took two in the chest, as did the other three.

When I looked back at the table, Nero was talking.

"Stand by, Aconcagua. Stand by..."

I put the rifle to my shoulder and took aim at his head.

TWENTY-EIGHT

GALLIN STEPPED in front of me, blocking my view of Nero, put her hand over the muzzle, and shook her head.

Nero said, "This is an emergency, Aconcagua. I repeat, this is an emergency, code twenty-three twenty-three. You are being scanned by satellite. Shut down all activity, but remain on standby."

Nero turned and looked at me.

"Were you about to shoot me, Alex?"

"No, sir."

"Well, you should have been."

"That would have been patricide, sir. I could never do that."

"You get that facetiousness from your mother's side."

He pulled his cell from his pocket and put it to his ear. "We need a cleanup team at Mount Row. We also need an interrogation team for Mr. Robles, though he may have some difficulty speaking for a while."

He hung up. While he'd been talking, Gabriel had been tying Robles' wrists and ankles with bootlaces taken from the dead guards. When he was done, we had a last look at the room and made our way out to the elevator. We climbed in and rode it to the first floor. As we stepped out, Nero's phone rang. We stood in the corridor outside the kitchen while he listened attentively. Eventually he nodded and thanked whoever it was.

"Combined operation between a Nimitz class carrier off Chile and a British nuclear submarine near the Falklands. Perfect strikes. Initial reports suggest the facility was completely gutted. We shall now have to carry out some serious diplomacy with the Middle East."

Gallin grunted, and Gabriel looked at the ceiling. Nero went on.

"Catastrophe was averted, but there are serious questions that need to be addressed. How did they get this far? How strong are they? With Robles taken out, what is their number?" He moved toward the hall and the front door. "I am returning immediately to Washington. Alex, I imagine you will be staying behind for a few days."

"If you don't need me. I could use a steak pie and some English beer. You look as if you could too."

This last I directed at Gallin. She smiled.

We had reached the hall. Gabriel slapped Nero on the shoulder. "Come, I'll drive you to the airport."

As he opened the door, a laundry van was pulling up outside. They spilled out, ascended the stairs, and brushed past us as we moved down to the sidewalk like we weren't even there. Gallin said, "Steak pie, huh?"

"And good English beer."

I hailed a cab. It pulled up, and I opened the door for Gallin. I gave the cabby the address and climbed in next to her. As we pulled away, she said, "You know how to make steak pie?"

"No, but I know how to buy one."

"Pah," she said. "I will sit and give you instructions while you wield the rolling pin."

"Each to his preferred skill."

"Exactly."

"I thought you were dead," I said after a while.
"I was, for a short while."
"I didn't like that."
"Neither did I, pal. Neither did I."
And she took hold of my hand.

Don't miss A VENGEFUL GOD. The riveting sequel in the Alex Mason Thriller series.

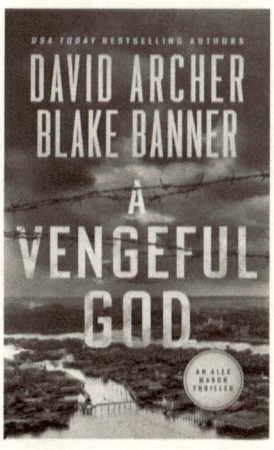

Scan the QR code below to purchase A VENGEFUL GOD.

Or go to: righthouse.com/a-vengeful-god

NOTE: flip to the very end to read an exclusive sneak peek...

DON'T MISS ANYTHING!

If you want to stay up to date on all new releases in this series, with these authors, or with any of our new deals, you can do so by joining our newsletters below.

In addition, you will immediately gain access to our entire *Right House VIP Library*, which currently includes *ORIGINS*—a full length prequel novel to *ODIN*.

righthouse.com/email

(Easy to unsubscribe. No spam. Ever.)

ALSO BY DAVID ARCHER

Up to date books can be found at:
www.righthouse.com/david-archer

ROGUE THRILLERS
Gates of Hell (Book 1)
Hell's Fury (Book 2)
Ice Burn (Book 3)
Judgement by Fire (Book 4)

JACOB HUNTER THRILLERS
The Kyiv File (Book 1)
The Bogota File (Book 2)
The Havana File (Book 3)
The Amsterdam File (Book 4)
The Saint Petersburg File (Book 5)

PETER BLACK THRILLERS
Burden of the Assassin (Book 1)
The Man Without A Face (Book 2)
Unpunished Deeds (Book 3)
Hunter Killer (Book 4)
Silent Shadows (Book 5)
The Last Run (Book 6)
Dark Corners (Book 7)
Ghost Operative (Book 8)
A Fire Burning (Book 9)
Dawnlight (Book 10)
Dead Ice (Book 11)

ALEX MASON THRILLERS

Odin (Book 1)
Ice Cold Spy (Book 2)
Mason's Law (Book 3)
Assets and Liabilities (Book 4)
Russian Roulette (Book 5)
Executive Order (Book 6)
Dead Man Talking (Book 7)
All The King's Men (Book 8)
Flashpoint (Book 9)
Brotherhood of the Goat (Book 10)
Dead Hot (Book 11)
Blood on Megiddo (Book 12)
Son of Hell (Book 13)
Merchant of Death (Book 14)
Extinction C-14 (Book 15)
A Vengeful God (Book 16)

NOAH WOLF THRILLERS
Code Name Camelot (Book 1)
Lone Wolf (Book 2)
In Sheep's Clothing (Book 3)
Hit for Hire (Book 4)
The Wolf's Bite (Book 5)
Black Sheep (Book 6)
Balance of Power (Book 7)
Time to Hunt (Book 8)
Red Square (Book 9)
Highest Order (Book 10)
Edge of Anarchy (Book 11)
Unknown Evil (Book 12)
Black Harvest (Book 13)
World Order (Book 14)
Caged Animal (Book 15)
Deep Allegiance (Book 16)
Pack Leader (Book 17)

High Treason (Book 18)
A Wolf Among Men (Book 19)
Rogue Intelligence (Book 20)
Alpha (Book 21)
Rogue Wolf (Book 22)
Shadows of Allegiance (Book 23)
In the Grip of Darkness (Book 24)
Wolves in the Dark (Book 25)
Olympus Must Fall (Book 26)
Children of the Empire (Book 27)

SAM PRICHARD MYSTERIES
The Grave Man (Book 1)
Death Sung Softly (Book 2)
Love and War (Book 3)
Framed (Book 4)
The Kill List (Book 5)
Drifter: Part One (Book 6)
Drifter: Part Two (Book 7)
Drifter: Part Three (Book 8)
The Last Song (Book 9)
Ghost (Book 10)
Hidden Agenda (Book 11)

SAM AND INDIE MYSTERIES
Aces and Eights (Book 1)
Fact or Fiction (Book 2)
Close to Home (Book 3)
Brave New World (Book 4)
Innocent Conspiracy (Book 5)
Unfinished Business (Book 6)
Live Bait (Book 7)
Alter Ego (Book 8)
More Than It Seems (Book 9)
Moving On (Book 10)

Worst Nightmare (Book 11)
Chasing Ghosts (Book 12)
Serial Superstition (Book 13)

CHANCE REDDICK THRILLERS
Innocent Injustice (Book 1)
Angel of Justice (Book 2)
High Stakes Hunting (Book 3)
Personal Asset (Book 4)

CASSIE MCGRAW MYSTERIES
What Lies Beneath (Book 1)
Can't Fight Fate (Book 2)
One Last Game (Book 3)
Never Really Gone (Book 4)

ALSO BY BLAKE BANNER

Up to date books can be found at:
www.righthouse.com/blake-banner

ROGUE THRILLERS
Gates of Hell (Book 1)
Hell's Fury (Book 2)
Ice Burn (Book 3)
Judgement by Fire (Book 4)

ALEX MASON THRILLERS
Odin (Book 1)
Ice Cold Spy (Book 2)
Mason's Law (Book 3)
Assets and Liabilities (Book 4)
Russian Roulette (Book 5)
Executive Order (Book 6)
Dead Man Talking (Book 7)
All The King's Men (Book 8)
Flashpoint (Book 9)
Brotherhood of the Goat (Book 10)
Dead Hot (Book 11)
Blood on Megiddo (Book 12)
Son of Hell (Book 13)
Merchant of Death (Book 14)
Extinction C-14 (Book 15)
A Vengeful God (Book 16)

HARRY BAUER THRILLER SERIES
Dead of Night (Book 1)
Dying Breath (Book 2)

The Einstaat Brief (Book 3)
Quantum Kill (Book 4)
Immortal Hate (Book 5)
The Silent Blade (Book 6)
LA: Wild Justice (Book 7)
Breath of Hell (Book 8)
Invisible Evil (Book 9)
The Shadow of Ukupacha (Book 10)
Sweet Razor Cut (Book 11)
Blood of the Innocent (Book 12)
Blood on Balthazar (Book 13)
Simple Kill (Book 14)
Riding The Devil (Book 15)
The Unavenged (Book 16)
The Devil's Vengeance (Book 17)
Bloody Retribution (Book 18)
Rogue Kill (Book 19)
Blood for Blood (Book 20)
The Cell (Book 21)
Time to Die (Book 22)
The Reaper of Zion (Book 23)

DEAD COLD MYSTERY SERIES
An Ace and a Pair (Book 1)
Two Bare Arms (Book 2)
Garden of the Damned (Book 3)
Let Us Prey (Book 4)
The Sins of the Father (Book 5)
Strange and Sinister Path (Book 6)
The Heart to Kill (Book 7)
Unnatural Murder (Book 8)
Fire from Heaven (Book 9)
To Kill Upon A Kiss (Book 10)
Murder Most Scottish (Book 11)
The Butcher of Whitechapel (Book 12)

Little Dead Riding Hood (Book 13)
Trick or Treat (Book 14)
Blood Into Wine (Book 15)
Jack In The Box (Book 16)
The Fall Moon (Book 17)
Blood In Babylon (Book 18)
Death In Dexter (Book 19)
Mustang Sally (Book 20)
A Christmas Killing (Book 21)
Mommy's Little Killer (Book 22)
Bleed Out (Book 23)
Dead and Buried (Book 24)
In Hot Blood (Book 25)
Fallen Angels (Book 26)
Knife Edge (Book 27)
Along Came A Spider (Book 28)
Cold Blood (Book 29)
Curtain Call (Book 30)

THE OMEGA SERIES
Dawn of the Hunter (Book 1)
Double Edged Blade (Book 2)
The Storm (Book 3)
The Hand of War (Book 4)
A Harvest of Blood (Book 5)
To Rule in Hell (Book 6)
Kill: One (Book 7)
Powder Burn (Book 8)
Kill: Two (Book 9)
Unleashed (Book 10)
The Omicron Kill (Book 11)
9mm Justice (Book 12)
Kill: Four (Book 13)
Death In Freedom (Book 14)
Endgame (Book 15)

ABOUT US

Right House is an independent publisher created by authors for readers. We specialize in Action, Thriller, Mystery, and Crime novels.

If you enjoyed this novel, then there is a good chance you will like what else we have to offer! Please stay up to date by using any of the links below.

Join our mailing lists to stay up to date -->
righthouse.com/email
Visit our website --> righthouse.com
Contact us --> contact@righthouse.com

facebook.com/righthousebooks
x.com/righthousebooks
instagram.com/righthousebooks

EXCLUSIVE SNEAK PEEK OF...

A VENGEFUL GOD

CHAPTER ONE

THE PHONE JANGLED me out of darkness, and I groped for it across my bedside table. I squinted at it, and the screen told me it was Gallin. I held it to my face as I collapsed back on the pillow and said, "What?"

She was quiet for a moment. Then, "I guess you're asleep."

"No. I *was* asleep. Now I am awake. Kind of. What do you want, Gallin?"

"Nah, forget it. It's OK. I'll call back later." But she didn't hang up.

"You know full well that if you hang up, I won't be able to get back to sleep because I'll be lying here, staring at the ceiling wondering why the hell you called me at..."—I held the phone away from my face—"one-thirty in the morning."

"The long dark night of the soul ain't till three, according to F Scott Fitzgerald. You're getting old. Guy like you should be out romancing some babe at this hour."

"Thank you. I'll bear that in mind in the future. What do you want, Gallin?"

"I wanted to talk to you. Past tense."

I had levered myself into a sitting position and was waking up. I was also becoming aware of a certain quality in her voice I couldn't pin down. I frowned. "Yeah, well, I had deduced that much from the fact that you phoned me. Are you OK?"

"No. Not really."

I rubbed my face and tried to sigh without making a noise. "What's up?"

"Is this a bad time? Are you alone?"

I eyed Manny Pacquiao curled up at the foot of my bed.

"No, I'm not alone."

"Oh."

"I have Manny Pacquiao at the foot of the bed. Of course I'm alone. Since I met you, I seem to have a sign nailed to my forehead that says—"

"Shut up, Mason."

"Fine. What's up?"

"Did I ever tell you about my mother?"

I was going to ask her if this was some kind of psychoanalyst joke, but something in her voice told me it wasn't. It was serious. So instead I said, "No, actually you've never mentioned her." As I said it, I rearranged the pillows behind me and got comfortable.

"She was murdered." I went cold inside. She said, "It happened seven years ago."

"Jesus, Gallin. I'm sorry. I had no idea."

"Yeah, I never talk about it. It wasn't political or anything like that. It was just some guy who used to see her when she went shopping or visiting friends in the neighborhood. He became obsessed with her, said he hated her voice." She was quiet for a moment. "She actually had a really mellow, gentle voice. But he hated it. He worked at the local supermarket. Apparently, one day he started stalking her, following her but staying out of sight. She never noticed." She gave a short, bitter laugh. "How would she? He was one of the guys you saw in the neighborhood. On top of that, he was the kind of guy you just don't notice. Dumpy, glasses, half invisible." She sighed. "So eventually he picked up courage and started to bump into her and engage her in small talk about the weather, just so he could hear her voice and hate it."

Without thinking, I said, "He was psychotic."

"I don't know. That's what they said. Paranoid schizophrenia. He used to hear voices, and they told him what to do. Anyway, it was January, when the days are really short in England, even in the south. By four p.m., it's already dark. She'd popped out to the shop for some avocados because we all decided we wanted avocados and smoked salmon. I had told her I'd go with her. I went up to my room to put on my boots, and she slipped out. She didn't want to put me to the trouble. By the time I'd brushed my hair, put my boots on, and got downstairs, she was at the supermarket. It was, really, literally just down the road.

"In the time it took me to put my coat and hat on and leave the house, she had paid and left the shop. I saw her. I'll never forget it, Mason, as long as I live. I saw her silhouetted against the big, bright plate-glass windows of the supermarket. I waved, and she waved back. As she was waving, I saw the figure come out of the loading bay at the back of the store. There was nothing strange or suspicious about him. He came out, and I recognized him. He called, 'Oh, Mrs. Gallin...'

"She stopped. It must have been all of thirty seconds or less. Then, it was weird, the two silhouettes seemed to fuse into one. I heard Mum say, 'Oh!' like she was surprised. I thought maybe she'd left her purse behind or something. After that, he was suddenly moving away, and I realized he was running. And she was going down on her knees. She died on that cold, icy pavement, while I was holding her. I'd called 999, that's our 911. I could hear the sirens approaching, but by the time they got there, she was dead."

"Gallin, I am so sorry. What—"

I was going to ask her what had brought this to mind. But she'd started talking again.

"I think he hadn't seen me because he went back into the store, back to work. When the ambulance and the cops had arrived, I went in after him. I found him in the fruit and vegetable department. He smiled at me, and I could see the gloating in his eyes. He thought I didn't know yet."

"Christ!" I barely whispered it.

"I castrated him."

"You—?"

"With my instep. I kicked him three times in rapid succession and ruptured his testicles. I didn't let him fall. I got behind him and put him in a chokehold, the naked choke, you know?"

"I know."

"I was killing him, Mason. I was squeezing, and he was going. But the cops were there and pulled me off him. They wanted to prosecute me, but there was no way they could prove my intent."

"What happened?"

"He pleaded guilty. The evidence against him was overwhelming. His prints were on the knife, staff had seen him go to the store room. So he pled insanity, and he went to Broadmoor, a mental institution, instead of prison. He was twenty years old. He was able to hold down a job, keep a small apartment, run a motorbike... But the court decided he wasn't evil, he was just crazy."

I had a sinking, burning feeling in my gut. Outside, through my window, I could see the moon, low on the horizon. It made black stencils of the treetops and the chimneys. I knew the answer, but I had to ask.

"What's happened, Gallin?"

"He's twenty-seven years old now, and he's been released. The shrinks think he's cured. Will *I* ever be cured, Mason? Will my dad ever be cured? What about my mother? Will *she* ever be cured? But Kingsley Gold has been pronounced cured, and he is back home with his mother and his father and his brothers and sisters. And the state will ensure that he is reintegrated as a healthy, productive member of society. The member who killed my mother."

"Kiddo, I have alarm bells going off in my head."

"It's not fair, Mason. That is not justice."

"You're right."

"He *killed my mother!* And he is out, free, with his family."

"Gallin, I need you to listen to me. Are you listening?"

It took her a long time to say, "Yeah, I'm listening."

"You cannot do anything crazy. You're in the UK, in London. You are not in an anarchic war zone, and you have not got the backing of ODIN or MI6, the IDF or the Mossad. You could wind up spending the next fifteen years in jail, and I *need* you on the outside."

"I know." It was an 'I know' that was heavily pregnant with a 'but.'

"At least promise me this: You won't do anything crazy without checking with me first. If revenge is an absolute imperative, we'll do it together."

She gave a snort. "You're a smart son of a bitch, Mason. OK, I am going to hang fire on any decision till we're on holiday. I'll be there day after tomorrow. You still meeting me at JFK?"

"I was going to call you in the morning."

"Son of a bitch! Don't do this to me!"

"Relax. It's no big deal, but it's beyond my control anyway, Gallin. You know how it is. I was told tonight. It's why I'm in bed so early. I have to fly to Finland in a couple of hours. Brass have arranged an exchange of prisoners. I have a pick-up in Helsinki at ten p.m. their time. That's three p.m. here."

"Why you? You're supposed to be on holiday, for crying out loud! Can't somebody else do it?"

I smiled. There was a tone in her voice I had never heard before. I decided I liked it. "Nero insists it has to be me. I have to go. I've known this agent since we were kids. Nero has some theory that I'll be able to tell if they've been turned."

She sighed heavily. "So you'll be a day late?"

"I'm afraid so. But I'll be there, Gallin. Don't go off half-cocked on me."

She was quiet for a moment. Then I kind of heard her shrug. "I won't. Thanks for talking to me. It helped."

"I'll see you in a couple of days. Look Out Inn, Freeport, Maine. Be there."

"You keep a martini chilled for me."

"Love you, Mason."

It gave me a start and a hot burn in my belly. I managed to hide it and said, "Back attcha, kiddo."

And the line went dead.

I looked at my watch. It made no sense going back to sleep, and I wouldn't have been able to sleep anyway. I got up, showered, and prepared my bag for Helsinki.

———

EXACTLY THREE THOUSAND six hundred and ninety-nine miles, one hundred and ninety-three yards and six feet away, it was six a.m., and Gallin rose from her armchair and went to stand at the window, gazing out at Campden Hill Square. The street was lined with trees, and the garden at the center of the square was fringed with an abundance of oaks, chestnuts, and sycamore. The streetlamps, among the few remaining Georgian lamps in London, were still burning amber in the early, pre-dawn light, casting a gentle, dappled glow through the leaves. She scanned the shadows for movement, however subtle. She knew she was a target, but in that moment, she didn't care. If he was out there, this time she would get him. This time she would send him to where he belonged: in hell.

Her phone pinged. For a moment, she thought it might be Mason sending a message of encouragement, but then she realized it was her private phone, not her secure phone. Mason only ever used the secure phone.

She picked her cell off the lamp table and looked at the screen. There was a text message. No name, just a UK number. She opened it.

Hello old friend

Her heart thudded hard high up in her chest. Her belly burned. She wrote: *Who is this?*

You were not easy to track down, but I had divine help.

She forwarded the two messages to the nerds at head office with, *Track this phone now!* Then she wrote: *You tracked me down? Where did we meet?*

Long time ago. It seems to me a very long time ago.

You want to tell me where?

Her secure phone pinged: *Call it.*

These have been crazy times, Aila. Really crazy times that have filled me with crazy feelings. I have missed you. You have no idea how much I have thought about you.

She typed rapidly: *How do you know I haven't been thinking about you? If you don't tell me who you are how can I know?*

She didn't wait for an answer. She dialed his number and heard it ring. His reply came through by text: *Don't call me. I'll tell you when we meet, old friend*

Her secure phone gave an alert. She snatched it up. The message said: *Outside your house. Corner of Campden Hill Square and Holland Park Avenue*

She ran for the door. It was sixty or seventy yards at most to the corner. She left the door open and vaulted the gate, scrambling to stay on her feet, and sprinted the seventy yards to the corner. There was just silent, empty darkness beneath the sighing trees. She put her secure phone to her ear and said, "Confirm."

"He's right there, Captain, at the corner. He's six feet away from you."

She switched her phone to her left hand, pulled her Sig Sauer P226 from her waistband, and scanned the area. Six feet behind her ahead and to her left was empty blacktop and an empty sidewalk. Six feet to her right was a redbrick garden wall, and lying on top of it was a cell phone.

"Son of a bitch. Send me someone to take a cell to the lab."

"On it."

She pulled a handkerchief from her pocket and carefully picked up the phone. As she did so, in her mind she saw her front door, open. She ran back and stopped outside the gate. It was unlatched, slightly open. Had she done that when she vaulted it? Into the phone, she whispered, *"Send backup. To the back of the house."*

She pushed through the gate, wondering if she was at that very moment being watched. She slipped her secure phone in her back pocket and climbed to the front door with her weapon in her hand. She inched through, scanning the stairs on her left, the passage ahead of her, and the open drawing room door on her right.

She eased the front door closed with her foot. If he was there, she did not want him getting away. Keeping her Sig trained on the stairs and the passage, she eased sideways across the hall to the living room. She scanned it fast, saw it was empty, and closed the door.

She moved then to the kitchen door, and keeping her weapon trained on the corridor and the bottom of the stairs, she opened it. The kitchen was empty, and the back door was locked. She closed the kitchen and made for the stairs, telling herself the ground floor was clear.

With her back pressed against the wall and her pistol held in both hands, she burst into the bathroom. There was nothing. She slammed open her study door. There was nothing there except the glow of the street lamps through the black glass of the window.

She moved to the guest bedroom and rammed the door open. It too was clear. That left her own bedroom and the en suite.

Keeping out of the possible line of fire, she eased open the door, then swung in on one knee. There was nothing, nobody. She scanned under and behind the bed and in the wardrobe. Nothing.

She went to the en suite bathroom and flipped on the light.

There was no one there, but as she heard the car arriving outside and the doors slamming, she stared at her face in the mirror with red lipstick writing scrawled across it:

HELLO OLD FRIEND
THANK YOU FOR THE MADDEST SEVEN YEARS OF
MY LIFE

Her front doorbell jangled, and she moved down the stairs. On her way, through the stained glass fan above the door, she recognized the form of her father, Gabriel, the head of the Mossad mission in London.

She opened the door.

"He's gone," she said. "The house is clear. But he left a message on my mirror, in my bedroom."

"David and Joe are checking the alley at the back of the house."

She closed the door, and they moved through to the living room. She poured them each a measure of whiskey. As she handed over the tumbler, she said, "I thought he was supposed to have below average IQ. What did they teach him in Broadmoor, Ninjitsu?"

"We must be very careful, Aila. Tensions are very high between us and this government of undergraduate cretins. If you kill this joker, it must look like an accident, or at the very least it must be untraceable."

"I'm going to be out of the country for a couple of weeks."

"Oh, yes." He nodded absently. "With Alex. Such a shame he is an atheist. Do you think he'll convert?"

"Papa, I have a stalker. Can we focus? Can you put someone on it while I'm in the States?"

"Yes, Aila, of course. I'll see to it. Maybe David and Joe have seen to it already." He settled himself in a chair while Gallin gazed out the window. "We'll stay until you go. You can pack your bag and get some sleep."

"Thanks, Daddy."

"You think Alex might think about a desk job? And you, Aila. You could make a good future for your kids."

She rolled her eyes, shook her head, and gave the black glass in the window a secret smile.

CHAPTER TWO

I TOOK the company Gulfstream from Ronald Reagan. I had an early breakfast of eggs and bacon, drank coffee laced with Jameson's, and read in the *New York Times* that Soleiman Khatyanatsov, the controversial Iranian-Russian billionaire oligarch, had bought the superyacht *Amadea* for three hundred and fifty million dollars. It had been seized by American authorities in Fiji as part of the economic sanctions taken by the United States government against Russian oligarchs. I guessed Khatyanatsov just managed to avoid being classified as a Russian oligarch because of his ties to the deposed Persian aristocracy.

I slept most of the way, and we touched down in Helsinki at ten o'clock at night, local time. I was fast-tracked through customs, collected a rental Grand Cherokee from Avis, and made my way down Highway 45 through a lingering silver dusk that just didn't want to go away. Eventually Highway 45 became the unpronounceable Mäkelänkatu, with umlauts over two of the three As, just in case you got overconfident.

Finland is a beautiful country, and Helsinki is a very attractive city. Mäkelänkatu was a long, very leafy avenue of the sort you don't often see in Europe anymore. It eased me gently toward the bay, past severely elegant buildings that seemed to say they had weathered many a severe winter and would survive many more, through the heart of the bizarre, almost nightmarish Hakaniemi interchange and finally through the ancient, cobbled prettiness of Holmnäsgatan, along the waters' edge and into the arms of the Hilton Helsinki Strand.

I parked outside and pushed into the bronze marble lobby. I told the very tall, very pale receptionist, "I am Alex Mason. I am here to meet Mr. Chen."

"Oh, yes, Mr. Mason. He told me to tell you he was in the bar, waiting for you. That was about fifteen minutes ago."

He pointed me in the direction of the bar. It was almost empty, but I found them sitting at a table in the corner. Chen was facing me, and as I came in, he stood and extended one hand toward me and the other toward a chair at their table. As I approached, Amy got to her feet and turned to face me. She came at me in a rush and flung her arms around my chest to bury her face in my neck, whispering, "*Alex! Alex! I have dreamed about this moment so many times! I can't believe it!*"

I gave her a tight squeeze and whispered back, "*Keep it together, sweetheart. We'll have plenty of time to talk on the way home.*"

She let go and smiled into my face with tears on her cheeks. "On the way home," she said. I gave her my handkerchief, and she gave a small, wet laugh. "I'm so silly."

Chen was watching us with an amiable smile. He gestured to the chairs again, and we both sat. He took out his cell and dialed a number. After a moment, he spoke quietly in Chinese. He glanced at me and grunted, then said, "Yes, Mr. Mason is here. Yao Ming is with you? I speak with him?" He was quiet for a moment, then spoke in Chinese for a bit again. Finally he hung up and stood up.

"It has been a pleasure to meet you, Mr. Mason. Our man has been delivered. I leave you with Miss Amy Lee. Good night!"

He gave a severe, terminal bow and walked away on stiff legs. A waiter came up and looked at me, waiting. I saw Amy still had her drink, so I told him, "Bring me a martini dry. Shake it, don't stir it."

He didn't get the joke, but he went away to fix my drink.

I studied her face, looking for something to read. It was a delicate, doll-like face with a trace of the orient about her eyes and her small, delicate mouth, inherited from her mother. Her dad had been a very successful American businessman, a real mover and shaker. Her mother had been a physically and emotionally fragile girl from Malaysia. He had chosen her from a catalog and married her so she'd take care of him and look good when they went to functions. Amy had inherited her looks but his aggression and courage.

"Howe are you? It's a stupid question, I know. But I mean it, how are you?"

"I don't know yet. What I feel more than anything is joy and relief at seeing you. It has been..."

She trailed off and looked away. I could see the light reflecting off the tears on her lower eyelashes. She bit down on her lower lip and gently steadied her breathing. She smiled with her mouth, but her eyes were still crying.

"...five years. It's been hard, Alex. Really hard. I had these stupid fantasies." She gave a faltering, damp laugh. "You remember when we were kids, and I always wanted to be a warrior princess, like Xena? But you always insisted you had to come and..." She pressed her lips together as the tears began to flow again. "You had to come and rescue me. And, in the darkest days, I used to fantasize that you'd show up at the cell door or look through the window..."

She bunched up the handkerchief and pressed it into her eyes. After a moment, she smiled. "I'm OK. It's all just been so sudden. I know you've been negotiating for months—"

"Years."

"Right, years, but we don't get to hear about that. They try to break us with despair. We get no news, we get no visitors, we get no relief. We get food and water, most of the time."

"Got."

"What?"

"Past tense, Amy. You *got* no news, visitors, no relief. It's in the past."

She nodded, then looked away, like the truth of it was somehow frightening.

"It's hard to believe. I keep thinking I'll hear the tramping boots, those ugly barking voices, I..."

She faltered. I waited, but she wouldn't go on.

"Amy, there is no hurry. When you're ready, you can tell me about it. If you want to. I'll be here."

She looked at me quickly. "You will?"

"Of course. You just give me a shout."

"Like when we were kids."

I smiled. "I've got the plane refueling, and we can get you another martini on board. You ready to go?"

She stood, I got the check, and we left.

Though it was past eleven p.m., the dusk was still lingering as we approached the airport. We were waved through security and were soon strapped into our seats and taxiing toward the runway. Amy gave a sudden laugh.

"Things must be going well. We didn't have our own Gulfstream back in the day. We used to borrow from Central Intelligence, if we were in really dire need."

"Yeah, Nero gets things done, and he gets what he wants. Nobody will say no to him."

"I never thought I'd say it, but I've missed him."

"He's hard work but worth it. He has a brain the size of a planet."

She gave a few small nods. The half-smile on her face said she was thinking about something else.

"What about you, Alex? Aside from work, what have you done with your life?"

I gave my shoulders a small hitch. "I adopted a cat. He is the meanest cat on Earth. I call him Manny Pacquiao, like the boxer."

"You know what I'm talking about, Alex. Don't be coy. Did you marry? Have you got a live-in girlfriend? Are you seeing someone?"

The whine and roar of the engines and the sudden acceleration of the jet saved me from having to give an immediate answer. There was the surge of weightlessness and then the illusion of the Gulf of Bothnia falling away beneath us.

It was as we crossed over the Swedish coast, looking down on Sundsvall that she said, "You haven't answered me."

I shook my head, asked the hostess for two martinis, very dry, and said to Amy, "No, I am not married. No significant other. The job makes anything like that impossible."

"Some people manage it, Alex. They get a desk job..."

"Nyeah, no. I'm not ready for that yet. In a few years, maybe."

"I remember you were always such a good analyst. You could focus on minute detail, then expand to a broad, global view of all the imponderables before making a positive, unfaltering decision."

"Keep going like that and you'll make me blush."

She covered her face with both her hands and looked at me through her fingers. "I'm gushing," she said. "I'm so sorry. I have been so long in solitary..."

"Don't sweat it, Amy. It's me, lifelong pal and pain in the ass, Al. Whatever you do is OK."

"I sometimes thought you could replace Nero."

I laughed. To my surprise, she laughed too.

A while later, they brought us a snack, and when we were done, as the hostess cleared the plates and glasses, I told Amy, "You take the bedroom. I'll sleep here on the sofa."

She stared at me for a moment. "Do you mind?"

I started to say, "No, not at—" but she interrupted me, and it dawned on me what she was saying.

"I mean, do you mind staying with me? Not, I don't mean anything..." She took a deep breath and sighed. "I just need to hold on to someone. I know it's a lot to ask. Do you mind?"

"Of course not. Hey! What are friends for, right?"

It was an awkward five minutes while we brushed our teeth and she put on a nightgown and got under the covers. I brushed my teeth a little longer than was absolutely necessary, took off my shoes, then lay down next to her, on top of the covers.

"Aren't you getting into bed?"

I wanted to say that she was vulnerable and we had to be careful and I should not take advantage of her, but how do you say that to someone who is vulnerable and beautiful and sensitive?

I slid under the covers, and she turned off the light and grabbed a hold of me. Two minutes later, she was snoring softly. I spent the night studying the ceiling and telling myself it was jetlag.

We finally began our approach to DC at about one a.m. I was up well before her, washed my face, combed my hair, and put on my shoes. She rose and showered, looking coy and shy, while I ordered breakfast. When she finally sat down and sipped her coffee, she asked me, "Will you be at the debriefing with Nero?"

"No. I can't be there."

She looked surprised and frowned. "Why not? Nero said he wanted you to be a part of it. I wanted you to be a part of it."

"I'll see you when I get back, Amy. There is something I need to do. I need to be away for the next two weeks. It can't be avoided. But you know Nero is going to take care of you."

She stopped dead with a piece of bacon halfway to her mouth. "*Two weeks?*" Then, "Oh." She stared out of the porthole at the approaching coast of New Jersey and Delaware. I followed her gaze and thought that just a couple of hundred miles to the north and a little to the west, Gallin was waiting for me at the Look Out Inn outside Freeport, Maine.

We landed shortly after that and were met at security by four of Nero's lethal bodyguards, all in XXXXXXXXL blue shirts that were too small for them, dark blue suits that were about to burst open over their biceps, and curly wires poking out of their ears, making them look not quite human.

I gave her a big hug and told her I would see her the moment I got back. She looked resentful and tearful. So I looked up at the walking boab trees and told them, "Look after her. She's extra special."

They gave no sign they had heard me, and the biggest of the boabs video-called Nero. I saw him on the screen, put my arm around Amy, and smiled. He didn't smile back.

"Good evening, Ms. Lee. Are you well?"

"Yes sir. Thank you for sending Alex to get me."

"These four intimidating gentlemen will take you to your hotel. In the morning, they will bring you to see me, and we shall chat."

"Very good, sir. Can't Alex come with me?"

I drew a breath, shaking my head, but Nero plowed on like an ADHD hippopotamus in a china shop on roller-skates.

"Mr. Mason is on holiday for the next two weeks. He did me the favor of postponing his vacation to go and collect you. I shall see you tomorrow, Ms. Lee. Good night. Alex, good night."

He hung up. Amy looked up at me. "Right," she said, as only women know how. "Well, enjoy your vacation. Are you taking Manny Pacquiao with you, or somebody else? Anyhow, whoever she is, have fun."

She turned and walked away with the four walking boab trees, leaving me to roll my eyes and groan before heading for the long-term parking lot to collect my TVR Cerbera. My bags were already in the trunk, and I was ready to go. From the car, I called Gallin. I let it ring for thirty seconds and tried again. She didn't answer. I figured she was asleep, so I left her a voice message saying, "At Ronny Reagan, on my way!"

CHAPTER THREE

IT IS, in theory, a nine- or ten-hour drive from DC to Freeport, in Maine. But I had managed to snatch some sleep on the plane while Amy snored, and I was motivated to get to where I was going. It was the early, wee hours of the morning, the roads were empty, and I was driving a monster that could go from zero to sixty in a little over two seconds and leave Porsches and Ferraris looking at each other, spreading their fenders, and asking, "What the hell was *that?*"

So by the time I rolled into the small hamlet of Hapsfell, sounding like a hundred Harleys thirsting for high-octane gasoline, it was just after seven a.m. There was a broad track leading off Harpswell Neck Road which I followed to the water's edge. There it opened out into a broad esplanade beyond which a light mist was drifting over the water. On the right was the Look Out Inn. It was a large colonial with three floors in cream clapboard and a black gabled roof. I could see dim light in some of the windows. Early risers rising.

I parked at the foot of the steps that led to the deck and climbed to the main entrance, where amber light spilled out onto the boards. I was about to push through in search of a good New

England breakfast of eggs, bacon, sausages, and rye pancakes, but a familiar voice stopped me.

"Boy am I glad to see you."

I turned and saw Gallin sitting in the shadows, holding a mug in both hands as though she was cold.

"You don't sound it," I said.

"I'm not. And I am."

I went and sat across the small, round table from her. "That's why Freud called you the dark continent."

"Screw Freud. He wouldn't understand."

"That was"—I gave a small shrug—"kind of his point. What's wrong, Gallin? I came straight from the airport. Nine hours driving, non-stop."

"Seven. I got your text when you left, and you were driving that beautiful beast." She jerked her head at my car. "Which was nice of you."

It was meant to be funny but failed miserably, and we both sat in silence, me watching her and her staring into her mug.

"Is this about that guy, Kingsley Gold?"

She nodded into her cup. "He was at my house." I felt the cold creep into my skin. She went on. "Dad has put a couple of men on it. They should be hunting Iranian spies. Instead they're trying to track down some crazy who broke into my house."

"He broke in?"

Now she looked up. "He tricked me, Mason. He's supposed to have an IQ of like eighty. But he lured me into an exchange of text messages. He knew I'd keep it going and have his phone traced. The guys traced it to the corner of my street. I went out after him. He knew I would. He guessed I might run out fast, without my keys, and leave the door open. He slipped in and wrote a message on the mirror in my bedroom."

"Son of a bitch."

"That's what I thought."

"Your dad's guys are the best. They'll find him."

Her smile was ironic and not very amused. "Again, that's what I thought."

She pulled her cell from her jacket, opened it, and slid it across the table. It was on her Whatsapp. The profile picture was of a row of butchered cows hanging from hooks. The name was KG. The last two messages read, first: *I'll tell you when we meet, old friend.* That was from the very night I had last spoken to her, and then, from that night, while I was driving from DC: *That's a beautiful view you have there, old friend, across the dark, dark waters of the bay, under that mist.*

I glanced at her. "He's here. He's followed you." She nodded. "Have you told your dad?"

She nodded again. "He's looking into who his friends were in prison, what he studied, what his background is post conviction. This guy has not got an IQ of eighty. He is smart."

"If he's here, he hasn't got many places to hide. The population is small, and available accommodation is scarce."

"He's devious, Mason. His thinking is unpredictable. He thinks like a chess player."

"Don't build him up too much, Gallin. He's just an asshole, and we'll get him."

"See? That's why I'm glad to see you."

I reached over and gave her wrist a squeeze. "C'mon, let's go get some breakfast. I've been driving for *at least* ten hours. It's been hell. Just to get here and see my best gal."

"Asshole."

But she said it with a smile, and we went in for breakfast.

Breakfast was everything you could have hoped for after driving seven hours through the night. After breakfast, with the sun sitting molten over the amber mist on the bay, Gallin helped me carry up my bags. Our rooms were adjoining. She slung my leather bag on the bed and dumped her ass next to it.

"I guess you're going to sleep."

"At some point in this life, it would be good to get four hours' sleep."

"I guess. You haven't slept much in the last..."

"Forty-eight hours. No."

"You didn't sleep on the plane?"

"Nyeah... No."

"K, I guess I'd better let you sleep."

"You can curl up at my feet if you like."

"It's all I ever wanted."

She stood, kissed me on the cheek, and left.

I stood a while in the silence left in the backwash from the closed door. Unconsciously I touched my cheek and went to brush my teeth. Watching myself in the mirror, I decided I looked smug and tried not to wonder why. I stripped, fell into bed still looking smug, and slept until just after noon. When I awoke, Gallin was sitting on the bed watching me. I gave a sleepy blink and said, "If a guy did that you'd say it was creepy."

"If a guy did it, it would be creepy."

She tossed her cell at me. I elbowed myself into a sitting position, then picked up the phone. It was open on her Whatsapp again.

Who's your boyfriend? You know you can never be as intimate with anyone as you're going to be with me, sweetheart. It doesn't get more intimate than what we are going to do.

I could feel the burn of hot coal in my gut, but a voice in my head told me we had to stay as cold as ice, or this son of a bitch would kill her. He was a narcissist with a god complex, and he had the audaciousness that comes with a total absence of fear. There was only one thing that could hurt him.

I said, "Don't answer him. Ignore him. Let him see the message has been read, but don't react. We'll walk on the beach, take out a boat, sit out on the deck like he doesn't exist. It will enrage him and lead him to make a mistake. Meanwhile, we'll look for him discreetly. Like I said before, there are very few places where he can be staying."

She nodded. "OK. Makes sense."

I copied his number and typed it into my secure ODIN phone. Then I sent him a message. My number and the origin of the message were untraceable, but he would know it was from me. I wrote: *Forget it. She doesn't even know you exist, pal. You're an idiot, a nobody, a non-entity.*

I showed it to Gallin. She arched an eyebrow. "Seriously?"

"He's a narcissist. It will drive him crazy, and he will show himself. We have to be very, very cool and stay very alert."

"OK, send it."

I pressed send. The message went. Nothing happened.

I got up and had a shower while she sat on my bed and stared at the window. I dressed, and we went down for lunch. We had a dozen oysters and a bottle of very cold five-year-old Arista white wine from the Russian River Valley. They were served by a girl with big pink glasses, buck teeth, and hair she had stolen from a merino ram. As she set down the plates, she made a noise in her nose that wanted to be a laugh and asked, "Are they really alive?"

Gallin arched an eyebrow at her. I said, "I hope so," and she scuttled away. I turned to Gallin. "You feel like renting a boat? There are lots of interesting islands around here. You got Sow and Pigs. That's got to be worth a visit. Then there's the Goslings Preserve, which is not edible but an island. Then there is Crab Island, which we might give a miss. I'm itching just thinking about it."

"Nero's right."

"Usually, but about what in particular?"

"You're facetious. I think it's a coping mechanism."

"Boy, you're going to be a scream on this vacation."

"Sorry."

"Don't be. Just imagine you're undercover hunting for Mohammed Sinwar."

She stared at me, pursed her lips, and gave a sideways nod. "Not a bad idea. It could work. OK, let's hire a boat."

An hour later, we were out on the dark water smacking across the small waves with the occasional crash of spray lifted by the breeze and hurled into our faces. Gallin had the tiller, and I had the sail close-hauled so at times we were heeled over and skipping fast over the water. It was good to see her laugh with the wind in her hair. It was three miles from the inn to Pettingill Island and the smaller Sow and Pigs next to it, connected at low tide by a strip of sand. Tacking as we were added another mile to the trip, and after we had messed around on the water for a while, it was past four p.m. when we finally pulled the small sailing dinghy up on the sandy west shore of Pettingill.

There we sat on the damp sand and cracked a couple of cold beers. For a while, we were quiet, listening only to the sigh of the breeze in the trees until Gallin said suddenly, "Mason, I haven't got a lot of respect for psychology, psychiatry, psychologists, or psychiatrists, with the possible exception of Freud."

"That's only because everybody else criticizes him because of his Oedipus Complex theory."

"Maybe. Shut up and listen. Having said that I have little respect for those professions, I will recognize that the people at the top of them are highly trained professionals."

I thought about Freud, women, contradictions, and the dark continent but said nothing.

"You've seen the messages that asshole sent me. KG is at the very least seriously emotionally disturbed. I mean, am I right or am I just being an hysterical, hormone-driven woman?"

"He is stalking you, and his messages are full of veiled threats. He is at the very least seriously emotionally disturbed. The only thing you've said that sounds like a hysterical, hormone-driven woman is the question whether you are being a hysterical, hormone-driven woman."

"Don't be an asshole right now, Mason."

"OK."

"Is that OK? Thank you. So here's my question. How come those highly trained professional psychiatrists at Broadmoor thought he was cured? How did they not detect that he was still emotionally very unstable?"

"You know yourself, Gallin, that sociopaths can be very persuasive."

She nodded laboriously and took a pull on her beer. She swallowed and smacked her lips. "But here's the thing: sociopath does not describe an actual pathology. It is not like a psychopath. It's an antisocial personality disorder that exists on a sliding scale and basically means you are indifferent to how other people feel. You can't relate to other people's suffering or joy."

"They have no empathy."

"That's what I said. They have a disregard for social norms and other people's rights. They are manipulative, and they lie to get what they want. The odd thing is that though they have no empathy, they can be very skilled at reading people and giving them what they want. Now at one end of the scale you have the kid who steals his classmate's lunch money, and at the other you have the ayatollahs and Adolf Hitler."

"Didn't you just make my point for me?"

"No, because what I am asking is, if you and I know this and can see what that asshole is about, how come those experienced professionals missed it?"

I shrugged. "It wouldn't be the first time it's happened. What's your point?"

"I don't know," she said absently, staring at the musty horizon. "I mean, if he is that kind of smart sociopath who is so clever at manipulating people, even top flight psychiatrists"—she turned and looked at me—"why did he wait seven years to pull the stunt?"

I frowned and grunted. She had a point. She went on.

"You know those people who wear sandals and hug trees?" I smiled. "They like to tell you that everything happens for a reason. I sometimes wish they could go and explain that to the newborn babies in the third world who have parasites eating them from the inside. 'Don't worry, everything happens for a reason.' Thing is, they are right, only not how they mean it. Everything happens for a reason because everything has a *cause*. Not a great purpose, but a cause."

I laughed. "That is a very long way of saying something prompted KG to go to work on the shrinks and convince them he was cured."

"Yup."

"It's a good point, and we should look into it."

"I'll ask my dad to pull some strings." A cool breeze wafted some stray strands across her face, and she fingered them away. She saw me watching and held my eye a second. "What?"

I spoke without thinking. "You're beautiful. I'd hate to lose you."

Her cheeks flushed, and she threw a piece of seaweed at me. "Take a hike!" But she smiled.

Something drew my gaze past her to the open water by Sow and Pig, where the small waves were lapping at the partially submerged sandbanks. There was a wooden dinghy bobbing beyond the bank, furling its sale. It was a stark silhouette against the glare of the water. I could just make out the silhouette of a guy in the boat. His spinnaker was down, and he was lowering his mainsail.

I glanced back at Gallin. She was frowning at me. "What?" she said again.

"Don't look," I said, "but I think he's here."

Her whole body jerked as though she was about to jump and spin around to look. I said, "Don't!" She froze, glaring at me. "Laugh and give me a hug instead!"

Her eyes narrowed, and she gritted her teeth. Then she let out a shrill, piercing laugh and hurled herself at me. In my ear she breathed, *"Squeeze me tight or I swear I'll pull my piece and I'll shoot the bastard!"*

Given the invitation, I squeezed and whispered back, "It might not be him." Glancing at the boat, I saw he'd set up a rod. "He may just be fishing."

She slipped out of my arms and stood. She was smiling, but her eyes were smoldering. My eyebrows rose high on my forehead as she stripped off her clothes and walked toward the water. "That is going to be cold!" I called after her.

She didn't flinch. She plunged in, disappeared for almost a minute, and erupted thirty feet away, screaming to the skies. "Oh my God! It's so cold!" Then she laughed out loud. "Come on, chicken! Come on in! Betcha don't dare!" She swam a bit and called back in a voice that was for some reason disturbing, "Oooh, it's nice when you get used to it. Come on, big guy. Come on in!"

What could I do? I stripped off and went in.

We frolicked playfully. Or perhaps we played frolicfully. Either way I was grateful for the very cold water, and in any case I was aware that the whole purpose of the playful frolic was so that she could get eyes on the boat, and as a bonus, if it was KG, let him see how much of a damn she gave.

We had no towels, so we dried ourselves with my T-shirt, and twenty minutes later, we clambered aboard our own dinghy and set the sails. For a moment, I hesitated, but Gallin grabbed the tiller and said, "We sail right past him. I want to see that son of a bitch's face."

We skirted the sandbank with the prow smacking into the small waves rolling in off the ocean beyond the bay. All the while I kept glancing at the other boat bobbing gently in the midst of the sun's reflected glare. Gallin would not take her eyes off him, though he remained completely motionless.

Finally, as we rounded the headland at the end of the sandbank, we were no more than thirty yards from him. He sat motionless with a large straw hat and heavy, black Wayfarers. Around his shoulders he had a large towel, like a poncho, that obscured most of his body. Only his hands protruded, holding his fishing rod.

On an impulse, I said to Gallin, "Stop."

She didn't hesitate. She turned us into the wind, and I

released the mainsheet. The boat eased to a halt. I grinned at the motionless figure and waved. "*How's it going? Are they biting?*"

If I hadn't seen him moving around earlier, I might have thought he was a wax figure. He didn't move. He just sat staring at us with his very black glasses. I waved again, got no response, and we got underway, back toward the inn.

Scan the QR code below to purchase A VENGEFUL GOD. Or go to: righthouse.com/a-vengeful-god

www.ingramcontent.com/pod-product-compliance
Lightning Source LLC
Chambersburg PA
CBHW030323200626
46816CB00006BA/1904